Maisy's Keeper

Club Drift, Volume 1

Saffron Hayes

Published by Saffron Hayes, 2018.

Maisy's Keeper © 2018 by Saffron Hayes. All Rights Reserved.
All rights reserved. No part of this book may be reproduced in any form or by any electronic or mechanical means including information storage and retrieval systems, without permission in writing from the author. The only exception is by a reviewer, who may quote short excerpts in a review.
Cover designed by Tom Thornton
This book is a work of fiction. Names, characters, places, and incidents either are products of the author's imagination or are used fictitiously. Any resemblance to actual persons, living or dead, events, or locales is entirely coincidental.
Saffron Hayes
Visit my website at www.saffronhayes.co.uk
First Released: April 2018
Second Edition: June 2018

For my extraordinarily patient family:

Please, never read this.

CONTENTS

- Disclaimer
- Chapter 1 | The Wedding
- Chapter 2 | The Fish
- Chapter 3 | Not a Pizza Place
- Chapter 4 | 101
- Chapter 5 | A Taste
- Chapter 6 | Perks
- Chapter 7 | How big?
- Chapter 8 | More
- Chapter 9 | Rope and Whips
- Chapter 10 | What Happens After
- Chapter 11 | The List
- Chapter 12 | Home
- Chapter 13 | Dinner Table Conversations
- Chapter 14 | Club Drift
- Chapter 15 | Sights
- Chapter 16 | Are you sure?
- Chapter 17 | Boutique
- Chapter 18 | Loose Lips
- Chapter 19 | Firecracker
- Chapter 20 | Just A Client
- Chapter 21 | Wax
- Chapter 22 | Bad News
- Chapter 23 | A Proposal
- Chapter 24 | Discovery
- Chapter 25 | The Bench
- Chapter 26 | Drop
- Chapter 27 | House

- Chapter 28 | Little Piggy
- Chapter 29 | The Difference
- Chapter 30 | Detached
- Chapter 31 | Office
- Chapter 32 | How Does It Feel?
- Chapter 33 | Airborne
- Chapter 34 | Heist
- Chapter 35 | Trespass
- Chapter 36 | The Main Event
- Chapter 37 | One Of Us
- Chapter 38 | Bad, Bad, Bad Cop
- Chapter 39 | Cards
- Epilogue
- About the Author

Disclaimer

I write BDSM Erotic Romance and I'm a part of the BDSM community in real life.

However, I don't write about real people in my fictional world. The characters, places, and events are all figments of my imagination.

Although my Club Drift novels are fictional, I hope they portray healthy and realistic attitudes to BDSM. If you see something alarming in my work that falls outside the suspension of disbelief required for these fast-paced romances to work then PLEASE tell me.

These stories are by their nature escapist fantasies, but I want everything I write to have safe, sane, and **consensual** play in mind.

The Drift heroes may be all knowing and preposterously attractive and things might move a little faster than in real life, but that's only because this is fictional fun.

In real life, you'll be extra careful, promise? If someone tells you they're an all-knowing pleasure God, then you can probably laugh in their face and walk away. If any potential partner demands you obey them without negotiations or without a safe word you will walk the hell away. If anyone treats your limits as an obstacle to overcome, then walk away. If some guy tells you he can only play during work hours that guy is married, mate. Probably walk away. Unless they're a poly couple and you're all into that, of course. Do your research. Be safe. Have fun, but please be safe.

"No." is a complete sentence.

Rule one in BDSM is mutual consent. Anyone who tells you otherwise is a potential hazard.

I'll be including some links to beginner BDSM information on my website because I hope my novels find their way into newbie kinkster hands one day. The kink community is big and broad and inclusive and fantastic, but it really helps to have your wits about you and some reading under your belt.

There are as many ways to be kinky as there are kinky people and my way isn't some ideal that should be upheld, but safe, sane, and consensual (SSC) or risk-aware consensual kink (RACK) are essential starting points for any kink relationship.

Have fun out there, you glorious kinksters, and take care of each other.

See you back at Club Drift,

~ Saffron

www.saffronhayes.co.uk

Chapter 1
The Wedding

The bride was radiant in her knee-length vintage tea dress. Her flame red curls were almost the same shade as her shoes. Neither the bride nor the groom could dance, but that didn't matter. The way they looked at each other, as if they'd discovered something secret and awe-inspiring behind their partners' eyes, made their dance more watchable than any choreographed waltz.

Their clumsy half steps did nothing to detract from the beauty of their obvious affection for each other. Even the bride's sour-faced mother-in-law managed to crack a smile when her son dipped his new wife at the end of the tune. Maisy watched from the sidelines with a smile, truly happy for them.

They might be clients rather than friends, but she liked them and hoped to see them again once her event planning duties were done. Everything had gone smoothly for them on the day. Well, everything had gone smoothly as far as the guests were concerned.

Maisy and the beleaguered bridal party had been up at 5 A.M. receiving the replacement flower order that Maisy'd been forced to organise last minute. The disastrous first delivery on the eve of the wedding had left the bride in tears and Maisy ready to scream at her incompetent boss. Maisy didn't hold with gender stereotypes, but gosh damn it, men like Michael who only cared about the bottom line shouldn't be allowed anywhere near a bride's floral arrangements.

Maisy had been so embarrassed when the florist's truck had arrived - so had the florist for that matter. Maisy'd used the company before and had never had a problem. This had Michael's fingerprints all over it. Apparently, he'd phoned around the contractors making changes to cut costs.

"He said it wouldn't matter if they were a bit small. He said it went with the theme and you'd made a mistake with the order before. I should have known to call you, but his name was on the business account. Oh God. Miss Sinclair, I am so sorry."

"It's okay." The bride maintained her composure throughout the ordeal. "Really, it's fine. It's not your fault."

"No, it's not fine." Maisy pursed her lips, staring at the sad bouquets and sparsely filled table arrangements. "Can you rush something through overnight? I wouldn't ask, but..."

"Say no more."

"I'll pay the premium rate, obviously-"

"No," the florist was adamant, "Standard rate. Hell, you can have a discount. I'll make this right. Let me get back to the shop. I'll call you."

Maisy was sure the new flowers would come out of her commission, but it didn't matter. Not when the alternative was letting a client down. Some people wouldn't see it that way - she could think of one person in particular, but flowers meant a lot to this bride.

The florist pulled it off somehow. They went over the possibilities, the vintage theming, and what could be done as quickly as possible during a rushed phone call that evening. Neither woman slept much that night, but it was worth it. The bride had wept again when the replacement flowers arrived. She'd wept several times throughout the day, in fact.

It seemed she was overwhelmed by the occasion in general. When Maisy saw the reverent way the groom kissed his bride's hand, Maisy understood why. They'd be happy together, she just knew it.

Soon after the first dance the bride approached Maisy, champagne flute in hand. "Come on, you must be off the clock by now."

"Oh, I really shouldn't," Maisy eyed the glass longingly, it had been a long day.

"I insist." Beaming, Miss Sinclair, well, Mrs. Thornton now, swiped a bottle from a passing caterer and topped the glass up to the brim, "You've earned it."

"Thank you." Maisy took a dainty sip, some unnaturally strong professional instinct keeping her from draining the glass and heading off to the nearest soft surface for a nap. "Congratulations, it was a beautiful ceremony."

"Thanks to you."

"Thank you, but it was all your ideas." Maisy looked past the bride at the unique floral arrangements that framed the evening garden party. Lush, full white roses nestling with burlap clones of themselves while silk and sacking fought for prominence in the chair covers and column shrouds. The couple had designed most of the decor themselves; Maisy had just helped make their dreams a reality.

The rustic and glamorous mash up shouldn't work, but it did. Maisy couldn't help but admire the Thorntons' commitment to their theme. "You're so good together."

The bride looked over her shoulder at her new husband, who was good-naturedly enduring a third waltz with his emotional mother, "Yeah, we're pretty great."

Job satisfaction can come in many forms, but Maisy thought she got a pretty good deal where that was concerned. Seeing that proud, adoring look on people's faces on a weekly basis? It was really something.

"Have you got anyone special in your life?"

Maisy's smile tightened a little at the edges. Weddings made up more than half of their business, and inevitably the question would pop up: 'When's it your turn?' Or 'How would you do your own wedding?' Or, most commonly, 'Are you seeing anyone?'

"No, not at the moment." There'd been a couple of dates recently, but Maisy had already decided she wasn't going to see him again. She never felt excited by these men. Maybe she just didn't like sex? No, she definitely liked something about sex, otherwise she wouldn't get through as many batteries and romance novels as she did, but in real life? It just wasn't doing it for her. Sex had always been perfectly pleasant, occasionally even orgasmic, but mostly? Just okay.

"Drinking on the job, Bennett?" The stench of whiskey assaulted Maisy's nostrils moments before her boss entered her field of vision.

The bride's smile faded when she caught sight of Michael, but she quickly recovered her polite façade. "How nice of you to make the evening party. Miss Bennett relayed your apologies for missing the set-up and ceremony."

Maisy masked a smirk behind her champagne glass, she'd done no such thing, but Mrs. Thornton clearly had a talent for backhanded compliments. In this case, her remarks translated to something like, 'Nice of you to show up for the free bar and dodge all the work.'

Michael, true to form, didn't notice any subtleties in her greeting, "Yes, yes! Bloody marvellous party. You'll have to hire us again."

Maisy winced at his forward approach to soliciting return business. The bride's raised eyebrow did nothing to dim Michael's clueless grin, "Yes, well, I'd hire Maisy to run every single day of my life if I could. She's a real star, really going places."

She squeezed Maisy's hand and, although she hadn't said anything, Maisy recognised a familiar refrain in her touch and in her eyes. The same thing her mother, her flatmate, and just about everyone else had been saying since Michael's father had died and his blockhead son had taken over: Run. Run now.

"Quite so!" He replied, not one to bother listening once he'd finished speaking. He winked at the newlywed, gave Maisy's glass a significant look, and wandered away. He would probably be heading for the buffet table.

"Pig." Cathy said, wrinkling her nose, "Maisy?"

"Mm?"

Cathy Thornton refilled Maisy's barely touched glass until the golden champagne bubbled over the glass's lip, "You ever consider, you know, moving on company wise?"

"Sometimes, but I do love the work." Maisy smiled, even more glad that they'd swapped personal phone numbers this month. She knew that leaving the firm seemed like the sensible thing for her to do now Michael was in charge, but every time she thought about it she baulked. She'd remember Michael Snr.'s kind face, how much the company had grown over the last ten years, how much she'd put into it all.

Not yet, she wouldn't leave quite yet. Besides, she might not admit it out loud, but she was terrified that if she left the company behind she wouldn't be able to do her job. Deep down she felt that without the contractors, the office staff, the support network she'd be revealed as a talentless nothing.

Maisy said goodbye soon after, confident that everything that needed to go well had gone well and all that was left was for the contractors to pack up when the last guest fell asleep on the lawn.

Chapter 2
The Fish

The morning after Cathy Thornton's wedding, Maisy rolled over, her fingers groping through the bedclothes in a blind search for her bleeping phone.

She wasn't sure how many times she'd already pressed snooze, but surely there was time for one more. A muffled thud told her that last night's paperback, which she'd devoured in a sleepy haze, had crashed to the floor. She had recently developed a bad habit of reading romance after romance in bed and waking up with the lights on and her face stuck to an open page. Still, there were worse bedtime habits one could have.

Last night's hero was much like all the others had been recently - perceptive, gorgeous, and Dominant with a capital 'D'.

The alarm went off again. Maisy didn't even remember pressing snooze the last time, but the phone was in her hand so she must have. 8:15 AM.

"Maisy! I made coffee!" Her roommate drew out the last syllable with a high-pitched perkiness that shouldn't be allowed before 10 AM.

"Coming!" Maisy jumped up and kicked the paperback under the bed with the others. She really needed to get the old ones to the charity shop; her bedroom was like a second-hand smutty bookshop. After the quickest shower she could manage, Maisy dressed in the clothes she'd laid out the night before. She might sleep in far too late, but at least she prepared for it.

Harry pushed a sweet, milky cup of coffee into her hands, "Don't be mad at me."

Maisy smiled, bemused, "What did you do this time?"

"You make it sound like I'm always killing your fish or something."

Maisy almost choked on her coffee, "You killed my fish?"

"No!" Harry looked mortified, "No, no, no. Hey, it won't seem so bad now. Remember: I might have set up an account for you on a dating website, but I didn't kill your fish!"

Maisy closed her eyes in pure exasperation. "Right. I'll be sure to remember that. Delete it." She downed her lukewarm coffee and started moving brightly coloured throw cushions around the sofa, looking for her make-up bag.

"Oh, please?" Harry's wickedly mischievous eyes couldn't quite pull off the manipulative puppy dog look.

"No! I don't like dating sites." She didn't particularly. She'd always found the number of unsolicited dick pics disconcerting. It was like turning up to a picnic and having whole salamis thrown at you from a distance rather than eating a carefully assembled sliced meat sandwich—painful and embarrassing for everyone involved, really.

The truth was, she didn't think she'd find what she really wanted on any old dating site, so she'd given up looking. It was horribly cliché to say that the men in books had ruined her for real life, but it was true. She'd never met anyone who made her feel the way the heroines in her books felt. She'd had boyfriends, sure, but she'd always felt uncomfortable or, if she was completely honest, bored in those relationships.

"Fine, I'll take a look." She didn't feel the slightest pang of regret about the lie. Harry would probably forget to check whether she'd looked anyway. Maisy's pocket-sized friend was very easily distracted.

"Great," her victory smile was a joy to behold, "I'm off. Don't forget to tell Michael he's an idiot today!"

"Mmhmm." Maisy rolled her eyes, waved Harry out, and checked her watch. Just over an hour until she had to be at the office. Maybe she'd have time to drop into the charity bookshop on her way in.

BY MID-AFTERNOON, MAISY was that special kind of bored that only comes from working on spreadsheets and costings all day. Her mind wandered back to the morning's conversation with Harry. She wouldn't be at all surprised if the dating profile was a joint scheme from her mischievous roommate and ever nosey mother.

Sure, it'd be nice to find someone, but the idea of a nice boyfriend and nice sex sounded about as appealing as a cold cuppa and she couldn't exactly explain that to her mum and oldest friend.

Maisy couldn't help but wonder if there were online dating websites for people with an interest in BDSM though. If they did exist, would she even be allowed on? She thought she was interested in that kind of thing because of the books and films and the feeling in her stomach when a man pushed her up against a wall for a rough snog, but she didn't really know.

She'd never met anyone she trusted enough to try it for real. She also got the feeling that if these websites did exist they'd be pretty heavy on hook-ups. There was no way the intense, satisfying, true love with kinky sex she'd been devouring in paperback form existed in real life; it was far too good to be true. Still, it couldn't hurt to look. She glanced around the quiet office before fishing her phone out of her pocket.

Well, she wasn't wrong about the hook-up thing. The first three hits on the search for "BDSM dating" were full of intimidating personal ads featuring an excess of close-up genital shots. She almost didn't click on the fourth result because it was listed as a forum rather than a dating site, then she realised that she had more questions than answers about the whole thing, so the site could be the most useful of the lot.

There were still far more genitals on display than she was accustomed to seeing at work. Maisy resigned herself to completing the search at home, but not before she asked a quick question in a thread helpfully titled 'Ask Stupid Newbie Questions Here.'

With a title like that, maybe she shouldn't have been surprised by the antagonistic responses she received.

Chapter 3
Not a Pizza Place

Maisy shut the front door with a happy sigh, it'd been one hell of a dull day. Thankfully, Harry was still out, so she had plenty of time to have a cup of tea and just slob out with a book - exactly what the doctor ordered. Before she settled in though, she remembered she had a forum to check.

The wonky kettle filled the kitchenette with steam as Maisy scrolled through the replies to her post.

All she'd asked was whether the kind of relationships she read about; the intimate, loving, kinky as all get out ones, even existed in real life and were there BDSM clubs in London as well as in her books?

She couldn't even get off by herself anymore without biting her own arm or cuffing her legs to the bed (something that feels very silly after the orgasm). There wasn't much point pretending she could just find a normal man and go off and have lots of normal sex like her girlfriends. She needed more.

Where on Earth were you meant to find a Dom anyway? The women in her novels were always swept off their feet by perfect men who knew how to make them scream with pleasure at the merest provocation, which sounded great, but hardly achievable.

The people on the fetish forum seemed to share her doubts. Several creepy guys offered to show her the ropes, wink wink, nudge nudge, if she'd just send them her address. Some, predictably enough, sent pictures of their dicks. A few accused her of being a man pretending to be a woman because she wouldn't meet those creepy guys. Some sneered at her for asking such a naive question and suggested she go back to her 'little books' if she couldn't be bothered to do any real research.

"Well," Maisy muttered, preparing to close the web browser and do just that, "Sorry I asked."

Before she could click on the little 'x' in the corner of the screen, the envelope icon started blinking red. One (1) new message.

"Please don't be a cock shot, please don't be a cock shot, please don't be a...phew." The message was blessedly free from any attachments.

"Dear JustCurious,

I hope you're not too discouraged by the replies you've received. It's always a shame to see derision towards those new to the scene.

To answer your question in the relative privacy not afforded on that message board: Yes. The kind of relationship you describe does exist, more or less, as do countless other intensities and variations on the broader theme of power exchange.

Relaxed BDSM clubs are also very real in most major cities worldwide. I'm sure your research led you to some sites advertising big club nights.

There are, however, more private places to indulge that side of your personality, many of which choose not to advertise.

I'm a member of a club in London which might suit your interests. It's relaxed, classy, and safe.

They run regular beginner's nights and all members are carefully vetted and monitored for everyone's safety.

It'd be an ideal place to get a taste of 'real' kink, as you put it. If you're interested, here's the address and the dates for the next beginner's nights.

I recommend bringing a friend to relieve nerves. Of course, if you like, I'd happily show you around myself.

www.clubdrift.co.uk
Hope to see you there,
Dan"

With a healthy sense of cautious scepticism (installed during her teenage years on the internet) she reread the message a few times.

He didn't seem to be sarcastic. His profile was sparse: no face picture, a generic suit wearing torso, an equally generic username, age (35), and the fact he was apparently single. Although, as the more helpful caustic comments on her forum post had pointed out, that didn't mean much online. Apparently married men posing as super-Doms online to lure in naive newbies was a common problem, who knew?

What's more, this Dan hadn't jumped straight into bossing her around, which was a huge plus compared to some of the other messages she'd received. He didn't even seem interested in her personally. The sensible advice to bring a friend stopped her worrying that he was after a hook-up.

He'd just told her politely where she could find actual answers to her questions. That's about as non-threatening as you could get in the circumstances.

She searched the address he'd given her. It came up as *Club Drift: Private Members Club*. The home page was black with nothing but a phone number and the address in a small and unassuming bronze type.

If she phoned ahead she'd know it was a real place and they could tell her more about beginner's nights.

She tentatively dialled the number, swearing to kick herself upside the head if it turned out to be a big hoax and she was just phoning the local pizza place.

"You've reached Club Drift, how may I help you?" The speaker's French accent was so strong it took her a moment to adjust.

"Yes, hello. I was just wondering...I was referred to you by... Sorry, I think I have the wrong number."

"One moment, if you please. Were you given this number by Daniel?"

"No," She clicked back to the tab with the forum, the message did say Dan. "Yes, I suppose so. He sent me a message online and I looked you up."

"Oui! Excellent. I'll just get him for you."

"No! Wait! I just wanted to-"

"Hello?" A deep and rumbling voice with a London accent.

"This is kind of embarrassing. I was just calling to see if, well, if this was a real place, to be honest."

The man chuckled, "A perfectly reasonable thing to do. I suppose Claude hasn't helped by passing you straight back to me."

"At least I know you're real." She cringed. What did that even mean? I thought you were a troll, but now you've got a voice I'm completely reassured? Glad to hear you're not a haunted computer emailing me to get my hopes up? For goodness sake, Maisy.

"Indeed. I sent you a message this afternoon inviting you to beginner's night, correct?"

"Yes, that's right. I'm, uh, JustCurious," She wrinkled her nose at the awkward introduction, "And I was wondering what 'beginner's night' actually means."

"Mostly what it sounds like. Claude - he's the owner by the way - Claude opens the club to non-members on a weeknight so they can come in, chat to some regulars, check out the equipment, stuff like that. It's just so people can get a feel for the place without the pressures of a full club night. Like a very relaxed munch."

What the hell's a munch, she thought.

"Right. Okay. That sounds less terrifying than I imagined."

"I'm glad to hear it. Shall I put your name down?"

"I guess so. First Tuesday of the month, right?"

"Next Tuesday, yes."
"Wow, so it is. I'll be there."
"And the name?"
"Maisy Be-. Just Maisy."
"I look forward to seeing you there, Just Maisy."
He hung up before she could respond.

Chapter 4
101

By the time Tuesday rolled around Maisy's mind was brimming with every excuse she could think of not to go to beginner's night. What were you supposed to wear to 'Intro to kink 101' anyway? Latex? She definitely didn't have anything like that in the back of her wardrobe and that was probably trying too hard anyway. Jeans? This place sounded pretty ritzy, maybe jeans were off the dress code.

A secretive, classy website was all very well, but sometimes people just wanted a dress code and some hard facts, damn it. She'd have to have a word with this Claude about her web developer contacts, surely he was missing out on business by... No, Maisy, no work. Definitely keep this weirdness separate from work.

She was suddenly struck by the delightful image of Michael sneering at the low cut black top she was trying on. "She's always been a little strange," Imaginary Michael said, the stench of whiskey strong even in her mind. Maybe she should take a leaf out of Claude's book with the privacy thing.

Maisy wasn't ashamed of this interest exactly, she felt like an adventurer about to discover uncharted territory, but some people were, well, some people were just Michaels. Best to keep it all separate. She settled on tight jeans in black, which took the casual vibe away a bit, and a red top in a draped silky fabric which showed some cleavage.

Not too casual, but not too dressy or revealing either. Maisy crossed her fingers in silent prayer that she'd guessed right. Then again, if she walked in and everyone was wearing fetish gear on the relaxed coffee night she wouldn't feel under-dressed - more like terrified. This was meant to be an easy introduction, like the kiddie pool.

She'd web-searched the term 'munch' after speaking to Daniel on the phone. Apparently it was a social event for kinky people that didn't involve actually doing anything kinky. That was the best she'd been able to come up with, anyway.

She couldn't help wondering what Dan and Claude looked like. Hearing their voices but having no reference for their actual physical appearance meant her imagined versions of them varied wildly day to day.

Claude went from a (frankly offensive) French caricature with a thin moustache and thinner legs to a rotund uncle-like figure, while Dan went from Mr. Darcy to Mr. Face-Like-a-Bag-of-Spanners. Strangely, the more she thought about it the more he turned into Mr. Darcy. No harm in hoping the nice helpful man was attractive. After all, he was the only person there besides the owner whose name she knew.

Maybe she could talk to him if she was brave enough. Ask him some questions. Maybe he'd show her the equipment, maybe even demonstra- Whoa girl. You're just going to see what it's about, don't get too worked up. It's not even a date, thank goodness. The last thing Maisy needed was a date to worry about as well.

AS FAST AS FIVE-FOOT-four Maisy could go without looking like she was running wasn't very fast at all, but she was desperate to get to Club Drift and inside before she could change her mind or be seen. Then again, there was no reason for anyone to think anything untoward was happening behind the little door in the huge black-boarded railway arch.

A bouncer in a dark suit stood near the entrance. She slowed to a halt when she spotted the imposing man, wondering again if this really was safe. A gaggle of giggling young couples sauntered past her in their office wear, waved at the bouncer, and went inside. Okay, so she wasn't a single woman wandering into a murder den. Probably. Almost definitely. Maybe.

Maisy took a steeling breath and approached the bouncer, trying to look calmer than she felt. She noticed a discreet bronze plaque on the door that read simply '*Club Drift.*'

"I'm here for, um, I-"

The man interrupted brusquely "Don't ask me, darling. The scary chick inside's got the list."

"But you're the - fine. Thanks." Maisy gave him a tight smile and pushed the heavy door open.

The small room behind the door surprised her, but she soon noticed the arched doorway beyond the reception desk, heard the not too distant clinking of glasses, and realised this was just a tiny partitioned part of the huge disused railway tunnels. Everything was gleaming glass and brass, a stark contrast with the bare stone floor.

"Good evening."

Maisy jumped, she'd been so distracted by the lush Art Deco chandelier she hadn't even noticed the woman in the shadows behind the desk. The tall and extremely attractive woman gave Maisy a warm smile, soothing her startled nerves. Scary, had the bouncer said? Surely not. "Are you on the list?"

"Yes, I think Daniel put me down. It's Maisy."

"Lovely to meet you, Maisy," She crossed Maisy's name out on a clipboard and came around the desk to shake her hand. She was wearing a tight-fitting black dress that was a touch too revealing to be office wear, but was still very proper somehow. "I'm Matilda, one of the house crew Daniel no doubt warned you about."

"Right." He hadn't, Maisy wasn't sure what she meant by that. "Nice to meet you," she tried to smile, but nerves got the better of her and it came out more like a grimace.

"Just fill in this tiny form for me and then you can go on in," Matilda passed her a booklet. "Just the first two pages, please." She filled in her name, address, telephone number, and, slightly unsettling, her next of kin. Matilda took the booklet back before she could flick through the rest of the pages.

"First time can be scary. This little box room doesn't help. Here, I'll show you into the main club. Get it over with then you can relax and chat some, it's like ripping off a plaster, you know?" Was that a Caribbean lilt in her voice? Everything about the woman exuded kindness, confidence, and good humour. Maisy realised through her nerve induced fog that she liked Matilda immediately.

"Uhuh. Sure." Maisy nodded, but although her gaze focused on the big doors behind the desk she didn't move her feet.

"Poor Maisy." Maisy frowned, but she found only understanding in the other woman's smile, her eyes held no mockery. "Come." Matilda took Maisy's cold hand in her own warm one and led her firmly to the doors, pushing them open before she could hesitate again.

"Oh wow."

Matilda chuckled and squeezed her hand before releasing it, "Wow is right, sweet thing."

Maisy wasn't sure what she'd been expecting. Maybe a strange, dingy room with red lighting and plastic seats. Maybe a dungeon with metalwork restraints and next to no lighting. What she hadn't been expecting was a lush and expansive underground bar straight out of *The Great Gatsby* with cavernous arched ceilings and decadent furnishings.

The seemingly endless space they'd entered was surprisingly warm for a bare brick room with a flagstone floor. Moustachioed men and precisely coiffed women in elegant period costumes manned the glass and brass bar that dominated the main room.

Maisy could see further tunnels that led beyond the huge space to areas bathed in shadow. Booths with burgundy upholstery in lush velvet or suede and dark wood tables framed the brick walls; women in beaded frocks with fringes that swayed tantalisingly with their hips moved among them serving drinks.

"Maisy? You okay with me going to get the next startled rabbit?"

"Hm? Oh! Yeah, thanks for showing me in, Matilda."

"No worries. Dan is on bar duty for the next hour or so if you're looking for him." She nodded then went back the way they'd came, leaving Maisy in the doorway.

Maybe I should have asked her to walk me to the bar, Maisy thought. Although it was early, the massive room was already heaving with intimate groups of friends and couples, all smiling and laughing. She felt like a gooseberry. After a deep breath she started walking towards the unusually large bar. It seemed much further away than it had a moment ago when she'd been admiring the antique water drip dispensers from a safe distance - were they the things you use for Absinthe? She was sure she'd seen that in a film once.

A lot of her surroundings reminded her of old films she'd seen, now that she thought about it. One foot in front of the other, Maisy, go on. No-one's looking. Okay, they are looking a bit. Is that guy wearing a dog collar? Oh shit, don't stare, now he's frowning. Keep walking. Hey, this floor is much too hard, I hope those girls are wearing kneepads. One, two, one, two - God, I hope they're serving alcohol tonight - one, two, one two.

DANIEL WATCHED THE little newcomer approach from behind his bar. The poor woman looked like a kid on their way to the head teacher's office for a telling off. It had to be Maisy, the girl from the forum. She'd seemed so curious, so articulate in her responses on the site. He hadn't been able to resist reaching out to her.

Claude had been nagging him to do some recruitment for a long time, so Dan had started keeping an eye on the popular forums. Maisy was the first person he'd encouraged to attend a beginner's event. Dan valued the privacy a carefully curated membership offered so, although he'd told Claude he'd keep an eye out for potential new members, he'd been slacking. Claude didn't really understand advertising and he too was concerned about privacy, but he insisted the younger side of the membership needed a boost.

She was obviously nervous, terrified even, and there she was, putting one foot in front of the other. When she reached the bar, Dan was delighted to see that she was only a few inches taller than its lowest point - damn cute.

Claude's oversize bar was an ingenious choice in a club that regularly entertained submissives who like to feel small. She blinked at the bronze bar rail that was just below her chin and shook her head before looking around the bar for help. Big brown eyes, full lips, lush curves, dark curls - damned if she wasn't the prettiest newbie he'd seen in a long time. Shame he'd have to behave himself so as not to scare her off. He approached quietly.

"Maisy?" She jumped, wide eyes turning to him.

"Yes? How did you-"

"It's Daniel. Glad to see you showed up."

Chapter 5
A Taste

Okay wow. Mr. Darcy can take a step back because this guy is something else entirely. Dressed in black jeans and a plain black t-shirt apart from a blue armband that read 'BAR', he was underdressed compared to the costumed staff, but still effortlessly stylish.

All the diversely attractive versions of Daniel from Maisy's imagination put together had nothing on the real deal. Tall, dark, gorgeous, stubbly, subtle muscle stretching out the thin t-shirt, and Dominant. Even if she didn't know that from his online profile, she'd have felt it. Something in the confident stance. Matilda shared that Dominant air come to think of it. There was something behind the eyes, something in the smile, something in the way he looked at her like he knew her deepest secrets - or at least intended to learn them. She didn't know exactly what it was that gave it away, but she knew this man was Dominant.

"Still with us, sweetheart?" His smile accompanied a slight narrowing of the eyes, as if he was trying to figure out what Maisy was thinking.

"Yeah. Sorry, I spaced out a bit there." Rein yourself in Maisy, he's just being helpful, no need to dribble over the poor man.

"Not to worry. I can take some time to talk if you like. Show you around maybe?"

She was going to say no, not wanting to take him away from his station, but all the small groups in the room were deep in conversation and she didn't want to interrupt them either. "If you're sure you don't mind."

"Not at all, Just Maisy. Give me a moment." He started to turn towards the other bar staff and paused, "What did you want to drink?"

"Gin and tonic, please."

"I'll be right back."

The small group of 1920s action figures jumped to attention when Dan approached. They all stood a little straighter and nodded earnestly when he spoke. Were they all wearing bangles or...? Oh, uncoupled handcuffs. Interesting.

One of the female waitresses ran up with a gin and tonic, her white beaded dress sparkling in the candlelight. When she passed the drink over Maisy saw that the blue padded handcuffs the waitress wore said 'BAR' just like Dan's armband.

"Thanks, how much do I owe you?"

"Oh nothing, it's all covered on newbie night. See you later."

She scurried away to serve someone else when she saw Dan returning, blue armband replaced with a plain black one that made it look as if one sleeve of his t-shirt was longer than the other. "Ready?"

"Sure." She walked with him to the gap in the bar that had steps down to floor level then followed him to a comfy looking booth on the main room's back wall.

She noted with approval that there were several thick rugs scattered around the seating areas and felt less concerned about the kneeling bar-goers. "What's with the armbands?"

He glanced at his as if he was so used to it he'd forgotten its existence, "That's Claude's idea. He likes to keep us well labelled. Sit, please."

She did, pleasantly surprised to find that while some of the burgundy chairs were plush velvet, others were leather or wood covered in throws. Somebody with an excellent eye for colour and texture had decorated this place.

He sat next to her and folded his hands on the table, a non-threatening, relaxed stance, "A lot of the more senior members volunteer their time to keep the place running smoothly. They might tend bar, monitor trainees, keep an eye out for any problems during scenes, or help new members think about their limits list. All kinds of things, really. Really we're here as the ones you ask if you need someone you can trust. Claude gives us these daft things so people can spot us."

"Right, I think I get that." She hesitated, "And the handcuffs on the others at the bar?"

"Trainee subs who help out in exchange for reduced membership and BDSM tuition."

"Wow, that's a thing?"

"Mmhmm. Interested?"

"Me?" She nearly spat out her sip of gin and tonic. "No, gosh no. No offence, but I'm just curious."

"Just curious, Just Maisy," he smiled, a cheeky glint in his eyes.

"Yeah. Just little old me." She blushed and scrambled for something to say to take the attention off her, "Aren't there trainee Doms?"

He rubbed his stubbly chin, "You know, I said the same thing when Claude introduced the programme. It's not that we're against the idea, there just hasn't been any interest. My theory is that some newbie Dom egos are so big they wouldn't ask for a full training thing, so we just answer questions and give them tips casually. Still gets the job done, more or less." He folded his hands back on the table and Maisy noticed that he was watching her intently - like one might watch the train timetable. Casually, but attentive and looking for vital information

"So," Daniel's easy grin revealed outrageously deep dimples which she was simultaneously very jealous of and a little bit in love with, "You want to find out how deep your submissive nature runs?"

She suddenly felt off balance. He put his hand palm up on the table, offering an anchor. She took it and was surprised to find she felt a little steadier right away.

"Don't panic, sweetheart."

"I'm not panicking." Her eyes were wide and darting around the cosy nook, looking anywhere but at him.

"I can see you're a little overwhelmed and that's fine, but you can relax," he watched her as though she was a startled animal, his voice low and calming. Maybe he was worried she was going to bolt. To be honest, she wasn't sure if he'd be mistaken in that concern. "Nothing is going to happen tonight, we're just talking. You can talk to someone else if you'd prefer. A woman, perhaps? You do want to learn more about Club Drift, don't you?"

She nodded slowly and leaned forward to take a long sip of gin and tonic from the straw. When she sat back she felt a little more centred. "You'll do. To talk to I mean."

He must have noticed she'd relaxed a little. "Good girl," he grinned and picked up his own drink, chuckling under his breath when his words sent an almost imperceptible shiver through Maisy.

"So," she said, watching him almost as closely as he'd watched her, "You're a... you do...we're sexually compatible."

He barked out a loud laugh that made her jump, "That's one way to put it, yes."

"And you're experienced with this stuff?" Her tongue felt thick and stupid in her mouth.

"What stuff?" He edged closer, his movements measured and unhurried. Slowly, so she could see him coming, Dan reached out to cup her chin.

"Um," all logical thought evaporated as she stared into his eyes. If she shifted towards him she'd end up on his lap, face clasped in his huge hand. What would that feel like?

The shiver was even more noticeable this time. He grinned broadly, "Oh, that stuff." He released her chin and brushed his fingers up her face, her neck, before wrapping them in her hair.

She pulled away; he let go immediately and leaned back, giving her space. Wide-eyed and flushed, Maisy felt herself lean into the space where he had been, missing the light pressure on her scalp.

Daniel was watching her with the same careful attention as before. She sat back, cheeks reddening.

"I'm sorry, I-" She didn't know what to say. She'd fallen at the first hurdle. Not to mention the fact she was behaving like a horny teenager. Why was he having this effect on her? He's hot, well, he's beyond hot, but she was usually pretty reserved on dates - and this wasn't even a date.

She thought she heard him tut before he spoke. "Sweetheart, rule one: Don't be sorry for what you feel. Be confused, aroused, angry, turned off, whatever, but don't apologise for it. Which one are you?"

"Confused," She muttered, followed by an almost inaudible, "Aroused."

"There you go, the tunnel didn't cave in because you admitted you liked something." His easy smile was comforting.

She nodded and took another big sip of her drink. Why was this so difficult?

"I told you nothing is going to happen. Not tonight. We're just talking. Do you feel like you can't get away?"

She shook her head.

"Do you want to talk about this, to figure out what you might want from someone like me in a place like this?"

She hesitated, then nodded.

"Well then, sweet little sub, let's just enjoy that without worrying about what happens next. If I do anything that you don't like, you tell me. That's how this works, whether I'm holding your hand or fucking you senseless."

For a moment she pictured him doing just that. Could he tell she was thinking that? How embarrassing. When he placed his hands palm up on the table she placed her hands in them again without hesitation.

"What do you want? Not from me specifically, like I said, we're just talking. What made you post on the forum?"

She gulped down a breath. His controlled gaze held her and, somehow, soothed her. Why not talk to him about this? She might not get the chance to talk to someone who understood again, she certainly wasn't sure she'd work up the courage to come somewhere like this again.

"I want to be... I am submissive, I think."

"Good girl. That's a big admission for you, isn't it? Why do you think that?" His thumb caressed her knuckles as she spoke.

"I want to be controlled," She felt herself flush crimson, "I know it's not normal, but I think I want to be controlled...you know, in bed. I want to be a good girl, to please someone. Not just any someone, but someone who it feels right with. Someone who I obey without hesitation, who wants to take care of me and give me pleasure."

She realised with a pang of confusion that she'd curled up on the seat and leaned towards him while she spoke. Her hands were still clasped in his, but now they rested on his lap. She started to shift away, troubled by how comfortable the intimate position was, but he shook his head and clenched his hands around hers a little tighter.

"No you don't, sweetheart. I'd like you to stay there if you're okay with it. So, you think you're abnormal?"

She relaxed into his arm, feeling more comfortable there than she'd like to admit. "Well, yeah. Most people don't want to be spanked and fucked and tied up and forced to come –"

He chuckled and released her hands so he could wrap an arm around her. "Is that what you want?"

"I - oh Christ." She groaned into his side. Why was she talking to this stranger about her desires? He must think she was a daft woman who'd been reading too many bodice rippers.

"Stop worrying, Maisy, it's doing you no good." He ran his fingers through her hair and she arched into the tingly touch like a contented cat.

"I don't know why I'm so comfortable with you, I shouldn't be-" She was interrupted by the rustle of a sequined waitress walking by to see if their glasses were empty. Maisy began to rise, but Daniel tightened his fist in her hair and she stilled. A wave of heat coursed through her at the possessive gesture and, seeing as the waitress passed by utterly unperturbed, she let herself enjoy the sensuous thrill of being held still by this powerful man.

"Aren't there usually machines and equipment and play stuff?" She ventured to ask when the waitress departed, not sure if she had the terminology correct. That's what they called it in the books, right?

"Yes, it's very different in here at the weekends. You wouldn't believe how well the high ceilings absorb screams and moans."

Her eyes grew wide and Daniel chuckled, "I'm mostly joking, sweetheart. Does the thought of equipment being used in here scare you?"

"A little," she admitted.

"Honest little Maisy," he pulled her hair gently, encouraging her to move to exactly the right spot until their faces were level. She was off balance, relying on his grip to stay upright. "I would like to kiss you, does that scare you?"

Her eyes widened even further. She tried to shake her head, but found that she was locked in place by his grip.

"No." She said, instead.

"No what?"

"No, it doesn't scare me," she fought to inch forward, eyes on his lips. She wanted nothing more than to kiss him.

He tugged her hair lightly and she refocused on his eyes. "'No, it doesn't scare me, Sir,'" he corrected, watching for her reaction.

Her eyes slipped shut for the briefest moment and a purely erotic thrill ran through her. Immobilised by his grasp, held by his gaze, made bold by the alien surroundings, she could almost feel her will bend to his.

"No, it doesn't scare me, Sir," she said, savouring each word, marvelling at how easily they came and how natural they felt in this place, with this man.

She caught a glimpse of an approving smile before he pulled her closer. The grip on her hair was just on the edge of painful, but it was a delicious pressure that fuelled her growing desire to feel his lips. She gave a low whine when he stopped just before their mouths met.

"That's a pretty noise. What do you want, Maisy?"

"I want you to kiss me," she scowled, wriggling in his grip.

"That's not very polite now, is it?" The smile that had warmed her moments before had been replaced with a cold authority that weakened her knees in such a way she was glad he was still holding her up.

"I want you to kiss me, please," she whimpered. His eyebrow quirked. "Please Sir," she added hastily.

"Since you ask so prettily," he finally ducked his head to take her mouth. His lips were firm but gentle, a direct contrast to his fist in her hair with which he controlled the angle of the kiss precisely. His free hand pinned her wrists to his lap and she was trapped. Held immobile by his grip, unable to do anything but be kissed, she melted.

She felt her helplessness, how he'd reduced her to putty in minutes, and in place of the confusion she half expected she felt only heat. She moaned into his kiss and he smiled before taking the opportunity to run his tongue over hers.

All too soon he pulled back, leaving her reaching for him with her mouth with humiliating eagerness. She blushed and he laughed. Infuriating man. Intoxicating man.

Daniel released his grip on her hair and gently tilted her face up by her chin, forcing her to meet his gaze, which was warm once again.

"You okay, Just Maisy?"

She rested her cheek on his palm and smiled. Okay was an understatement, this man didn't only understand her strange desires, he knew how to tap into them with a few words and gentle touches. There was none of the shyness or, worse, clumsy violence that she'd experienced with hapless lovers who'd tried to fulfil her needs in the past. Daniel was utterly in control, dominant. It was his nature, just as submission was hers.

"I'm good, thank you. Really good."

"Good." He settled her so she was leaning into him comfortably with his arm around her shoulders. "This main room is a social hub even on club nights. Most weeks the equipment is kept in the other tunnels, apart from the really big stuff, so everyone can still come here to socialise and drink."

"What sort of big stuff?"

"It's mostly whipping posts that need the space," he said.

"Jesus," she muttered. For a moment there, snuggled under the nice stranger's arm, she'd forgotten that she'd wandered into a whole new world.

"The club is open every night, but it's mostly vanilla drinks and BDSM workshops apart from Friday and Saturday. Claude runs special events on weekends sometimes though."

"What kind of events?" Maisy's work brain switched into overdrive. Just look at the ceiling height, the decor, the exposed brick – she could throw one hell of a party in a place like this.

"You'll see. He's quite imaginative, our Claude. What are you thinking? Your eyes just lit up."

Maisy blushed, "They did? I'm an event planner, I was just thinking about the potential this place has a venue."

"I see. You'd best not tell Claude, he'll try to rope you into the subbie training scheme in exchange for borrowing your skills.

"He could try!" She laughed, but she could just imagine the main room filled with circular dining tables, a brass band on a platform above the bar, is fetish-formal a dress code yet? It could all be so amazing.

"So, will you come back? We'd love to have you."

Maisy blinked, his choice of pronoun reminding her that yes, other people did exist outside this booth, "Yes, of course. I mean, why not?"

"Good. I have to get back to work soon or Claude will have my guts for garters. You'll be alright? That table is full of beginners and other people on Claude's team of regulars if you wanted to mingle?"

"No," She shook away the strange urge to cling to him as he stood up, "I need to get up early in the morning, so I'll be off. Thanks for, you know, everything."

His absurd dimples deepened when he smiled in response to her awkward gratitude, "My pleasure. I'll see you soon, little Maisy."

He kissed her cheek and was gone, leaving Maisy feeling like she'd been frisked by a whirlwind. She was determined not to look back at the bar as she walked away. Play it cool, girl.

Yeah right, she'd been putty in the guy's hands. Was that like snuggling a double-glazing salesman when he's explaining his wares? Had she made a complete fool of herself? No, he'd just been giving her an example, a taste, a friendly introduction with a very friendly kiss. No harm in it and *wow* had he sold the goods.

Matilda was behind the desk sorting paperwork with a distinguished looking gentleman in a blue three-piece suit. His short dark hair and substantial beard was flecked with grey. She noticed now that they both wore black armbands like Dan's.

"Thanks again, Matilda." She said with a wave.

"One moment, please." The French accent told her that the distinguished man was Claude, the club owner who she'd heard so much about, "How did you enjoy your evening."

"Very well, thank you," she said, wondering why she sounded like a schoolgirl thanking a kind adult. Why did she feel the urge to call him 'Sir' too? Something about these people just radiated bow-to-me dominance, but in an entirely unobnoxious way. Impressive, really, she could use that effect at work when she was trying to hurry contractors into getting their act together.

"Did you see Dan?" Matilda asked, waggling her eyebrows in a goofy suggestive manner that shattered the scary broad image entirely. Maisy failed to conceal her laugh and Matilda gave her a questioning stare that just made Maisy giggle even more.

"Oh, I really must know what's amused you so much, little Maisy," she grinned, poised to get the secret with her no doubt exceptional interrogation skills. Luckily, Claude interrupted.

"Wait! This is Maisy?" Claude clapped his hands together as if Maisy had just been introduced as a long-lost cousin, "Why did you not say so! How was it with Daniel?"

"I don't know, I just-" Maisy stepped back, "He just sent me a message online, we don't really know each other."

"Getting ahead of yourself there, boss man."

"Yes, thank you, Matilda." Claude sighed, but his kind blue eyes held no real disappointment. "Forgive me, I have been hoping my friend would find someone for some time."

"Don't worry about it," she smiled, thinking about the way her mother behaved every time Maisy mentioned a man's name.

"So, should I get some membership forms?" Matilda batted her eyelashes, earning another giggle from Maisy. It wasn't like she'd been expecting to wander into a vampire den, but she was still relieved that she could imagine being friends with these perfectly ordinary, nice people.

"Sure," Maisy said, "Why not?"

JESUS CHRIST ON A SPANKING bench - that is why not. She'd managed to smile politely and say goodbye after receiving the forms, but all she could see was the annual fee flashing in neon type in her mind. Sure, the place gave off an exclusive and ritzy vibe, but wow. She could buy a car with that fee. A good car. She needed a lot of things more than she needed spankings or friends that understood her cravings or whatever it was she might get from Club Drift.

But if she didn't go back she wouldn't see Daniel again. She couldn't exactly go back to the forum and awkwardly ask him out for a drink without revealing why she couldn't return to Drift. How embarrassing would that be?

He was just being Mr. Welcoming Recruitment Drive anyway. Talking with him, kissing him, feeling herself respond to his mere presence with easy, calm submission - it'd all been amazing. But it didn't, couldn't, mean anything beyond that. He was, well, he seemed extraordinary, but he'd just been introducing her to the club. He'd given her an idea of what to look for. Just because it'd made her newbie stomach tie itself in knots doesn't mean it'd been anything other than a brief lesson for him.

Why would he be interested in someone so naive anyway? He could have his pick of members there with his looks and obvious experience, why clueless little Maisy?

Maybe she'd send him a message and ask if there were any less astronomically expensive clubs in the area, however humiliating that could be. Or maybe she'd go back to books. After tonight she wasn't sure she wanted to go out into the world and discover a bunch of Doms who weren't even Mr. Darcy let alone Dan levels of sexy. Lightning doesn't strike twice, after all.

Chapter 6
Perks

Dan was polishing glasses at the bar. Not because the glasses needed polishing, he just wanted something to do with his hands. Claude sat alone nearby, nursing a whiskey as he often did towards the end of an evening. He was watching people as they left, taking satisfaction from the happy faces. The owner tended to keep close tabs on what went on in his club. He treated the members as friends and some of them even as family. Claude was generous that way.

Dan kept polishing the glasses as he asked, "Did any of the newbies sign up tonight?"

Claude didn't turn around, but Dan could almost hear the knowing smile in his voice, "Maisy took the forms away with her."

"I didn't say anything about Maisy."

"You didn't have to, my friend."

"Your imagination gets better and better as you age, Claude."

"Forgive an old man his fancies, hmm?"

Dan snorted. Forty-something year old Claude was far from an old man and he was fitter than most of the younger men in the club. Still, 'Old Man Claude' was a running joke at Drift. He tended to act like a father figure to the house Masters and Mistresses, maybe it was the protective Dom in him or maybe he was just a bit of a control freak. Opinion varied depending on who you asked.

"Has William done any shifts this week?" Claude still didn't look around.

"Nope," Dan shook his head. William was one of the few other Drift Masters actually on the payroll, but recently he'd been AWOL more often than not.

"I'll deal with it." Claude turned his stool around, reached over the bar, and topped up his whiskey.

"Sure." Dan knew he wouldn't. William wasn't Claude's biological offspring, but for as long as he'd known them they'd acted like father and son. Whatever William's problem was this time, it'd sort itself out before Claude got around to confronting him and everything would go back to normal for a while.

"Your Maisy -"

"Not my anything, Claude," Dan threw the tea towel over his shoulder, listening attentively despite his protest.

"Your Maisy looked a little uncomfortable when Matilda gave her the forms."

"The fee?"

"Oui, I believe so."

"Thanks for letting me know."

"You could always nominate her. You've not availed yourself of that perk for, oh, it must be five years now."

"Four and eight months, yeah."

"You're not going to tell me how many hours?"

"Claude."

Claude held his hands up in apology. "I am sorry. I should not mock you on this."

Dan nodded, accepting the apology, and carried on polishing glasses, "I could nominate her, I suppose. Would you second?"

"No. As the one who decides if the nomination is valid I should not. Matilda might, though."

"Right." Dan had been polishing the same glass for a good two minutes now. The nomination perk had been designed to let dedicated Drift Masters and trainees get free membership for their partners, but it had been used charitably before.

He was pretty sure all of Matilda's annual nominations had been used to help less financially able wannabe members get in. That woman had deep pockets and a heart as big as her stilettos. Shame she was Domme to the bone, she'd be a good match for Claude in another life.

"She is inexperienced though." Claude said, in such a carefully measured tone that Dan immediately grew suspicious.

"So? She's not the first newbie you've taken in."

"Still, it would not be fair to give her the membership with no training or partner to guide her through."

"For fuck's sake, Claude."

"What? I merely thought that-"

"No."

"You don't even know what I was going to say."

Dan put the glass down on the bar far too hard. "You," he pointed at Claude, his anger spilling out in the gesture before he could rein it in. He started again, carefully, "You are trying to force me to spend time with someone because you're an interfering bastard."

"Did it ever occur to you that I'm trying to help?" Claude was infuriatingly calm, as usual, which made Dan feel like a small boy losing his temper with a teacher. He forced the anger down completely and lowered his voice.

"You always are."

"I was merely suggesting that you take on Maisy as a trainee for the first six weeks of her membership should you chose to nominate her. She is, I believe, too timid and inexperienced for the trainee programme and she'd benefit from one-on-one lessons."

Dan grunted, fighting the urge to shout several obscene variations of 'meddling git.'

"And Daniel, I hate to put you in this position, but if you refuse these terms I will reject your nomination of Maisy when you make it." Claude drained the last of his whisky and stood up to leave, paying no attention at all to Dan's furious expression. "Please, give it some thought." He said, and then he was gone.

"Interfering, bossy, domineering, nosey bastard wazzock," Dan hissed, throwing the tea towel into the under-bar laundry bin with so much force it fell off its supports.

LATER, ALONE IN HIS sitting room, Daniel rifled through Maisy's paperwork for the fifth time. Matilda had agreed to co-nominate her; all he had to do was phone and ask if she wanted the membership. Of course, he also had to broach Claude's ridiculous conditions. However much he'd like to just gloss over that part, he knew Claude wouldn't forget and it wasn't fair to Maisy not to mention it.

Dan glanced at the half-read paperback he'd thrown on the coffee table earlier, a pulpy thriller full of bad guys and zingy one liners. He could just go back to reading that, maybe get an early night, consider calling Maisy tomorrow lunchtime.

No, he was too riled up about this whole thing now. He'd sleep better if he got it over with tonight. He hated that he'd lost his temper with Claude, especially at the club. Dan prided himself on being patient and calm with all things in his life, but although Claude was an old and dear friend he sometimes poked Daniel's sore spots with a marksman's practised accuracy.

Five years since he'd used the nomination perk, not since Alicia. Damn Claude for bringing it up.

With a gruff sigh he looked over the nomination form once more. It couldn't hurt to help Maisy get a membership, he was old enough and wise enough to keep his distance and she was obviously a natural submissive. It'd be good for her. He glanced at his watch. Still a civilised enough hour to make a phone call. Just as it had been the last four times he looked and wouldn't be if he left it much longer.

Claude was a sly bastard, he must've seen how easily they'd slipped into a comfortable dynamic earlier. It was obvious to anyone watching how willing and eager Maisy became once her wariness had faded. And obvious how Daniel had responded to that transparent need in her.

They were compatible for these kinds of games, maybe even for more. Or they could be if Daniel had any intention of ever dating again. He'd love to be the one to coax that submissive side out of Maisy. She had so much potential.

He remembered the way her eyes had widened when his fingers had tightened in her hair earlier, her surprise fading to submission and lust. Her emotions as legible on her face as her phone number on the form. Gorgeous. So sweet and open in her responses.

A good-hearted newbie like Maisy did not need his baggage dumped on her. He'd introduce her to the club and its members, maybe do some light play if she really wanted to, then he'd kiss her goodbye and give Claude a good talking to.

Chapter 7
How big?

"How big is his thingy?"

Maisy groaned as she slammed the front door. Harry stood with her arms crossed in the narrow hallway of their home, her bright eyes scanning Maisy expectantly.

"Evening. Can I sit down?' Maisy gave the petite blonde a breezy smile and dropped her bag by the hall cupboard.

Harry pursed her lips, turned sharply on her heels, and stalked through to the living area.

"Sit."

I was sure I'd just left the Dom behind, thought Maisy, biting down on a chuckle.

"What? What's funny? Was there sex? Was there funny sex?"

Maisy chucked a throw cushion at the pint-sized chatterbox's head, "It wasn't even a proper date, let alone a shag fest."

Harry caught it and smirked, "Okay, at least a snog then?"

Maisy groaned again and slumped further into the sofa, but she didn't bother hiding her grin.

"Finally! I was about to ask if you'd donate your tits to me seeing as you weren't using them. For reals though, did you have a good night?" Harry dropped her interrogative stance, curled up besides Maisy, and unselfconsciously rested her head on her shoulder.

"Yeah, I really did. Went to this cool bar, maybe you'd like it." Maisy spoke before she could consider what Harry might think of Drift's weekend identity. "You need an expensive membership or a friend who has one though," she added hastily.

Harry snorted, "Sod that."

Thank goodness for cheap friends, Maisy thought.

"I thought you'd given up on men?"

"I had!" Maisy smiled down at the tufty golden head on her shoulder. Maisy and Harry had been friends since their first day at university. In fact, they'd lived together since university too. "But it was just a drink."

Harry found dating easy. She was funny, effortlessly likable, pretty, and nigh-on fearless. She was never shy of dusting herself off after a break up and getting back out there. Harry also seemed to attract the most attractive and eligible singles in any bar without lifting a finger which, despite her chesty assets, Maisy had never achieved. Not that she minded; she couldn't handle that kind of attention.

Anyway, nowadays she had some idea what she was really looking for in a man and it seemed less and less likely that she'd find it in any old bar.

Harry knew most of this as well, the only reason she teased Maisy about her persistent singledom was because she knew that it was more or less by choice. The teasing that ran through most of their conversations was a sign of long lived affection, as was the incessant nosiness. Harry still peered up at Maisy, waiting for any gossip that was as yet unshared.

"Okay. One, none of your business and I don't know; two, there wasn't any sex, sorry; and three...' She paused, enjoying Harry's interest, "Holy shit, he's just about the most attractive man I've ever seen."

"Well, in that case I'm jealous." Harry stretched her leg out and yawned, "You're seeing him again then?"

"I don't know. Maybe. Probably not." As she said it she realised that she really did want to see him again. Shit. Maybe he'd want to go for a drink outside the club? Maybe she could brush any questions about membership under the rug.

Harry sat up, forehead crinkled, "Why the fuck wouldn't you see the most handsome man in the world again?"

Before Maisy could think of an answer that didn't involve saucy acronyms and pricey clandestine clubs, the theme tune of their favourite drama started playing.

"Later," she said, knowing that Harry would abandon the investigation for the period drama. Maisy needed to figure out just what exactly she was going to tell Harry about Dan and Club Drift.

MUCH LATER, WHILE THEY were watching a rerun of Harry's favourite soap and sipping decaf coffees, the phone rang. Maisy fished it out of the sofa. Unidentified caller. She held the screen up to show Harry who responded by saying, as she often had before, "Answer it. It could be a gorgeous prince proposing to one of us."

Maisy rolled her eyes and pressed the answer symbol, "Hello?"

"Hello Maisy."

Oh gosh, that voice. That deep, dark voice that tonight had commanded her to obey. She must have been gawping, because Harry, her own eyes wide, poked her knee, reminding her that she hadn't spoken yet.

"Yes, sorry, yes this is Maisy."

"It's Dan," she thought she could hear a knowing smile in his voice. Did he realise the effect he had on her even over the phone? How embarrassing.

"I know." She said, pulling a disgusted face at her own stupid answer. Harry, smothering giggles, gestured for her to say something else. "How can I help you?"

At home, Dan grinned. He might not be able to see her, but he knew a flustered subbie when he heard one. Christ, he wished she was there in front of him, maybe kneeling on that patterned rug in front of the fireplace with those big, expressive eyes looking everywhere but at him. How would those eyes change when he ordered her to meet his gaze as she stripped?

He jeans grew uncomfortable at the mere thought of it.

"I just wanted to follow up on membership and see if you'd gotten home okay?"

The pause at the other end of the line was slightly too long to be natural. Claude was probably right about the fee being a problem, he was right about most things, damn him. He interrupted Maisy's silence to save her thinking of an excuse, "I just wanted to let you know that if you did enjoy tonight and if you were interested, you could have a year's membership on the house."

"Why? I mean, thank you, but why?"

Would she get the wrong end of the stick if he said he was nominating her? Maybe he should skirt the truth for now. "It was Claude's idea. We have a limited number of free memberships every year and we thought you might appreciate one."

There, close enough to fact.

"Okay, that's... that's really great. Thank you."

"Is that a yes, little Maisy?"

"Yes, definitely."

"Great. There's one more thing, not a big deal, but it might affect your decision."

Harry was distractingly mouthing the word 'yes?' at Maisy from the other end of the sofa.

"Okay, hit me." Maisy held back a grin. Did that count as an innuendo when discussing membership to a place where spanking was a regular occurrence?

"It's a prerequisite of the sponsored membership that you are..." He paused, apparently searching for a word, "Supervised by one of the house masters for the first six weeks. I'm the only one available at the moment. Will that be a problem?"

Supervised? What did that mean? Would he just follow her around while she awkwardly chatted up Doms? Instruct her on the proper safety precautions for each piece of equipment like a kinky high-school sex education session? Maybe, just maybe, he'd show her more of what he'd hinted at tonight, more of how submission could feel with him in control.

She swallowed, mouth suddenly dry. "No, no problem."

"Great." What was that odd tone in his voice? Relief? Disappointment? She couldn't place it at all.

"Are you around on Thursday evening? We could meet at the club to discuss it further. There's nothing much going on Thursday, so it should be much like tonight. Very low key."

"Yeah, that'd be great. Seven?" She gave Harry a thumbs up. Yup, definitely seeing him again, even if it probably wasn't the dinner date her friend might imagine

"I'll see you then. Be good." He hung up, leaving Maisy reeling for the second time that night.

"I'm seeing him on Thursday." She said, in response to Harry's questioning glare.

Even Club Drifts' lauded ceilings would have had trouble absorbing her answering squeal.

Chapter 8
More

Maisy was surprised to see a young blond man at the reception desk when she arrived at Club Drift on Thursday evening. Uncoupled diamante wrist cuffs glinted in the candle light when he waved at her and she flashed a nervous grin.

"Hi, I was sort of hoping to see Matilda. It's my first time and I'm just not sure, you know, about-" she spread her arms and gestured at the outfit she'd agonised over.

"Oh, well, let me set you straight there," he fanned himself in a comically lascivious pantomime then grinned at her, "You look perfect, honey, perfect. Don't you worry. It's Carl by the way, with a 'C.'"

"Thanks Carl. Maisy" She took the hand he offered, wondering why a handshake was necessary. A weird kink formality, perhaps?

Instead of shaking her hand Carl bowed and kissed it, showing off the turquoise glitter in his roots in the process. "First time, right? So, you'll need the booklet?"

"I think so. I filled out something on the open evening thingy, but Dan said something about a limits list?"

"'Dan said,' huh?" He fluttered his unnaturally long eyelashes as he passed her a neatly stapled booklet of forms, "Would that be Master Daniel the High and Mighty?"

Maisy pursed her lips, enjoying a vision of serious Dan in a crown and goofy cloak, "Uhuh, unless there's two of them."

"Oh no, honey, there's only one of him, no doubt about that." He winked cheerfully, but there was something unusual about the tone he used, like he was thinking about something other than Dan's indisputable attractiveness.

"Okay, what is it?" she asked after a moment, unable to shake the feeling.

"Nothing! Nothing! Shhh, you'll get me in trouble for gossiping."

He waved a pen at her, placed it on the forms, and turned to stamp an arriving couple's hands.

Maisy frowned and bent to fill in the forms. Page one was the same as before. Name, date of birth, next of kin, health concerns etc. However, when she turned to page two and saw the first part of the limits list she faltered. She had to decide all of this now? She didn't even know what some of it meant. What is a violet wand, anyway?

"Um, Carl..."

"Hmm? Oh! Don't you worry, honey. You can take that in with you and have a think. No sense in rushing, right? Our illustrious leader says it's more 'to 'elp le submissives think about their desires' rather than some necessary admin thing anyway."

Maisy laughed at his terrible French accent then froze as Claude emerged from behind the tall cabinet that screened the main entrance from the reception desk. Carl saw her expression switch from laughter to apprehension and chuckled.

"Ee is behind me, non?" He asked, laying the dodgy accent on even thicker and ignoring Maisy's appalled expression.

"You have never had any manners, Carl." Claude said, good-naturedly.

"Never, darling," Carl agreed, turning to bow to Claude as he had to Maisy.

"Never 'Sir,'" Claude corrected, mildly. "It's after nine, Carl. The club is open."

"And so I must degrade myself by being polite to you, I know, I know." Carl sighed, then winked at Maisy.

She noticed Claude was smiling as he shook his head. The pair seemed to be friends. Nonetheless, Maisy wasn't sure she'd dare to speak to Claude like that. There was something about his bearing that suggested he'd be proficient with the canes that were mounted on the wall in a striking attempt at decoration.

"Hello, dear Maisy," Claude smiled and kissed both of her cheeks.

"Hello - uh- Sir," she said, stumbling over the moniker, "I hoped I'd see you. I just wanted to say thank you so much for letting me have the membership. It's so kind of you, really."

"Not at all, little one. Besides, you must thank Daniel and Matilda. It was they who nominated you."

Carl's mouth dropped open as if he'd just overhead Claude confess his secret love for licking raw octopus tentacles in bed rather than a small detail like who nominated a newbie for sponsorship.

"What's the matter?" Maisy asked.

Claude turned to see what she was frowning at, before sighing exasperatedly, "Carl. Behave."

Carl rolled his eyes and mimed zipping his mouth up and locking it. He waved Maisy over using theatrical hand gestures because, presumably, he couldn't very well call her over with a locked mouth.

He leaned over the counter and stamped her hand, then, seeing that Claude was greeting a new arrival, whispered in her ear, "Find me later. Gossip." He winked and mimed locking his mouth again before passing her the invisible key.

"Ready to go in, Maisy?" Claude was by her side again, giving Carl a not so subtle silencing glare.

She nodded and waved at Carl, smoothing her frown away before she looked up at Claude.

"Thanks again, Sir."

"No problem. Maisy, do not listen too much to Carl's gossip, yes? He has good intentions, but he is, uh, how does Matilda put it? 'Addicted to drama.'"

If Carl heard him he didn't react and although she'd didn't know him well, Maisy couldn't imagine Carl not reacting to such a slight.

Maisy laughed, "I see. I'll be sure to remember that."

As Claude opened the door to the main club they almost walked into Daniel coming the opposite way.

Daniel grabbed her arm as she stumbled backwards, caught by surprise.

"Maisy," Daniel didn't release her arm when she steady again. "I was coming to find you."

Maisy felt his eyes on her as surely as his hand. Unable to find a proper greeting, she said, "Thank you for the nomination."

Daniel flashed an impenetrable look at Claude, who ignored it and placed a gentle hand on Maisy's shoulder. "I'll leave Daniel to see you in. Enjoy your evening, Maisy."

Claude returned to the reception desk to greet another newcomer without a backwards glance.

Daniel shook his head as if dispersing an unpleasant thought and took Maisy's arm in his properly. "Come on, sweetheart, we're blocking the door."

She was grateful for the support; she was sure that the impact of Club Drift's main room wouldn't be softened by her single previous visit.

It was a little quieter than it'd been on Tuesday, or at least it seemed to be; she later realised that people were just spread over a larger area than they had been before.

The shadowy tunnels that led to who knows what were partially lit tonight and a handful of people migrated that way as they entered. It seemed that the rules were a little looser than they'd been on newbie night because some of the outfits were...unusual to say the least. It still felt like walking into a secret underground London to Maisy. A woman wearing shimmery wings and a sequined bikini bowed her head respectfully at Dan.

On their way to the bar Dan greeted a man whose sharp, angular face Maisy didn't recognise. He was focused on setting up a wide rope barrier around a freestanding post that hadn't been there on Tuesday night.

The blond man nodded tersely as they passed, engrossed in his work. At the bar a red headed man wearing a full beard and a plaid shirt poured drinks and passed them to costumed waitstaff. His black armband seemed too tight on his thickly muscled bicep.

"Maisy, this is Master Matthew, Matthew, Maisy. A new member."

"Hi," she said, peering up at him over the preposterously over-sized metallic bar.

"It's a pleasure." His accent was American, but Maisy didn't know enough about the States to place him exactly. He winked as he shook her hand, "What are you drinking?"

"A gin and tonic, please."

"Just water for me," Dan paused, considering, "and my bag when you've got a minute, mate."

"No problem." Matthew tossed him a plastic bottle from under the bar and passed the mixed drink order to a passing barmaid before disappearing around the back of the bar's central brass column.

"It's busy, huh?"

"The location helps. A lot of members come in from the city after work."

"Makes sense." No matter what was going on over in those tunnels apart from drinking, and Maisy was trying hard not to speculate too much, Club Drift was a good bar. The kind of quirky good that you might find further East in London, but with extra benefits.

It would never get so uncomfortably busy you couldn't get to the bar to order a drink, partly because of the exclusive membership fees and partly because the place was so cavernous you'd need several buses full of people before you came close to capacity.

Maisy caught herself thinking about her company's biggest client and their annual Christmas party. With a room this size she could really go to town with theming and entertainment and still have over-sized tables. Maybe Claude would be open to hiring it out... No. Maisy redrew the line between Club Drift and work in her mind. Big important line - Do Not Cross.

Matthew returned and placed a sizable black leather holdall on the bar in front of Dan. "I hope I don't have to remind you of weeknight rules, Master Daniel," Matthew said, one side of his mouth curling up in a wry smile.

Daniel rolled his eyes, "I don't know, you give them a black armband and they think they're everyone's ma."

Matthew had one of those big booming laughs that only come from huge and merry men. He laughed so loudly on this occasion that a young waitress who'd been about to pass him a drink ticket squeaked. Still chuckling, he took it from her, "Sorry darling. Have fun you two!"

Maisy trailed a footstep or so behind Dan as he looked for a free area, "What are weeknight rules and why are they funny?"

They stopped to watch the man at the post finishing his preparations, "He thinks it's funny to remind me of the rules because he's been knocking around eighteen months while I've been here at least a decade now."

A decade? Wow. That's a long time to work anywhere, Maisy thought.

"I haven't always been on the payroll though. Used to just be advisory 'cause I've known Claude for -" He wrinkled his nose as he did the maths in his head, "Christ, about twenty years now."

"Did you go to school together."

He nodded, "Sort of, but we'll save the sweaty rugby stories for another day."

She flushed, "I didn't mean -"

"I know," He squeezed her arm and nodded at the blond man, who was now unravelling a long coiled... Oh wow, a long coiled whip. "Looks like William's doing a single tail demonstration tonight. You want to watch?"

Maisy quickly shook her head, "No, thank you." She noticed that Dan was watching her with that astute closeness again, trying to read her reactions, perhaps? She stood a little taller. She didn't want to seem afraid because she wasn't, she was just... Okay, maybe she was a little afraid, but bloody hell, a whip is a whole different thing from a spanking.

Dan's brow furrowed, "We'll see. Maybe it'd do you good to watch him work. He's very good, you know."

Before she could argue that even if he was the Beethoven of whippings, she still wouldn't want to watch, Dan had taken himself off to a nearby row of tables with benched seating.

Maisy looked at the intimidating man - William, apparently - who was testing the stability of the post by jumping on it with all his weight. Well, it looked like he wasn't getting started quite yet, she could always make Dan move tables when the demonstration began.

Dan threw his bag on the unoccupied table and leaned against it, the very picture of relaxed confidence. "Let's establish some rules for the evening."

"Rules?" Maisy placed her untouched drink on the table and tentatively accepted the hand he offered her.

"Absolutely." He tugged her closer and wrapped his arm around her waist, still holding her hand. With her back pressed against his chest, he was in the perfect position to whisper into her ear.

"We don't know each other yet, little Maisy, so we're going to have to talk to get things started."

Maisy's mind hesitated over that 'yet' for a moment. Just how well would they know each other?

He continued, his voice low and steady, his hand holding hers firm against her own hip, "I'm not your Dom, sweetheart, but I am your mentor, so I'll act as your Dom when we're at Drift for these six weeks. As such, I expect your behaviour at the club to be exemplary."

She shivered a little at the tantalising subtext to his words: if you don't behave there will be consequences.

Maisy felt his chest rumbling as he chuckled, "I won't punish you for making mistakes, but if we've discussed a rule and you've already been reminded... well then, sweetheart, I will take great joy in paddling your beautiful arse."

In her mind's eye she saw herself bent over his knee on one of Club Drift's many soft benches, his hand rising, her hands clenching in anticipation...

"That's acceptable," she said, her voice hoarse.

"Good." He brushed his lips across her cheek, "Rule one, little Maisy. You will use a safe word if you need to. That is non-negotiable. Do you understand?"

"Sure, I think so." She hesitated, wary of appearing even more naive than she was. "It's a word that stops everything, right?"

"That's right. The club uses the traffic light system, so even if you have your own personal safe word, everyone around will understand if you say 'yellow' or 'red.'"

"Traffic lights? So green for go, red for stop, and…"

"Yellow is, usually, a cue for the top to check in with the sub and make sure everything's okay. Maybe make some adjustments to play. All clear?"

"Yeah, I understand that."

"It's non-negotiable because it's the most important thing with power exchange, Maisy. You must be able to communicate any discomfort to me at a moment's notice. That's the only way I can give you everything you need."

Surprised by his serious tone, Maisy turned her head a little, so she could look him in the eye, "It's okay, I'll tell you if I don't like something. Of course I will."

His jaw tightened slightly, but all he said was, "Good."

Dan released Maisy from his gentle grip and sat on the burgundy bench that filled the wall near the table. He plucked a velvet covered cushion from its place and put it on the floor between his spread legs. The hot and commanding look he gave Maisy made her knees wobble slightly, so she was almost relieved when he gave her the simple order.

"Kneel."

Maisy took a step forward then stopped, caught between thoughtless obedience and the strangeness of the action. She looked at Dan, who just sat back and waited, exuding quiet strength and confidence. Somehow, that was enough for Maisy to kneel at his feet.

The cushion went some way towards protecting her knees, but she still felt the cold floor on her bare ankles. She looked at the floor, conscious that if she looked up she'd be staring directly at Dan's crotch.

Instead he leaned forward, resting his elbows on his knees, "Look at me."

She raised her eyes and met his. His irises were brown, almost black, in this light, even darker than his hair. She must have been smiling because he smiled in return. "How do you feel?"

She shrugged, "A little strange, I guess."

"Did you want to obey me?"

Embarrassed, she merely nodded.

"Words please, sub."

"Yes," she said, then quickly added, "Yes Sir."

"Good girl. And why is that, do you think?"

She squirmed under his intense gaze and equally intense questioning. "I don't know, it just... it felt like the right thing to do. It's fun, I guess."

"Good enough." He leaned back, "Place your hands behind your head. Yes, like that, but spread your elbows wider. Sit up straighter. Straighter than that."

Maisy obeyed the quick-fire orders, blushing as the position made her already prominent breasts look even bigger. From the corner of her eye she watched a pair of women walking by, holding hands and chatting. They both gave her appreciative glances on their way past which made her blush even more.

"Now, spread your legs for me."

She frowned at him, he merely returned her gaze with the same quiet calm and confidence.

Maisy looked down at her skirt, it was stretchy and long enough that she shouldn't reveal anything much. She lowered her arms, so she could support herself, but he said, "Keep your arms in that position please, sweetheart."

Scowling, she did as he said and awkwardly shuffled her thighs apart, all too aware of the cold stone floor and the less than graceful jiggle of her breasts.

Eventually, she managed to nudge the cushion to one side and spread her legs as far as her skirt would allow. She glanced up at him, half expecting him to tell her to lift her skirt. She wasn't sure if she'd object or obey.

"Sit up straighter. There. Beautiful."

The way he looked at her sent a spark of arousal right through her body. She'd never felt so exposed in so many clothes. The way her elbows were spread made it feel like she was framing her breasts, putting herself on display.

It was exciting, especially when he was so clearly attracted to what she was displaying. She shifted her back a little, determined to sit as straight and proud as she could.

"Many Doms, myself included, like to teach their submissives positions like this. Positions that they should perfect and display when asked. How do you feel about that?"

"I think I like it," she smiled shyly, her heart beating faster in her chest. How did she feel turned on just from this?

The crooked smile he wore as he watched her reactions was sinfully sexy, "May I touch you, little Maisy?"

Maisy nodded, skin tingling with anticipation.

He smoothed his hands down her arms, easing the goose pimples away with his tender touch, "Don't forget your safe words. Your only job is to relax and obey. Don't worry about anything else."

She realised she had tensed up and took a deep breath. It was strange, being touched by a near stranger in a public place. Even though he'd only touched her arms so far, her position made even the most chaste touch seem intimate. Her arms relaxed under his touch.

"Brave girl," he said, his approval evident. Why did that approval feel so valuable to Maisy? She hardly knew him, but obeying his orders gave her a deep thrill that she couldn't quantify. It was turning her on, sure, but it was something more than that too. "We're going to have to talk about whatever it is that makes you frown so adorably at some stage, sweetheart."

She scowled at him briefly before remembering where she was. "I'm not adorable, Sir."

Amusement lit his eyes, "Is that so?"

She bit back her reply, sure that it'd come across as rude no matter how she phrased it.

"Hm. Can I touch you more?" He asked, his line of sight telling her exactly what he wanted to touch.

"Yes," she said, subconsciously pushing her chest out further.

DAN CUPPED THE LITTLE sub's breasts, enjoying her startled squeak. She was shy alright, but she was new so it was to be expected.

"Push your breasts together for me, that's it." Her little hands pushed her cleavage up beautifully. She hadn't hesitated, although her brow wrinkled again now as if she wasn't sure why she obeyed so easily.

Dan bent to take a kiss, over-leaning to push her off balance. Her right hand shot out to his chest to support herself. He steadied her then growled in her ear, low and dangerous "I said push your breasts up, subbie."

He smiled as he watched a deep pink blush roll up her cheeks, her eyes darken, her hands quivering as she pushed her heavy breasts up for him. She was definitely submissive. She was enjoying carrying out his orders, even if she didn't understand why.

"Good girl." Christ, there was that shy, proud little smile again. That smile was catnip to a Dom. Sweet surrender willingly offered and control gratefully accepted - all in that simple expression. "Stay where you are, sweetheart."

He stood, watching to see if she moved her head to follow his movements. No, she sat perfectly still. She would be a joy to train properly, shame he wouldn't get the chance.

He hadn't been sure what, if anything, he'd use from his toy bag when he'd asked Matthew to pass it over. He'd merely intended to ask Maisy what she thought about using various toys at a later date. However, now he'd seen her ample breasts jutting out from under the flimsy fabric of her dress, he knew exactly what he wanted to do to her.

"You said you liked bondage, little Maisy?"

Her lips parted involuntarily and he thought he saw the colour in her cheeks deepen. "I like the idea of it."

I'll say you do, Dan thought to himself, but out loud he said, "Good, let's find out what you think about it for real."

Chapter 9
Rope and Whips

Maisy looked up, forgetting the previous order to stay still, and was startled to find he was now holding a neatly coiled length of rope.

The line of his mouth turned hard when he saw her move. The rope thudded onto the table and he gripped her chin between finger and thumb. "I said to stay still, sweetheart. Don't make me remind you again."

Maisy's breath quickened, "Sorry Sir."

He kissed her forehead, accepting the apology, and forced her face back down to its proper position.

Maisy felt sure that she shouldn't be aroused by Daniel manhandling her like this, but she was. What's more, knowing that he was watching her so attentively that even the smallest deviation from the rules would be observed and punished... well, it was just hot.

She tried to sit straighter, to push her breasts a little higher, spread her legs a little wider, knowing that he was watching.

"There's a good girl. You learn quickly."

She thrummed with pride, eager and ready for whatever was next.

"Stand up."

She stood, keeping her hands on her breasts as she did so, certain she'd earn some sort of reprimand if she didn't. He stepped closer, looming over her. She grinned at him, every order and correction made her feel more comfortable, less nervous in these strange new surroundings. His eyes crinkled at the corners, as if he wanted to grin back but had taught his features not to display his feelings. She adopted a less gleeful expression.

"You can smile, I like you smiling." He undid his cuff buttons and neatly rolled his sleeves up to the elbow before picking up the loop of hemp rope again. Her smile widened and she forgot all about her nerves as he stalked towards her.

He really was a sight to behold. His broad shoulders and thick arms flexed beneath his tight t-shirt as he unwrapped the rope with easy, practised movements. The hair on his arms was thick and dark like the unruly mop on his head. Everything about him from muscles to gait to confident smile screamed strength and power.

He swooped in for a brief kiss then spun her so she was facing away from him and the table.

"Give me your arms, Maisy."

She moved her arms behind her, stretching away the slight stiffness from holding her arms in one place for so long. She hoped that the rope was for what she thought it was for. She had so many fantasies about being immobilised by rope and strong hands.

A joyful shiver shook her as he gripped her wrists firmly and arranged them one on top of the other behind her back. With deft movements that betrayed experience he carefully bound her wrists with loops of rope. Then he added another separate rope which encompassed her shoulders, waist, and each breast.

She rolled her shoulders experimentally, she could move, but only a little. It was snug, but not uncomfortable. Daniel went around each loop slipping his fingers between the rope and her blouse to test the tightness. His obvious care and attention was almost as arousing as his skill. Her breasts jutted in little peaks, pushed up and out by the bondage. She felt beautiful.

"Thank you, Sir," she said, grinning widely.

"You like that?" He returned the smile and ran his hands along her waist and around to her breasts. When he pinched her nipples, she moaned aloud at the rush of pain and pleasure.

"What...?"

"The bondage lightly restricts blood flow to your breasts, makes them swollen and sensitive. Now make sure you behave or I'll add a clit knot."

A what? She must have looked appalled, because Daniel chuckled. She almost wished her hands were free so she could swat at him.

"You look beautiful bound for me, Maisy," he said as he turned her towards him by pulling her tied wrists. "Kneel over here for me, please, on the cushion again. Face this way."

She took a step forward, but she wasn't used to being bound like this and she staggered slightly. "Please Sir," she said, feeling shy about asking for his help with something so simple, "Will you help me?"

He nodded and she saw something like approval cross his face before he helped her down to the cushion. She arranged herself as elegantly as she could with the new impairment.

"How do you feel?" He knelt in front of her, a kind hand on her cheek. "Your knees holding up okay?"

"Yes, thank you. I'm comfortable."

"Good, but make sure you speak up if you get stiff, little Maisy."

Daniel moved to sit on the bench behind her. He tugged her cushion back towards the wall and she giggled as she briefly tipped into his thigh.

"There, we'll both be comfortable for William's demonstration now."

"Daniel, I really -"

He tugged her hair gently and pushed her head onto his thigh, encouraging her to relax, "I know it's not your thing and that's okay, but you're going to see a lot of stuff you're not into on a weekend here. You'll need to figure out how to cope with that. Maybe you'll learn something about yourself too."

Maisy leaned into him while she considered his words. She was half pissed off that he'd tied her up before bringing this up, but she knew in her heart of hearts that all she had to say was 'red' and they'd be out of there. And, truly, deep down she was a little bit curious.

"Okay."

"Okay." He stroked her hair as she leaned into his knee.

Kneeling there with him was surprisingly peaceful. The hand in her hair and the ropes on her body both restrained her gently and she felt comfortable. She was at his mercy and it was fun and relaxing, not scary at all.

While they'd been talking, William, his set up complete, had disappeared from the main area. Now he returned with a topless young woman in tow. Maisy recognised her as the barmaid she'd spoken to on newbie night. One of the trainees, then.

The trainee smiled at the various people who stood and sat around the fenced off post; a small crowd had gathered to witness the demonstration. Maisy saw Claude and Matilda talking to Matthew at the bar on the opposite side of the cavernous main room.

Although there were still some hushed conversations going on, everyone's attention was on the couple making their way to the centre of the room.

Daniel leaned down to speak quietly in her ear, "They'll just get right into it out here, but they've just come from negotiations. Claire's a masochist and an exhibitionist. Everything's agreed upon."

Maisy nodded, trying and failing to keep an open mind. She accepted that Claire had agreed to it, but she couldn't quite get her head around why or how she could possibly enjoy it. A whipping was a whipping, right? A painful punishment, surely. How could it be for fun, too?

William fastened Claire's arms to the post at a point above her head using the soft black handcuffs she already wore and some chain. He stepped back to take in her position then pushed her legs open a little further. From where she sat Maisy could see Claire laugh at the unexpected adjustment. William embraced her from behind, saying something that Maisy couldn't make out, but she did see Claire nod. When William walked away and picked up his coiled whip the huge room fell completely silent.

William was an imposing figure. He was average height, only a couple of inches taller than Claire, but the way he held himself made him seem taller. He wore a tight, plain black t-shirt with short sleeves that made his pale skin and blond hair seem almost white by comparison. He had a lithe, powerful build; all muscle and no fat.

Maisy was reminded of a tiger stalking its prey as he prowled around the whipping post's make-shift enclosure. The prey, meanwhile, had closed her eyes. Claire seemed poised and ready. Maisy saw the bound woman smile a little wider when the footsteps behind her stopped. The lash landed on her shoulder blade or at least Maisy gathered it had from the way Claire's shoulder moved. The whip moved faster than her eye could track.

A pause, thick with tension, then the thunderclap of the whip again. Maisy winced, the cracking noise alone was enough to turn your stomach. Claire, however, tensed when the blow hit then immediately relaxed with a tiny groan of pained ecstasy.

Maisy watched, fascinated, as William set to work. From where she was sitting she couldn't see Claire's back, but she figured the blows must be much lighter than they sounded. Although the whip was obviously hurting, Claire's expression became increasingly serene between groans and grimaces. Maybe she was drugged. Maisy glanced around the bar then up at Daniel. No, it wasn't like that. They didn't even let you have more than a few drinks here, it said so behind the bar. Whatever high she was on it was natural.

Maisy wriggled her shoulders, slowly becoming aware of the stiffness there. Dan placed his finger and thumb on the back of her neck, applying light but persistent pressure.

"What should you be saying, sweetheart?" He said, quietly so as not to disturb the performers.

"Um." Her mind had gone completely blank. She was focused on William's taut muscles and fierce countenance, his concentrated and skilled wielding of a vicious weapon that she'd never seen outside of a picture book before. A weapon that he was using to give what Maisy could only assume was a twisted kind of pleasure, given Claire's reactions.

Maisy was vaguely aware of Daniel muttering under his breath before she realised he was loosening the ropes on her wrists and shoulders. She was going to protest, but when she realised her breasts were still happily wrapped in pretty rope she let it go.

"Roll your shoulders, sweetheart. Come on, move."

If she'd been anywhere else she would have shushed him, she wanted to watch the performance. After a slow beginning, lashes dished out with tension filled lulls holding them apart. The whip was cracking in a more regular rhythm now, building to a crescendo.

Gently, Dan moved her arms to a more natural position. Maisy hissed so loudly that several people in the crowd turned to look. Carl, who was nearby with a statuesque blonde Domme, laughed then gave her a sympathetic look. He received a sharp swat on the arse from a be-ringed hand in retribution.

Thankfully, William either hadn't heard or was above distraction. Claire was completely oblivious to her surroundings. Her skin was lightly sheened with sweat and her head was bowed, a small smile played on her lips.

Still entranced, Maisy did as she was told and moved her shoulders and arms until they felt natural again.

"Now the legs. Keep stretching out until you can sit up here." Dan's hands rubbed her shoulders encouragingly.

Maisy managed not to hiss out loud when she unfolded her legs, but Christ did they burn. She must have been sitting like that much longer than she'd realised.

Eventually she managed to stretch her rebellious limbs out enough to sit beside Daniel. Before she could settle he pulled her onto his lap and held her tight. She didn't think to protest, because really it was exactly where she wanted to be.

She nuzzled into him happily, feeling the after burn from her frozen joints fading away. He shifted her slightly so she could see the performers again. Maisy had missed the grand-finale while she was settling in Dan's arms.

Now, William was taking Claire down from the post. He rubbed her shoulders and arms just like Daniel had rubbed Maisy's. William, however, took care not to rub his sub's back. Claire's face was streaked with sweat and tears, but she was still smiling, laughing even, as William spoke to her and made sure she was steady on her feet.

While William folded his whip and gathered his belongings, she waved at the gathered people as if she'd only just become aware of them.

William raised a hand to Daniel, who nodded in return, before taking Claire's hand and gently steering her towards one of the quieter areas in a tunnel.

"So, little Maisy, what do you think?"

She saw the livid marks on Claire's retreating back. Maisy thought about it, but was unable to come up with a meaningful sentence to describe how she felt about what she'd witnessed. Claire had obviously been in pain, but she'd been relaxed and happy as William helped her down from the post. She'd looked peaceful when she was up there, even when the whip made that awful noise. How did that work?

"I don't know," she said, honestly.

"You flinched a couple of times."

"I did? It's the noise, I think. It's so loud."

Dan nodded, absentmindedly stroking her arm, "It is that. It's a skill many admire, making the whip crack like that loudly, but still controlling the strength of the lash. Making the blow featherlight. He's very good."

"Mm."

Dan paused a moment then tried a different approach, "How do you feel about what we did?"

"What we did?" Maisy frowned, they'd just been watching the performance.

"I bound you, took away your freedom of movement. It hurt after a while, didn't it? You got sore because you're not used to it, but you still liked it."

Maisy nodded slowly, "Yeah, it did hurt a bit, but I liked it. It felt... peaceful. And it's a totally different thing."

"It is and it isn't." He pulled her closer to him with the ropes that still bound her breasts. "You and Claire both gave your bodies to someone else to play with and you both enjoyed it, even though it hurt. Your limits and experience and desires are vastly different, but trusting me or William to use your body in any way requires a similar power exchange, you see?"

"I guess," Maisy said, doubtfully. Various groups who had gathered to watch the demonstration now settled in free seating areas. The bar felt busier than before because the silence had been filled with echoing talk and laughter.

"Get over my lap, Maisy."

"Excuse m-" Daniel cut her off by pushing her head down and arranging her over his lap himself. His hand caressed her neck even as it held her down. Her arse was up in the air and the ropes around her torso felt tighter in this position.

"No hesitation." He said, his steady voice seemed at odds with his actions, "We agreed, did we not, that if you broke a rule you would be punished like this?" His lips brushed against her ear making her shiver even as she bristled in outrage.

"I didn't break any rules! This is ridiculous!" She kicked under his hands, feeling helpless as she realised he could hold her for as long as he wanted to.

"Shh, sweetheart. People are looking. Do you want to get spanked with an audience?"

She froze, mortified.

"There we are. Now, I'm not going to hurt you, but we agreed that if you were in pain or uncomfortable in the ropes you'd let me know. We agreed that you'd use a safe word if you needed to. Instead I had to figure out myself that you were hurting. That's fine, but I'm not a mind reader. I've got to know you're going to look out for yourself."

"Oh." Maisy said, realising that she had sat there in pain, then going numb without saying anything, too distracted by the show to pay herself any heed. "I'm sorry. I'll remember next time."

"I'm sure you will." He kissed her cheek and sat up, then spanked her left arse cheek hard. She cried out, surprised by the sting in the blow.

"Hey! I apologised." She twisted in his unshakable grip.

"I accept your apology." He said, then spanked her again, lighter this time. "But we didn't agree on an apology, we agreed on this." Another blow, and another, three sharp hits in quick succession.

Maisy felt like she would cry from the unfairness of it all. It didn't hurt that much and in any other context it might be exciting, but she resented being punished like a toddler.

Daniel was watching her face as anger began to turn into angry tears. "Oh sweetheart." He pulled her up into an embrace, "You've got to understand, Maisy. I need to be able to trust you to safe word or at least speak up when things aren't 100%. What if it was something more serious?"

"I would say something!" she said, wetly.

"I don't know that until you prove you can. You're putting a lot of trust in me, but I've got to put trust in you too, for both our sakes."

Maisy shook her head, but the logic of what he was saying got through to her. He'd given her one rule. Just one. And it had been a simple rule about safety. She'd agreed to this, hell, she'd been turned on by the idea earlier and now she was crying.

Unable to speak without spluttering all over him she loosened the embrace and placed herself back over his knee.

Chapter 10
What Happens After

He looked at her wordlessly for a moment, then nodded. "Good girl." He spanked her five more times, rounding it up to ten. Not too hard, but not limp handed swats either. She deserved more for her bravery.

He couldn't remember ever seeing a newbie accept she'd been wrong and admit it with her body so eloquently. It was alluring to see a submissive present her arse for punishment, sure, but seeing her vulnerable eyes full of tears as she acknowledged that she'd earned that punishment - it tugged at his heart. He wanted nothing more than to scoop her up and hold her for the rest of the night.

He knew, though, that it was risky to hold her for too long after a scene. The heightened emotions and sensations that came from even light scenes in the early days could easily be mistaken for other feelings. He didn't want to cause this sweet, brave little subbie any unnecessary heartache. Although, if he was honest, it wasn't her heart he was worried about.

No. He'd hold her until she stopped feeling unbalanced, as any Dom should, and then he'd let her go.

Until next week. Fuck, Claude had put him in quite a position here. However appealing Maisy was, he couldn't afford to get too close. He'd promised himself he'd never go beyond casual dating again, not after Alicia ripped his heart out and trampled all over his career in the process.

Seeing as Claude had sentenced Dan and Maisy to six tantalising weeks together, he'd have to be up front with her to prevent any sort of attachment forming. He'd have to be more disciplined with himself too. The urge to reward her bravery with affection had surprised him, but maybe it shouldn't have.

He'd stuck to demonstrations and casual play with experienced submissives, mostly trainees, for so long. How long since he'd done something slow, intimate, or training focused like they'd done tonight? It was a different kind of domination. A restrained waltz instead of the wild tangos he'd grown accustomed to. He'd missed it.

He signalled a passing waiter and pushed the troubling thought away. He mouthed 'basket' at the man and shifted his focus to taking care of Maisy. She was overwhelmed and confused right now. He should be taking responsibility, not going around in circles in his own mind about things that couldn't be changed.

He helped the still sniffling Maisy sit up on the bench beside him. He smirked a little when the cold hard bench met her pink backside and she winced. She didn't notice because she'd turned her head away, apparently embarrassed by her tears. He put an arm gently around her shoulder and drew her closer.

The sub waiter returned quickly, placed the basket on the table in front of Dan, gave a little bow, and departed.

MAISY WATCHED THE PERFORMANCE with ill-disguised fascination. "Does everyone have to bow to you?" A thought hit her and her noise wrinkled, "Do I have to bow to you?"

He chuckled, "Glad you've got your insolence back, sweetheart. No. I don't go in for much high protocol stuff. Xavier there is just a bit...formal. Good bloke though. Great goalie on our five-a-side team."

Well, that response raised more questions than it answered.

The basket that Xavier had fetched for Dan had a folded blanket on top, concealing its other contents. Dan lifted it, shook it out, and threw it over Maisy's shoulders. Before she could protest that she didn't need a blanket he passed her a handbag sized packet of tissues and a bottle of water.

While she blew her nose he rummaged in the bottom of the basket. She got the feeling he was giving her privacy more than he was looking for something, but he did emerge with a small bar of chocolate.

She reached for it, feeling more herself now her eyes were dry. He pulled it away at the last second. "Water first, subbie."

She rolled her eyes and pouted, enjoying playing the brat now they were... what did you call it anyway? He was obviously still in control, but they weren't doing anything bondagey. In recovery? She did have a shock blanket, for goodness sake.

Once she'd taken a few big sips he passed her the chocolate and relaxed into the bench, pulling her back into his side at the same time. "I once told Claude that I thought chocolate was an essential part of aftercare. The subbie baskets have had some ever since. Can't say the man doesn't listen."

She leaned into his comfortingly solid torso, too tired to feel any surprise at how secure she felt there. The rich, dark chocolate was like a restorative elixir. "It's exactly what I needed, I know that much. What's aftercare?"

He squeezed her shoulder through the blanket, "This. More or less. Everyone's different, just like everything else in kink, but for me and a lot of Doms I know play ends with a cuddle and a chat about how the scene went. Some people just do the chat, some people have a nap, some feel like they need to exercise, others just shake hands. I think it's best to do the chat thing, at the very least. In fact, it's another non-negotiable of mine: No play without a debrief after. The cuddle is optional."

She snuggled deeper into his chest. After the bewildering array of sights and sensations she'd just experienced the anchoring cuddle was very welcome. "That wasn't a scene though, right?"

He shrugged, "Depends how you look at it, sweetheart. You let me take control. I punished you. You were turned on, in pain, confused, and all sorts of other things in a short space of time. Seems to me it's a scene for all intents and purposes."

She was quiet. It'd been almost disappointing to think that was a scene. Shouldn't there be more...stuff?

But he was right, she had been turned on by the orders and the ropes, some of which still encircled her. The spanking had been painful and she still didn't know how to feel about it, but she did know she'd deserved it and taking it had felt right.

How comes she was crying and being swaddled in a blanket whereas Claire had just walked away smiling? Was she really that pathetic?

Dan sighed, "New rule. Stop thinking whatever you're thinking."

She snorted, "Good luck enforcing that."

Dan followed her gaze and saw the tunnel William and Claire had vanished into. "They're probably having a cuddle too, you know. Master William is an avid snuggler, don't let it get around or I'll let him snuggle you."

Maisy giggled at the absurd threat, but her eyes still seemed troubled.

He gave her hair a playful tug, "Out with it, little Maisy. What's bothering you?"

She shook her head, dismissing him, "I'm fine. Just a bit hormonal."

HE HADN'T MEANT THE tears, but that's what her mind jumped to. Interesting. Maybe she was bothered by showing emotion during a scene. He wanted to push her on the issue, get a straight answer, but he hesitated. She'd had enough for the moment. Chances were she didn't know exactly what she was thinking yet. Some bloke who wasn't even really her Dom nagging her immediately after her first public scene, however light it might have been, wouldn't help her tumultuous emotions.

"What do you think about saving the debrief until later. Your drink's ruined, we could go get another?"

She nodded, grateful for the reprieve.

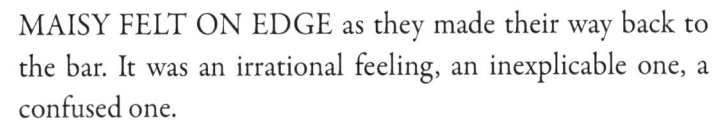

MAISY FELT ON EDGE as they made their way back to the bar. It was an irrational feeling, an inexplicable one, a confused one.

She was aware of Dan's arm around her waist. As they reached the bar she noticed William and Claude were having a quiet, but obviously intense, argument. She couldn't hear their words until William loudly stated, "Bollocks" and stalked away in the direction of the whipping post. A small group greeted him, evidently they'd been waiting to ask questions about the demonstration.

Claude shook his head and then, as if nothing had happened, smiled broadly at Dan and Maisy. "How are you, little Maisy? The ropes suit you well."

She blushed to her bones. She loved the ropes and how they clung to her curves, how they made her feel more womanly, and somehow erotically connected to the man who'd bound her. Having someone else comment on them, however, felt extremely odd.

Claude was friendly and generous and... well, he was gorgeous. If ever a man deserved the moniker 'silver fox' it was Claude. The compliment was thrilling and confusing in equal measure.

"Thank you, Sir. I'm well." She said with the formality she was slowly becoming accustomed to. Claude's bright blue eyes scanned her face closely then glanced up at Daniel.

Whatever Claude saw in Daniel's expression seemed to satisfy him, because his smile returned. "I must go deal with some paperwork. Please excuse me."

Matthew placed a gin and tonic in front of Maisy with a warm, "Here you go, pet." She grabbed it and took a refreshing gulp, she felt like she needed it.

"That's her first drink, Matthew," Dan said.

"No worries." The big redheaded barman adjusted his mental tally effortlessly. He leaned forward on the big metallic bar. "You busy? I've had a thought about the trainees."

Daniel glanced at Maisy. She nodded, hoping for some time to think. He paused for a few moments then kissed her forehead. After securing his arm around her waist he turned back to Matthew, "Go ahead."

Maisy almost sighed with relief. She'd never have guessed that just being under Daniel's keen scrutiny could be so tiring. It was exciting too, of course. Everything here was just so...much. So much more real and intense and strange and satisfying than she could ever have imagined. She ran her fingers over the smooth rope around her waist, following its path up her breast and over her shoulder.

He'd said he wanted to talk more about what they'd done that evening. A 'debrief,' he'd said. Maisy clung to her glass, grateful for the cool soothing beads of condensation. What would she tell him? What could she tell him?

It was amazing. It was scary. It was everything she hadn't understood she needed. A booth near the bar housed a quiet couple. The willowy submissive knelt, her head resting on her Dom's knee. His hand rested gently on her shoulder. They looked so peaceful, so at home. Maisy realised that without even knowing what to call it, she craved whatever it was that couple was enjoying. Peaceful submission?

She didn't know how to describe it and she was sure she couldn't ask Daniel to explain, but she wanted to be where that serene submissive was. Not just on her knees, but more honestly herself somehow.

Slowly, she tuned back into the conversation. She didn't follow all of it and there were a lot of unfamiliar names, but the gist of it was that the trainees on early evening bar shifts were often too tired to play afterwards and were missing out, so there needed to be a fairer system for divvying up work. Something like that. She wasn't entirely sure how the trainee system worked. She'd have to ask when she wasn't so full of her own feelings.

"Ready for drink number two, love?" Matthew said.

Both men had turned their attention to Maisy when they heard the embarrassing gurgling noise her straw made at the bottom of her empty glass.

Suddenly under the intense gaze of two Drift masters, Maisy understood how the proverbial deer in the headlights felt. "Yes please," she said, in a voice that was nearly a whisper.

Matthew gave another of his echoing laughs, "Look here, Dan, we've scared your girlfriend."

Maisy felt Dan's arm leave her waist as she saw Matthew's face fall. "Sorry pal, didn't mean to..."

"It's fine." Dan snapped. Maisy scarcely dared look up at his face. All the warmth and care and thoughtfulness had vanished to be replaced with icy nothing.

Without his comforting arm around her she felt a lot colder. Within a minute he'd smoothed the hard look from his face and replaced his arm around her waist, but Maisy was shaken.

What was so bad about the implication she was his girlfriend? What could cause a reaction like that? Matthew was still nearby, chopping limes while waiting for his friend to recover himself. He kept shooting glances at Maisy as if he'd like to explain, but he kept quiet.

Eventually, after a long and awkward moment, Dan's shoulders relaxed and he spoke. "Forgive me, Maisy. Matthew is an arse," He gave the American a wry smile, "and so am I." Matthew nodded as if accepting both statements as true and carried on chopping limes. "Look, we should take our drinks somewhere quiet and talk. I really should explain and -"

"It's fine," she said, even as her rational side protested that it really wasn't fine at all. "Maybe I should call it a night anyway, it must be getting late and I have to work tomorrow."

"No chance, sweetheart. Not until we've had that chat."

Non-negotiable he'd said, damn it. "Maybe we can-" Maisy's disagreement was interrupted by a flurry of shouting and frenzied activity from the nearest tunnel.

A man wearing a florescent armband ran out and waved in their direction. Matthew vaulted over the bar and ran towards the disturbance without a backward glance.

Daniel grabbed Maisy's hand and pulled her to a booth in the shadows near the bar. "I'm sorry, sweetheart, I've got to go help. I'll explain as soon as I get back." He paused, as if debating whether to leave her at all, but a female voice shouting from the tunnel Matthew had disappeared into decided him. "If anyone approaches you tell them you're under my protection."

She nodded vaguely, her own attention focused on the increasingly loud disturbance in the darkened tunnel. Dan kissed her then ran towards the commotion.

Maisy's hands gripped the edge of the seat. She considered leaving without hearing Dan's explanation or giving him his damned debrief, but she'd agreed to his terms. Anyway, she'd love to hear whatever his excuse was for that rudeness at the bar. Maybe the suggestion he'd date some incompetent newbie was inherently insulting.

Dan and the man with the glowing armband emerged from the tunnel first, an unfamiliar man struggling in their unbreakable grip. They moved towards the private staircase that Claude had indicated led to his office amongst other things. Matthew followed, his arm around a young woman with a furious expression and a livid bruise on her cheek.

As the unruly procession passed Maisy she saw that the woman wore trainee handcuffs and a t-shirt that had been ripped down the back. Maisy's faint irritation at Dan's behaviour faded with concern. What on Earth had happened? Thank goodness they'd reacted quickly, but it looked like that man had hit the woman hard, and obviously without consent judging by the fury in their eyes as they led him away.

Maisy was suddenly very glad that she had Dan as a mentor. She easily could have ended up meeting someone less kind if left to her own devices.

"Hey! Hey, new girl!" Bewildered, Maisy looked around for the source of the whisper.

"Carl? Where are you?"

"In the corner behind you. Don't make it obvious you're looking!"

"What in the world... Wow." She stifled a giggle. Someone had obviously got bored of Carl's attitude and ordered him to stand in the corner facing the wall. "No dunce hat?"

"Well sure, darling, but it's not on my head."

She spluttered.

"Bless your innocent heart. I just wanna wrap you in cotton – shhhhh."

Maisy was going to ask what was up, but stopped when she saw William coming in their direction, fierce prowling mode turned up to the max. He was still in a mood after his conversation with Claude, by the looks of it.

"Evening. Where's your Dom, newbie?"

It took her a moment to gather the courage to answer him. "Daniel? Daniel is assisting with a disturbance, Sir." William was looking past Maisy at Carl. She noticed his riding crop twitching. "Actually, I think they said they could use extra help. All hands on deck, you know?" She pointed towards the staircase.

His alarmingly bright blue eyes focused on her properly, "Oh yeah? Sounds fun. Thanks for the heads up." He tilted his head, catching the faint sound of a man shouting, before loping in that direction.

"You lie to him, new girl?"

"Not really, the guy who kicked off did look like a handful."

"Well, it's your arse on the line, I guess. Can you hear me alright?"

Maisy curled her legs up and shifted further towards the back of the couch, "Yeah, just about."

"Good. I'm glad we're getting the chance to talk, I didn't think the house crew would leave you alone, honestly."

"They're just being friendly because I'm new." She blushed. Was she receiving special treatment?

"Oh, I know, I didn't mean ought by it."

Maisy watched a woman in the opposite booth pour little droplets of wax from the table's tealight onto her partners hand while whispering something. Judging by the other woman's glazed expression, it was something filthy.

"You need to know what he's like, okay? I don't like to gossip, but it's just not fair if you don't know."

Goosebumps prickled up her arm. She hadn't wanted to listen, but really, it was only self-preservation. What if Daniel was secretly a violent arsehole and she was turning down friendly advice?

Come on now, Maisy. Don't make it some noble thing, you know you're just curious. "Don't know what?"

"I don't know what's been said, but you can't give than man anything, you hear? He's a major commitment-phobe. Usually refuses to play with anyone more than once. Never plays outside the club. Really touchy about subs getting attached, you know? I just thought I should warn you. A nice newbie coming in without a clue how he is might take him the wrong way, especially as he nominated you."

"It's okay, he explained that he's just helping me settle in. It was Claude's idea, I think."

Carl actually turned around, "Okay no, that is some bullshit. Papa Claude is going to get you hurt and I am *not* going to sit around and watch that."

"Trainee!" Matilda had heard the last bit at least, who knows what else. Carl turned white and dropped to his knees, apparently forgetting Maisy entirely.

The imposing Domme looked down at Carl as if he was a particularly ugly worm that had been crawling among her roses. "I'm too angry to discipline you twice tonight. Go find Master William. Go!" This last was barked when Carl gave her a dismayed glance. "Stay on your knees."

Matilda watched him leave the corner on all fours then sat opposite Maisy. Maisy watched her, awe filled at the transformation from friendly receptionist to devastatingly beautiful leather clad Domme. The other woman took a deep breath before smiling at Maisy, "Where's your Dom hiding?"

"He's in the office with Matthew and William and some arse who caused a problem, uh, wait, I can't call you 'Sir.'"

She laughed and relaxed into the booth, flinching when the boning in her corset poked her rib, "Ma'am is fine."

"Ma'am, cool. About Carl-"

"Ugh, do not get me started on that drama queen. I nominated him last year and he's been nothing but trouble. Sweet as sin and fun to play with, but he likes to stir the pot."

"Yeah, I'm hearing that a lot tonight." Maisy's expression must have said more than she meant it to, because Matilda scooched closer.

"Don't listen to him. He's right about Dan being a commitment-phobe, but Dan's not some player, okay? He's got his reasons and he'll do right by you. He always does."

"It's fine, honestly," Maisy smiled, but she was still a little unnerved by Carl's stark warning and Dan's behaviour at the bar.

"What do the fluorescent yellow bands mean?" Maisy asked, keen to change the subject.

"They're for the dungeon monitors, the DMs, who patrol the scene areas and make sure everything's safe. There's usually only one on a weeknight because there's no nudity or heavy play until the weekend. All the masters pitch in on Fridays and Saturdays though." Matilda glanced around, "Actually, if Joe got involved in the same thing as Dan I should step in now. Claude hates leaving the scene areas unwatched."

She put an elegantly manicured hand inside her bustier and rummaged for a moment, it emerged holding a fluorescent band.

"Stop gawping, newbie. Fetish wear never comes with pockets." She winked and fastened the band around her arm. Somehow the absurd colour didn't detract from her impressive appearance in the least. "Be good."

"You too, Ma'am," she replied, earning an eye roll. Maisy could see the Domme becoming a firm friend, given the chance. She hoped she'd get the chance to make friends here.

As she watched Matilda walk away into the gloom of the tunnels she thought over what she'd said. No nudity or heavy play on a weeknight, huh? That must be what Matthew had meant by weeknight rules.

Chapter 11
The List

Across the room, Maisy saw Dan's amusement as Carl descended the stairs on his hands and knees. Neither Matthew nor the DM had emerged yet, maybe Dan had excused himself to get back to Maisy. She almost snorted at the absurdity of the thought. No, they must have had no further need for Daniel once they got the violent man upstairs to Claude, especially with William following.

Dan detoured to the bar on his way over to the shadowy booth. He didn't bother ordering drinks from the remaining bar staff, choosing instead to pour them himself. Maisy could see the tight-lipped smile of the closest barmaid. The trainee apparently objected to his behaviour but didn't have the authority to speak up. It was fun to watch her trying to wipe the disapproving expression from her face.

Luckily, Dan didn't notice the bar staff at all. He was focused on returning to Maisy.

"Sorry about that, sweetheart." He put the much delayed second gin and tonic in front of her.

"No problem," she said, grabbing the drink eagerly. "Is she okay? What happened?"

Dan sat down beside her, glass of whiskey firmly in hand. "Kelsey's fine, just pissed off. He was a new member this month, didn't catch the name. He won't be back again."

"Gropey arsehole?"

Dan shrugged, "More or less. Not a Dom anyway, just a pushy, entitled, handsy prick."

"Do you get a lot of that here?" The atmosphere of safety that Maisy had begun to value in Drift suddenly felt a little unstable.

Dan shook his head, "Absolutely not. One slips through the vetting process occasionally, it's inevitable, but only once in a blue moon. New members are watched pretty closely too, people like that guy get caught out quickly. Most of them leave when they realise they have to put some effort in anyway. You're safe here, sweetheart."

She smiled; he'd seen her concern then. He was certainly observant.

"There's something you should know, Maisy."

"Oh yes?" She sipped her drink, keeping her expression neutral.

He hesitated before he spoke, appearing to choose his words as excerpts from a longer script. "I am out of practise."

"Okay?"

"It's been a long time since I played with anyone new to the lifestyle, even longer since I trained anyone. You understand?"

"I think so, yeah." Was he going to explain why? There must be a reason the word 'girlfriend' makes him flinch and everyone knows him as a commitment-phobe.

"I'm not-" he hesitated again, "I am not used to seeing the same submissive multiple weeks in a row. I don't date because I don't do attachments. I don't want you to think I don't want you. You're a beautiful woman and I'd be honoured to continue helping you to settle in to the club, but I don't want to lead you on." He kept breaking eye contact. The relaxed man she had been obeying all night had vanished.

"That's fine. Really. I assumed you were just doing it as – I don't know. I'm not expecting anything." Never mind Harry's double date plans then. "So why do we have to do this, if you don't want to?"

"It's not that I don't want to. It's just complicated and Claude interfered, as usual."

"So, how long do we have to-"

"You don't have to. If you want to be a member here I'll help you settle in in any way you like. I'll give you my full attention for the next six weeks, unless you decide you don't want it, in which case I'll bugger off and Claude can stop playing games. You'll still get your membership, I'll make sure of it."

Maisy nodded and glanced around the busy bar area. Having someone she knew help her settle in had seemed unnecessary, but now she was ankle deep in this strange environment she recognised the value of a mentor.

She knew, rationally, that all of these people were perfectly normal and probably very friendly, but if she had to introduce herself to the people in lizard make-up over by the bathroom or that guy with such a large cage on his genitals she could see it through his pleather trousers she'd wuss out and just sit in the corner the whole night. And that's without worrying about looking for someone to make her feel as aroused and safe as Dan had with the rope earlier.

So what if Daniel was only doing this as a favour to his boss, she'd never expected someone as green as her to catch a Dom like Dan anyway and it was nice to have someone to talk to.

"On board, little Maisy?"

"Why not?" She grinned as if it was nothing. "Will you help me with this list thing then, Sir?"

He grinned when he saw the booklet that contained the limits list, "That thing is a whole lot of fun. I should warn you, if you let me be your Dom while you're here I will work with you to make sure you are honest about your limits. If you are being far too timid you will not get anything out of the experience here, understand?"

She frowned, "Yes sir."

"But?"

"But?"

"Why do you look so unhappy, Maisy?"

She made an effort to smooth her forehead "I'm fine, Sir."

He sighed, "Remind me at some point that I owe you a spanking for lying. If you forget to remind me you'll get double."

She gulped, her bottom still stung from the last time. "It's just, don't take this the wrong way, but limits are so I can protect myself, right? That's the one thing I don't want you...I mean anyone to control."

He nodded and pulled her into his side, a position she was starting to like very much. "Sorry. I can see why you'd misinterpret what I said. Like I said, it's been a while since I've had a sub of my own or even been trainee Master here."

She wanted to ask why. She'd assumed all the 'house crew', as Carl called them, helped with the trainee programme, but something told her that Dan wouldn't share his reasons.

Maybe Carl would fill her in another time. Dan affectionately tweaked a lock of her hair and she felt a pang of guilt. No. No more gossiping about him. That wasn't on, especially as he'd ended up telling her everything she'd heard himself.

"What I meant to say was more that I'll help you consider your limits so you understand how serious you are about them, yes?"

When she frowned again he swore and rubbed his head with his free hand. "Sorry, sweetheart. I'm not going a good impression of an all-knowing Dom today, hey?"

She chuckled and shot him a cheeky look from under her eyelashes. "Third time lucky, Master Dan."

He gave her hair a less gentle tug, "Watch it, subbie." But she saw the corner of his mouth turn up.

"Okay let's try an example. I once knew a sub who walked in here with her limits list already filled out. She didn't want any pain beyond a gentle spanking, and no full nudity, no public sex, humiliation, no anything. And that was fine. She made a good show of knowing what she wanted and we won't turn a trainee submissive away because she isn't kinky enough.

"If all someone needs is a firm hand, some gentle orders, and a Dom to kneel for that's more than fine with us. Hell, sounds like a perfect Sunday, right?"

"So what happened?" She noticed that she was stroking little circles on his arm with her fingertip while he spoke. He didn't seem to mind.

"She was miserable," he said. "She watched the other scenes and longed for them even as she refused to explore anything new. She'd brat like no-one's business hoping to goad someone into hurting her more as punishment. She'd rub herself up against the Masters hoping to get fucked."

Maisy nodded, "She was wrong about what she wanted?"

"In a way. She ticked the boxes that made herself feel safe and acceptable. That's common in new subs, but for me to give you what you need I need to know more than that. I need to know what turns you on, what scares you a lot, what scares you just a little, what little itch you have deep inside you that's just begging me to scratch it."

The dark rumble of his voice was hypnotising. He reached his arm further around and placed his hand on her breast, heavy and possessive. She jumped, but settled after a breath. It felt oddly comfortable.

"I understand," she said in a husky whisper.

"I hope so, because we're going to test some limits next time. I want you to think about what you want between now and then. Now, let's revisit how you feel about bondage after trying some ropes..."

Chapter 12
Home

The sunlight came through Maisy's haphazardly drawn curtains in the usual way. Dappled light and shadows drawn by leaves danced across her bedspread bringing the embroidered flowers to life. The gentle hum of Harry's radio in the room next door and the less gentle rumble of her snores.

Maisy stretched in the usual way, legs first - down with pointed toes, then wide like a starfish. Usually she'd stretch her arms out next, encountering her phone or a paperback abandoned somewhere under the covers in the process. Today, however, Maisy stretched her legs out wide and was confused by an unusual twinge of pain.

In an instant she was reminded of the events of the night before. She hadn't realised that he'd spanked her hard enough to feel it the next day, but the faint sting as she pressed her arse into the mattress confirmed he had.

She wondered if she had a bruise in the same way one might wonder if they'd caught the sun. Like a traveller hoping for a suntan as a souvenir.

In her bed, in the warm morning breeze, Club Drift felt more like a dream than a memory. The unassuming door in the disused railway arch was like a wardrobe portal to her own secret Narnia.

She'd wandered from the streets of London into a place that was as friendly as it was alarming. The people there were strangers to Maisy, but now she'd been inducted into their world, they all shared a secret.

Maybe that was why everyone smiled at her if she caught their eye. They didn't know each other yet, but they were friends by default. Bound by their passports to this subterranean fantasy world.

Does that make Claude a religious sermon masquerading as a lion? Maisy rolled her eyes at her own ridiculous train of thought. Drift was no dream. Neither were its inhabitants and owner. Neither was Daniel.

Maisy rolled over and hugged her pillow, giving her sore arse a little breathing space. Daniel was something else entirely. Not a dream or a fantasy, although he looked like he belonged in one.

The way he'd focused on Maisy's every reaction, watching her carefully with those intense dark eyes, made her feel safe. It was partly because of his attentiveness, she thought, that she'd been brave enough to try things out last night. She hadn't realised how daunting it'd feel, even the simple things like kneeling, but he'd taken away her fear every time.

He had a straightforward way of speaking that pleased her. It wasn't bluntness, although it was close to it at times; it was just unfiltered honesty so far as she could tell. He explained things that she had no idea about, and half the time was too nervous to ask about, without patronising. He seemed to enjoy sharing knowledge about the club as much as she enjoyed learning. As for the rest, his enjoyment of that was without question.

It was strange, but kneeling for him, being bound for him, just following his orders was more arousing and intimate than some sex Maisy had experienced in the past. And that was just the taster. A sip before the full glass.

She'd certainly been right about her desires; they were more than a mere fantasy, but how would she handle more when the taster left her feeling like she'd been kissed for the first time?

Harry's alarm went off, shattering the birdsong and Maisy's peaceful thoughts. They had a family dinner to attend and Harry wasn't one to be late for free food.

———◆———

"WE'RE HERE!" MAISY shut the door haphazardly and breathed in the welcoming scents of home - freshly cut grass, cinnamon, and leather.

Her dad's muddy boots were in the hallway instead of the porch again and her mum's collection of scarves had upsized from the hall stand drawer to a huge freestanding basket. A new photo of her brother's tiny son had appeared on the wall. There were always little changes from week to week, but this house still felt like home to Maisy. She suspected it always would.

Maisy's mum came running from the kitchen covered in flour from blonde bob to fluffy slipper toe. She hugged both girls at once, not bothering to apologise for the powdery mess she was making of their clothes. Harry was a second daughter to Carol and often filled the gap left at the table by Maisy's busy brother James and his little family.

"Did you make crumble?" Harry asked the moment she disentangled herself from the motherly hug.

"I'm fine thank you, Harriet." Carol tutted and patted Harry's shoulder affectionately. "Of course I did. I couldn't forget my favourite girl's favourite pudding."

Maisy stepped back from the huddle in mock outrage. "She's your favourite now? How dare you. I'm a better baker and I have fewer ripped tights."

"Come here, girl, you'll always be my favourite." Maisy's dad, Geoff, emerged from his den wearing a wide grin. He must have been hiding from the kitchen havoc with a book. The walls of his little room were lined with well-stocked shelves. Maisy hugged him happily.

"Dinner's nearly ready. Do you want to settle yourselves at the table...?" Carol let the end of the question linger a little longer than was necessary.

They all decided to help her finish up in the kitchen instead.

Chapter 13
Dinner Table Conversations

"So," Geoff leaned back and rested his hands on his ample stomach, "What's new with you girls?"

They'd polished off the pork, twice as many roast potatoes each as any human should eat in a week, and a large portion of rhubarb crumble with custard. They were the very image of sated gluttony; each slumped in their chairs and grinning slightly at nothing in particular.

"Nothing much." Maisy took a tiny sip of water, "Work's the same, living with this human jack-in-a-box is the same..."

Harry reached to the empty chair to her side and raised a cushion threateningly, grinning when Carol tutted.

"About work, have you...?" Geoff didn't need to finish the question. The three of them had been nagging her about looking for a new position for weeks, but Maisy hadn't yet found the courage.

"Oh, you know. I've not really had time what with the wedding season."

Geoff nodded glumly, "Right-o."

Maisy had begun to wish she'd never told them how bad Michael had been recently. She'd just been so frustrated after another day of the idiot undoing her good work and sleazing about the office she'd needed to unload.

Immediately, they'd been outraged. What's family for if not a bit of supportive outrage? However, they'd also demanded that she take action. Get another job, start her own business, stage a mutiny (Harry's pitch, obviously). Honestly, it'd been a bit much.

"Your brother wouldn't put up with this," Carol said, not for the first time.

"Mum -" Maisy bit her tongue. Maisy's brother had a big temper and a wilful streak that'd cost him several jobs when he was younger. He might have it under control now, but Maisy did not like the implication that she should be more reactionary, like her brother, rather than biding her time as she was now.

She'd look for another position when everything settled down a bit. Michael Snr. had only been in the ground a few months; it seemed wrong to abandon the company she'd loved for so long so soon after he passed.

"Fine. What about you? Anything new, Harry?" Carol asked, an easy smile replacing the motherly frown that clearly said, 'this conversation is paused, not over.'

"Maisy's got a boyfriend!" Harry shrieked before hiding behind the cushion with a peal of laughter.

Stunned silence met this announcement. Both parents stared at the girls, mouths agape, trying to work out if this was another of Harry's jokes.

They weren't prudish, in fact they were well used to discussing Harry's escapades over the dinner table. Generally, Geoff kept his mouth shut and his eyebrows raised during those conversations. Maisy's love life, however, was so barren it rarely warranted discussion.

"Maisy?" Carol couldn't disguise the hope in her voice. Bless her, apparently one grandchild wasn't enough. She always sounded a tiny bit disappointed when she had to respond to well-intentioned enquiries about Maisy's love life with a cheery 'Nothing to report!'

She'd had flings of course, but nothing serious enough to mention. Maisy had been more interested in work than dating for some years as her mother knew very well.

Speaking of which so did Harry, and what had happened the night before with Daniel definitely did not constitute 'dating.'

Maisy glared at Harry when she peeped out from behind the cushion, "That's not quite true."

That clearly wasn't enough for her parents. Her mum smiled encouragingly and her father seemed keen to learn more too, even if his eyebrows had started to creep towards the ceiling.

"I went on a date." Maisy crossed her fingers behind her back knowing full well her second encounter with Daniel in a London BDSM club wasn't exactly what her parents would call a date.

"He seems nice and I want to see him again. That's about it."

Carol and Harry exchanged a loaded look.

"Shall I put the kettle on?" Maisy asked with a bright smile. She didn't wait for an answer before striding off to the kitchen.

She wasn't cross with Harry, not really. It was just the sudden thrusting of Daniel as a possible partner into her consciousness that had riled her. She'd considered it briefly last night, when they'd been cuddling, but she was still convinced that that he was more interested in marketing the club than seeing her.

Why would an experienced, gorgeous guy like him be interested in a clueless newbie? Anyway, everyone at the club, Dan included, had made it very clear that dating wasn't an option.

She loosened her grip on the kitchen counter and took a deep calming breath. It wasn't as if anyone here knew what Daniel was to her and if they asked after the six weeks were up she'd just say it had fizzled out. It's natural for them to be curious. It wasn't a big deal.

He is a big deal though, she thought to herself before pushing the troubling thought away.

The kettle clicked off the boil and Maisy realised that she hadn't even got the coffee pot out of the cupboard.

"Maisy?" Harry's wide eyes peered around the kitchen door. Maisy smiled, determined not to make a fuss.

"Sorry, I think I ate too much." She started pulling the coffee pot and cups from her mum's meticulously ordered cupboards.

Harry fetched the tray from its usual place and sidled up alongside Maisy.

"Sorry," she said, giving Maisy's hand an affectionate squeeze, "You just seemed so giddy last night I thought you must be smitten with the guy. I was only teasing."

"It's fine," Harry was a jokester, but her good nature ran deep. How was Harry to know that her smile was more to do with experimenting with light BDSM than any grand romantic emotions? And if Maisy thought that there might be more to it than that then she certainly wouldn't say so to Harry, not if she couldn't even admit it to herself.

MAISY TOSSED ANOTHER ripped pair of tights over her shoulder. The laws of sod dictate that when you're in any kind of rush you'll never be able to find clean, intact underwear. She decided to forego tights in the end. It wasn't a cold day and she'd be entrenched at her desk for most of it in any case.

"You okay in there?"

Harry. They hadn't spoken much since they got back from Maisy's parents place on Friday.

Maisy opened the door and smiled brightly, "Fine thanks!" It sounded false even to her own ears.

Harry looked even shorter than usual, her bounce temporarily diminished to make way for contrition. She held something behind her back and for a moment Maisy had a strange feeling that she was going to present her with a bunch of flowers or a kitten.

"Look, I know I ballsed up." Maisy shook her head, but Harry interrupted, "No, I did. I shouldn't have teased you like that at home. I thought your dad's ears were going to fall off."

"It's fine, really." It was fine. Maisy hadn't even realised she'd still been a bit cross until Harry turned up just now. "You didn't do anything wrong I'm just..." Just what? Hormonal? Confused? Having a tiny sex-fuelled identity crisis?

"Doesn't matter." Harry said, her infectious smile returning full force now she'd been forgiven. "So, I was going to save this for your birthday, but I thought you might like it now. Close your eyes."

Maisy closed her eyes and held out cupped hands. Harry placed what felt exactly like a book in them.

"Okay. Open." Harry was still holding the book that was now in Maisy's hands. It was a new copy of her favourite romance novel. The one that she'd loved and reread quite literally to shreds.

Before she could thank her for the much needed replacement, Harry opened the book to a few pages in.

To Maisy, May you always have a book in your hands and love in your heart. Carrie Ridley x

"Oh wow." Maisy didn't know what to say. Her big mouthed friend had a big heart to match.

"She was in town the other week. And before you say anything, no I didn't ask when the sequel is coming out. The woman ahead of me in the queue asked and I got the feeling she was the 999th to do so. That author lady has an excellent death glare."

"It'll come out eventually." Maisy said, running a finger over the inscription.

"I'm glad I've sent you in to rapture, but you're late."

"Crap. Thank you, Harry. Really." Maisy put the book carefully on the bed then gave Harry a bruising hug. "See you tonight."

Chapter 14
Club Drift

Maisy found herself sitting opposite Club Drift's owner just after opening time, both of them nursing a cold drink.

Claude had been in reception when she arrived. In fact, it was almost like he'd been waiting for her. Claude had swept her through to the main club before Carl could say hello. Maybe Matilda had reported back to the boss about Carl's gossiping.

Every time the door that led to the offices and changing room opened Maisy started. Was it Daniel this time?

"I don't know what is taking them all so long. Talking about me, I expect." Claude stood, looked over at the bar, towards the main entrance, then at the stairs in the far corner that led to a door marked 'private'.

Maisy felt a twang of guilt. Claude should be supervising his business, not babysitting her. She was trying to think of an appropriate way to tell him it was okay to leave her when he called out a greeting.

"William!"

Maisy recognised the lithe figure with fierce eyes and almost white blond hair as the whip wielding man from Thursday night. He was loping towards them at an alarming speed.

She instinctively leaned in behind where Claude was standing, some subconscious part of her eager to conceal herself from this intense man. She noticed that he gripped a riding crop very tightly in his right hand.

"I'm here. Happy now?" He practically barked at Claude. Despite the man's alarming appearance, she couldn't help being reminded of a teenager stropping at their parent.

She looked between the two men – father and son perhaps? No, no way was Claude old enough for that, William had to be over thirty. Maybe a wayward brother then?

Claude's expression remained impassive. "Perhaps you could introduce yourself to our new member instead of parading around in a temper."

William's fierce blue eyes focused on her for the first time and she sat up a little straighter.

The man pushed past Claude and knelt before Maisy in one smooth motion, his expression softening in an instant. How'd he get to be so elegant anyhow? She'd look like a stumbling kitten if she tried that (she should know, she'd practised kneeling in the mirror). Speaking of which -

"I thought you were a Dom," she blurted out.

Claude tried, and failed, to stifle a laugh. The man in front of her merely raised an eyebrow. That cool intense gaze still held her motionless and she belatedly realised that he was wearing a black Master's armband just like Dan's.

Of course he was a Dom, what else could he possibly be?

"Sorry, I just meant, because you were kneeling. Um...nice to meet you properly, Sir."

He chuckled and bowed his head, hiding his crinkled eyes. "Mistress Maisy, it's a pleasure."

She blushed down to her heels, "I really am sorry, I'm just..."

"Nervous," Claude interrupted, "And no wonder. Maisy is new to our way of life and to your teasing, my friend."

The strange man took her hands in his and kissed each reverently. "Call me William. I apologise for storming over here like a pit bull, but not for teasing you because I like the way you blush, love."

She giggled tentatively and Claude sighed. "Need I remind you that you're on duty tonight, William?"

The younger man rolled his eyes, not bothering to look up at Claude. "It's good to meet you properly, Maisy. I'm not as bad as the other subs say, promise." William gave her a wink and pulled himself onto the seat beside her with another display of impossible grace. "Alright, fill me in," he said, instantly affecting a business-like demeanour.

Master Claude sat down at his other side and the men discussed the nights rota. William was going on DM duty in the main tunnel first, then someone called Ben was going to take over, then Matilda was taking the last shift.

Daniel wasn't going to be on bar tonight. Was that because of me, Maisy wondered. Claude was going to pitch in, something that William found hilarious for some reason.

His informal London accent clashed almost comically with Claude's rich French lilt. She hadn't noticed it when he'd been kneeling in front of her. Strange. She cleared her throat discreetly.

"Yes pet?" William's eyes turned on her and she froze. His focus was so intense, it was like there was nothing else in the room but him and her. She had no idea what she'd been about to say next.

"Dial it back, friend, there's plenty of time for that." There was laughter in Claude's voice.

William faux bowed at Claude before turning back to Maisy. "What was the question?"

His eyes were the same striking blue as before, but the hold they'd had over her faded away. How did he turn that on and off? She'd have to ask him one day. "Sorry, I was just going to ask how many of you there are. House Masters, I mean?

William paused, working it out "I think there's about a dozen at the moment. Changes a lot though. Claude keeps adding people and people drop out sometimes. Seems to me he needs to slow down though, we'll end up with a club full of arrogant wankers with fancy armbands at this rate."

"Thank you, William." Claude gave him a stern look and the younger man shrugged. It looked like keeping his mouth shut was hard for him. He'd be a terrible sub.

Maisy giggled at the thought of him wearing a ball gag. He caught her eye and winked at her again, "I like laughing subbies, it's extra fun to make them cry."

The colour drained from her face and he laughed again, but there was no cruelty behind his eyes this time. Christ on a bike, he would be scary as hell to play with. She had no idea when he was serious and when he was joking.

"Stop scaring Mistress Maisy and go change your armband," Claude looked at his watch then gave her a warm smile. "I believe Daniel will be here any moment." The crowd around the bar was growing rapidly.

William stood, stretched like a cat, and waved the riding crop in a farewell gesture, "See you later, love. Let me know when you get bored of Daniel."

He swept away as quickly as he'd arrived. Claude rested his hand on her shoulder for a moment before he followed. "If it becomes too overwhelming come and find me or Matilda, oui?"

Maisy didn't have time to nod before she was alone on the velvet sofa, holding a glass of gin flavoured melted ice.

Chapter 15
Sights

Maisy heard boots approaching from behind her sofa and stood up. Dressed in head to toe black and gorgeous as ever, Dan smiled when he met her eyes. "Sorry sweetheart, been on the phone to a supplier for ages."

He leaned over and grabbed her hair, forcing her to kneel up on the sofa and kiss him or risk falling over. "I've been looking forward to that all day."

"Same," Maisy replied. Just a simple hand in her hair and a kiss and she was right back to that half-aroused and half-nervous state that domination, or maybe just Dan, consistently inspired in her.

He lifted her effortlessly over the back of the sofa and tucked her arm in his, "The club has a big anniversary coming up so Claude's doing a celebration event for members. It's a nice idea, but I'm sick of organising it to be honest with you."

Maisy made a non-committal interested noise. She'd jump at the chance to arrange any event at this venue, let alone some glitzy thing for lovely Claude, but she had promised herself she'd keep it all separate. Anyway, she liked it here and if she made a mess of the event she'd feel awkward coming back.

If Daniel had expected her to say anything about helping he didn't press the issue.

"Might I suggest water, Maisy? You may want to save your next gin for later on." Maisy might have been intrigued by the naughty glint in his eye, but she didn't notice it. She'd just seen a pair of naked male slaves with cages on their cocks kneeling for a majestic woman in a wheelchair.

Meanwhile a man in aged brown leathers rested a hand on one of the slaves' shoulders. Maisy didn't mean to stare, yet again, but she couldn't take her eyes off the anticipatory smiles the slaves wore.

Maisy averted her gaze when the male Dom started unzipping his leathers.

"Having fun, sweetheart?" Dan asked, offering her the bottle of water he'd procured from the bar.

She blushed, "Sorry, am I being really rude?"

"Nah," Dan glanced towards the scene himself and nodded at the Domme when she saw him looking, "A bit starey perhaps, but you're new so nobody'll mind much."

Maisy groaned and squeezed the plastic bottle until it crinkled. "So embarrassing," she muttered.

Dan laughed and wrapped an arm around her shoulders, "Don't worry, love. They won't think anything of it. If they didn't want to be watched they'd go to a private area."

She nodded, "That sounds nice. Can we go to one of those, maybe?"

"Not feeling the exhibitionism, hmm?" That assessing gaze of his always seemed to lay her thoughts and feelings open to examination.

"I don't know if it's really me." She glanced again at the happy group and was disconcerted to feel a stab of arousal when she heard a low sexual moan coming from one of the slaves. Oh God.

Dan's mouth turned up at the corner, "We'll see. We're going to see how you feel about following simple orders for a bit, okay?"

She dragged her eyes away from a naked man in a zebra mask covering his eyes. Was it Xavier? It was hard to tell with the mask, but she thought she recognised him as the formal submissive from Thursday evening.

He had painted white stripes over his deep brown skin. Somebody must have helped him do that, especially down…oh my. They really had painted every inch.

A petite black Domme in a leopard print body suit, a black armband, and fuck-me heels pushed a bottle of water into the zebra man's hand and said something that made his eyes light up.

Dan's hand gripped Maisy's chin and forced her to look at him, he looked like he was trying not to laugh. "Seeing as you're having trouble keeping your eyes to yourself today let's start with this. I want you to walk behind me with your eyes lowered to the floor."

She nodded and complied immediately, only for her chin to be lifted again, more gently this time.

He kissed her again, fiercely, and leaned in to whisper, "I wonder how red you'll turn when I parade you around naked like that."

She flushed deeply at the mere suggestion, but didn't refuse. How would that feel? If the growing stripes on a certain part of the zebra's anatomy were anything to go by, it was an arousing experience. At least it didn't have a fluffy tip on the end like a zebra's tail.

She nearly burst into giggles, but Dan's raised eyebrow stopped her. She really didn't want to explain that thought. She returned her eyes to the floor.

Satisfied that she'd regained control of herself, Dan squeezed her hand and started walking at a slow and leisurely pace so she didn't have to worry about tripping over in blind haste. Maisy concentrated on the heels of his boots, letting the welcome feeling of his control wash over her along with the scent of leather and polished wood.

Maisy chanced a look at the bar when she was sure Dan wasn't looking. She saw Claude engaged in conversation with Matilda, who had her arm slung casually around a tall brunette trainee's waist. She caught a glimpse of a red beard as Matthew pushed a tumbler towards the chatting pair and a shimmer of sequins as a waitress hurried up with an order slip.

Claude made eye contact with Maisy for a split second and she flinched. She looked back to her feet, wondering if Claude would tell on her.

She jumped as Dan's hand gripped her wrist, thinking she'd been caught out, but he just said, "Nod if you're okay, Maisy."

She nodded then lifted her chin slightly so he could see her relaxed smile.

"Good girl," he wrapped her hand in his and pulled her to his side. She'd half expected to walk behind him all night, so the change was welcome. Made brave by his gesture, she leaned into him, resting her head on his shoulder. He gave her a quiet grunt of approval. Aha! So he was a secret snuggler.

Maisy heard feminine giggles from her right and voices raised in chatter. Now she stood with Dan rather than behind she couldn't get away with peeking, a fact she was thankful for a moment or so later.

"Who's that with Master Dan?"

Was that one of the trainee's voices? It was hard to tell without looking and she didn't know many of them, only the ones she'd met briefly at the bar.

"Nobody. One of the charity subs."

She felt the cruel words like a punch in the chest. Charity? Well, yes, she'd been nominated for subsidised membership, but so had loads of other people, right? She'd never thought about it in that light, but the faceless voice made it seem so obvious. Kind Master Dan taking on the charity sub.

If Dan didn't have her hand grasped so tight she'd have run out of the club.

"Don't be such a spiteful bitch, Jenna."

The matter of fact London accent seemed familiar too. Claire maybe?

A different voice, whispering, "But he doesn't do those. Didn't you say, Jenna? Didn't you tell me that-"

"Master Dan!" The woman's - Jenna's - already cloyingly sweet tones somehow got even more saccharine as they drew level to the table.

Dan stopped. No, no, no! To Maisy's relief, Dan guided her to stand behind him, still holding her hand.

"Did I ask for you, sub?" Maisy jumped, for a scary moment she thought the question was directed at her, then she registered Jenna's surprised squeak. Dan's voice was positively icy.

"I'm sorry, Sir. I was just hoping to -" She'd winched up the high pitched 'I'm such a sweetheart' tone in her voice until it was on the edge of babyish.

"If you were a well-behaved trainee I might be interested in what you were hoping." Maisy smothered a smile when she heard Jenna's shocked gasp.

"Sir, I have never-" She was practically spluttering.

Maisy kept her eyes on the floor, the picture of demure submission. In her head, however, she was giving Jenna the finger and cheering Dan on.

"Enough. I don't have time to deal with rude subs tonight. Who is trainee master this week?"

"Master William, Sir." Claire supplied, a little too helpfully.

"Jenna. Go to Master William and tell him you're a... what was it again? A 'Spiteful Bitch.'"

Claire actually giggled and clapped her hands.

"I'm sure he has an appropriate punishment. Claire, go with her and explain what happened to Master William. Protecting your fellow trainee will not be rewarded."

Claire made a noise like an outraged cat, but didn't argue. Nobody argued with a Drift Master for long.

As they moved on Maisy felt Dan give her hand a reassuring squeeze. Apparently that had been for her benefit. She grinned. To hell with revenge being served cold, smoking hot with a side of gorgeous Dom was absolutely fine by her. Then again Master William seemed like a bit of a hard ass, and he had that whip...

"Sir?"

"Yes sweetheart?" He pulled her closer again as they walked towards one of the back tunnels so he'd be sure to hear her.

"William, I mean, Master William, what will he do to them?"

His chuckle echoed in the tunnel, "He's all front, pet. Well, not all front, but he won't do her any harm if that's what you're worried about."

"A little." She just about resisted the urge to look over her shoulder to see what had become of Jenna and Claire.

"Seeing as she was nasty about a fellow submissive I'd hazard a guess at tickle torture."

"Tickle..." She shot him an incredulous look, then remembered herself and looked back to the ground.

He laughed again, "You'd be surprised. I'm no masochist, but I'd rather take an hour long whipping with a single tail than ten minutes merciless tickling. She's got it coming anyway, sweetheart. She's been a trainee for ages. She should know how to behave."

Maisy couldn't bring herself to be concerned about the mean woman after that, tickling didn't sound so bad. Although, Maisy really hoped Claire didn't get in trouble for being the bearer of bad news.

"We'll sit here for now." He sat then pulled her easily on to his lap. "You've done very well. You can have your eyes back now."

She lifted her gaze to his dark brown eyes and smiled her thanks.

"Have you thought about that limits list yet?"

Had she thought about it? She hadn't thought about anything else since she'd left Drift on Thursday. That didn't sound like an appropriate reply, but she had a feeling he knew as surely as if she'd said it out loud.

Instead she said, "I have, but I'm still not sure on most of it. I know I don't want to be whipped."

"So, whipping is a limit for you?"

She nodded, "Absolutely, Sir, hard limit."

"Hm." The noncommittal noise cranked her anxiety up several notches.

"Sir?"

He caressed her knee, pushing past her skirt and up her thigh with firm hands. His confident touch made her shiver with anticipation, but his hands never reached the place where all her attention was now focused.

"I think the best way to make this point is to demonstrate, so I'm going to ask you to trust me to show you something now. You're not going to like the idea, but I promise it won't hurt beyond what you can handle. You can say no now or safe word at any time. Deal?"

She nodded tentatively and slid her legs slightly apart, silently begging him to touch her a little more intimately.

He grinned and pinched the inside of her thigh just enough to make her squeak. "Hey!"

"I'll give you exactly as much as I want to give you, little Maisy. No more. Do you remember your safe words?"

The serious question brought her back to Earth. He was going to do something to her, something she might find scary. Something erotic?

"Yes Sir," she answered quietly.

"Good girl," he bent to kiss the spot he'd pinched. Maisy felt his unruly dark hair tickling the inside of her thighs and considered asking him to kiss a bit higher. She held back, partly because she was eager to find out what he wanted to show her and partly because somehow it didn't seem very submissive to brazenly ask for cunnilingus.

Chapter 16
Are you sure?

Soon after, bound spread-eagled on a wood and leather contraption that Dan called a St. Andrew's Cross, she wasn't so sure she wanted to know what he was planning.

He'd secured her so that she was facing away from him, tits poking provocatively through the upper v-shape of the cross.

There was enough space around the damned thing he'd have access to every inch of her, but for now he stood behind her.

"How do you feel about nudity and sex?"

"Excuse me?"

He walked around the cross to face her, the sound of his boots echoing through the tunnel, "How do you feel about being naked in the club?"

She shivered involuntarily, not sure whether it was from arousal or the thought of baring her skin in a place with stone floors.

Most of the people, at least the submissive people, she'd seen since she arrived tonight had been in a state of undress. She felt more conspicuous being fully clothed than she would probably feel if she was naked.

"That's okay by me." She said.

"Nudity is okay? Good." Dan reached around the cross and lifted her skirt, swiftly tucking it up into its waistband. Then he pulled her knickers down until they were stretched tight between her bound thighs, adding another level of restraint.

"Beautiful," He said, leaning back to take in her bare legs and exposed pussy. Dan stroked her thighs as he had earlier, running his palms firmly over her skin. They crept higher, but never high enough. "And how about being touched intimately or fucked?"

Distracted by his hands, she hesitated, her eyes closed and focused on the sensation of being naked and touched just a few feet away from the crowded bar.

He stopped and dug his fingers lightly into her thighs instead. Her eyes flew open and she finally focused on the question.

"Um, only you, right? Not other people?"

He smiled easily and resumed stroking her sensitive thighs, creeping ever closer to her pussy, "That's entirely up to you, sweetheart. You don't have to be touched intimately by me either, if you don't want."

"I do want!" She protested, trying and failing to push her bound hips towards him.

"Me too," he said. He tapped two fingers hard directly over her clit then withdrew his hands completely. It wasn't painful, although it sent a jolt of unusual sensation through her like nothing she'd ever felt before. It was, however, cruelly frustrating.

"But-"

"No buts, sweetheart." His boots echoed off the stone floor again and Maisy heard a long zip being undone. Now he'd moved away her arse and damp pussy felt cold.

She gathered from the noise that he was rummaging in that big holdall that he called a toy bag. Honestly, she'd seen set builders at work with less gear. He took a few echoing steps towards her and stopped.

Then there was silence. Well, not quite silence. She heard the murmurs of conversation from nearby members, indistinct laughter, and the tinkling of glass at the bar.

Here, however, in their little bubble, there was silence. Both of them listening to the other breathe, waiting for the scene to begin.

She flinched away as something landed on her right shoulder. Instead of a whip he seemed to be stroking her with something silky soft.

"Sir, wha-"

The same object struck her waist with a crack. She squeaked, but the sensation wasn't pain, more like tiny fingers tapping her.

"Silence unless you're addressed Maisy, understand?"

She nodded.

The thing cracked down again in the same place, harder. This time it did sting. "I was addressing you, little one." He said, matter of factly.

"Yes Sir," she said through gritted teeth.

"Good girl." she could almost hear the laughter he was keeping back. "This is for the attitude."

She squeaked indignantly as he flicked his wrist and whipped the same spot again, much harder.

She let out a slow shaky breath, swallowing the cross words she'd just love to shout at him.

When she remained still, silent, and obedient he began in earnest. Every stroke was as soft as the first one. The little fingers tapped her all over in a sensuous, rhythmic assault. He increased the pressure slowly and her skin warmed under his attentions. It was like receiving a massage from a thousand tiny hands. She sighed happily.

"You like that, sweetheart?"

"Feels nice, Sir," she smiled and let her head sag to her arm. Her eyes drifted shut and she let the smells of the club wash over her. Leather, sex, pain, perfume, gin.

He kept building the pressure up, never breaking rhythm but pushing until the blows started to sting again. When she began arching away from the blows he stopped and approached the cross. She hissed when the fabric of his shirt brushed roughly against her lightly pinkened skin.

"Shh, I know." One hand gripped her breast and the other stroked her arse. "Now then, little Maisy, is whipping still a hard limit for you?"

"But that's different, sir!" She turned her head to face him as well as she could, "I meant like, um, what's it called? What William used the other day?"

"That big single tail?" His gruff chuckle caught Maisy off-guard. "Yes pet, I can see why that would be a limit. But you're no masochist, and I'm no sadist, so we don't have to worry about that."

"But I don't-"

"You didn't know that. You don't know me, you don't know your own limits, or what that scary whip thing is called."

She looked away, embarrassed. What was she doing playing dress up with her wimpy little submissive desires here? This place was serious business, she should have known that she wouldn't fit in here.

Dan's gentle cupped her chin, "What on Earth is going on in that head of yours?"

"Nothing, Sir," she said, but to her utter horror she felt tears pool in the corner of her eyes.

"Oh, sweetheart," he kissed her forehead affectionately, "None of that is a bad thing. Remember what I said before? We don't understand all that to start with, no-one does. That's why we need to talk about it and try things out."

She nodded, blinking away the tears before they could fall. She wasn't going to wimp out over a little soft flogging.

He frowned slightly, "So, Maisy, we're going to talk about what just happened then start again."

She nodded. Her skin thrummed with recently lost sensation. She wanted more.

He continued, "You said that whipping was a hard limit, but I just flogged you for a good ten minutes and you look about ready to come for me, pet. So I'd say you were mistaken."

Her eyes widened at his crude assessment, but she couldn't say he was wrong, "Yes, I suppose I liked it, but I meant I didn't like pain."

He nodded, as if that's what he was expecting her to say, "Alright, that's almost true."

"What is that supposed to mean?"

The hand on her breast began to tighten, until it was just on the edge of pain - she wriggled under his touch, not sure if she wanted to pull away or beg for more.

He bent to tongue her neck and pinched a nipple cruelly. She moaned and thrust her hips towards him, her arse pressed against his jeans for a moment, but to her frustration he leaned back until the cross held her and blocked her access. He chuckled at her frustration. The brush of cold air where his mouth had been made her moan again.

"It means that you like some pain, pet."

She couldn't really disagree, but she frowned regardless.

He pinched her nipple much harder and she squeaked, then glared at him. "Hey!"

"You don't like all pain," he said, matter of factly, "But you do like some when it's paired with submission and pleasure." He pinched again, stopping at just the point where she gasped, just the point between pressure and pain.

His other hand skirted downwards and she shook her head even as her arousal shot through the roof. To have him touch her was all she wanted, but still she shook her head, confused.

"Overwhelmed, sweetheart?" His hand stopped at her waist and held her easily, "We can stop."

"Don't stop." She said.

"Right." He watched her for a moment with quiet, intense consideration. "We'll continue, but I want you to remember your safe words."

She nodded and gave him a small smile. He didn't find it quite as reassuring as she intended it to be.

"Does it bother you that you like pain, Maisy?"

She nodded again, "Some, Sir."

"Brave girl. Why is that?"

"I don't know. It just does."

"I'd like you to think about that if you can. I know it's hard, but I think it'd serve us both well if you understood why you don't like that you enjoy something so much. For now, can you agree that your body likes a little pain when I give it?"

Her skin was still warm from the gentle flogging, her nipples still tight from his fingers - "Yes Sir."

"Would you be willing to explore it further?"

Her gaze drifted to a nearby display that housed several impact toys. Was that why he'd chosen this area? "Maybe Sir."

"Good girl. Maybe is good. Do you understand what I was saying about limits now? That sometimes what your body wants is different to what your head is saying you should have and it's okay to change your mind in both directions?"

"Yes, I think so."

He kissed her forehead tenderly, "That's a good girl."

He loosened the straps on her right side and gently placed her hand on the sturdy frame, so she knew to hold on in case she was wobbly. As is turned out she was a little unsteady, but it was more to do with the confusing and overwhelming arousal than the brief time in bondage.

He pulled her underwear back up, but left the skirt tucked up in its own waistband. When he'd released her properly she drew her legs together, suddenly feeling exposed.

Something told her she wasn't allowed to pull her skirt back down. At least her boobs were still firmly away - oh. She noticed as she glanced down that her right breast was on a scouting expedition for freedom, aided by Daniel's enthusiastic manhandling. Her bra and a sliver of nipple was visible. Maybe she'd be able to tug that up when Dan wasn't looking.

Dan kissed her cheek and tidied his flogger back into his holdall. He even wiped down the cross with the provided disinfectant spray even though they'd only been there a short while and fully dressed at that.

Daniel threw the bag over his shoulder and took her hand, "Right then, sweetheart, about those private rooms-"

Before he could finish that very intriguing sentence, William and a sour faced woman with chopsticks pincering her tongue rounded the corner, "Scene over, mate?" William asked.

Dan nodded and put the holdall back down. He put his arm around Maisy's waist and pulled her in front of him. Maisy was very, very glad that she'd worn pretty knickers.

William nodded and gave her an appreciative glance, "Alright, Mistress Maisy? Jenna here's got something she wants to say."

Ah. So this was Jenna. She was gorgeous. Her uncoupled handcuffs were plain black like all the other trainees, but her other jewellery sparkled in a way that said they were inset with real diamonds. Honestly, Maisy felt sorry for her. Those chopsticks looked painful and this was only going to get more awkward before it got better.

"Get on with it, pet," William batted her arse gently and she stepped forward. Her eyes spat venom at them both, "I'm thorry about twhat I said."

The chopsticks were an embarrassing impediment, but Maisy understood well enough.

Maisy started to speak, but Daniel squeezed her wrist gently to stop her. He spoke instead, "Sorry, Jenna, I didn't catch that."

Jenna glared at him, then at Master William, and finally at Maisy, who recoiled from the ugly look. "I thaid I'm thorry."

Daniel squeezed Maisy's wrist again, so she kept quiet. "Top tip, you're not getting forgiveness or your tongue back until you apologise with the dignity and humility we expect of a Drift trainee."

If a human being could explode from internalised fury, Jenna would have in that moment. With what looked like a colossal effort, Jenna schooled her features into something like contrition, although it was honestly hard to tell with her tongue protruding between the chopsticks.

"I really am thorry," she said, bowing her head slightly.

"Very nice," Daniel said.

Maisy saw William shaking his head, apparently he didn't buy Jenna's performance. Before the embarrassing spectacle went on any longer Maisy said, "That's okay. Thank you for apologising."

Dan kissed her head gently, perhaps he approved of her preventing William from continuing the punishment.

"Oh, alright then, come here." Jenna went back to William who removed the chopsticks and dismissively waved her away. "Be kinder next time, trainee. I've got plenty more where these came from."

Jenna left, but not before shooting a final cross glare at Maisy. Great, she thought bitterly, making friends and influencing people on my first proper night. Dan didn't seem to notice, he was shaking his head at William. "Chopsticks?"

"Caught me having my dinner, didn't she? Had to improvise."

"Fair enough."

"He treating you well, Mistress?" William winked.

"Very well, thank you, Sir." She said, feeling shy under his scrutiny and very aware that her skirt was still tucked up, exposing her scanty underwear.

Daniel looked between them, eyebrow raised, "Right then. The mistress and I have plans. Thanks for sorting that for me."

"No worries. She's a gobby one, ain't she? You'd think she'd have learnt by now." William shrugged. "Ah well. More fun for me if they don't learn fast I suppose." His boyish grin belied the sinister intent in the remark. He gave them a quick salute and went on his way, graceful as ever.

"Mistress Maisy?" Dan asked, eyebrow raised.

Maisy groaned, "Don't ask."

Chapter 17
Boutique

Dan held her hand firmly as he led her back into the huge main room of Club Drift. "Okay, sweetheart, what sort of private room would you like to see?"

Maisy glanced at the many tunnels that led to areas of the club she hadn't seen yet. "There's options?"

"Mmhmm." He secured the holdall on his shoulder and used his newly free hand to point down the nearest tunnel, "Medical, secretary, and couples room."

He pointed to a tunnel across the way, "Brothel, dungeon, and cowboy."

She pulled a face, "Cowboy?"

"Yeah, Western, cowboy, whatever. There's usually a bale of hay."

Maisy giggled, "Not sure about that."

"There's a couple of normal bedrooms on the office floor, but they're not particularly well equipped. Might I recommend the room of mirrors, the water bed, sensory deprivation, or the kinky hotel experience," he pointed at another tunnel.

"You're just making these up now."

He shrugged and gave her a lopsided grin, "Only a couple."

"Hotel room doesn't sound too scary?"

The grin turned slightly evil, "Good choice."

"Which ones were you making up?" She asked, peering into one of the tunnels he'd indicated to see if she could figure out what was down there.

"That would be telling, sweetheart." He started towards the last tunnel he'd pointed at, "I'll give you a proper tour sometime. Or we could just fuck our way through all of the rooms..."

She laughed, "There's always that."

"Claude refits them quite often, to be honest. For all I know there really is a water bed in one of them now."

The tunnel became a narrower corridor as they entered it, less brightly lit than the main room. Maisy could tell that the large original space had been partitioned to create private rooms.

There was enough light to read the small sign on the first room they passed, 'Sensory Deprivation.' A small 'Occupied' sign hung on the door handle. Maisy stared as they passed, what was going on behind the closed door?

She dragged her eyes away when she realised Daniel had stopped. The plaque on this door read, 'Boutique.'

"Luckily for us, our first choice is unoccupied." He let go of her hand so he could rummage in one of the side pockets of the holdall. "Sorry, should have done this earlier."

He steadied the bag against the door as he fished in the bottom of the pocket, which must have been bigger than it appeared. "Right."

A set of keys. She almost laughed. They looked like any old house keys, not the keys to the secrets of a subterranean sex dungeon. Surely they should be on a rusty iron ring and look like the keys to a fairy kingdom?

He didn't notice how unimpressed she was with the keys, he was too busy rifling through them for the correct one. He swore under his breath, "I really need to remember to do this beforehand."

She leaned against the back wall, waiting patiently. Honestly, Dan being normal and disorganised was reassuring after the all-knowing-Dom stuff he'd been pulling tonight.

As Dan found the key and turned it in the lock, the sensory deprivation door swung open. Maisy briefly heard laughter from within before she was pulled into the boutique room and the door was shut behind her.

For a moment they were in darkness. Daniel pulled her close and kissed her roughly, missing her lips at first in blind haste. She wrapped her arms around his neck and kissed him back eagerly.

Was this the first time they'd just kissed like this? No control or restraint, just two people kissing because they can't keep their hands off each other.

It was almost a shame when Dan reached out to switch on the light, breaking the intimate moment.

She looked around the room, a quizzical expression taking over her features.

"Not what you were expecting?" He asked, swinging his holdall onto the blanket chest at the end of the bed.

Honestly, Maisy wasn't sure what she'd been expecting, but it wasn't this. It appeared to be a perfectly ordinary room. Something you'd expect at a four-star hotel, perhaps.

There was a small door at the back which was ajar, so she could see it led to a shower and toilet like any other hotel room. The main room contained a small writing desk, a chair, and a large four poster bed with pristine white sheets.

She was starting to wish she'd picked the cowboy room when Dan opened the top dresser drawer.

"Oh."

He smiled and opened the next one, then walked around the bed and opened the wardrobe. "What do you think we should play with?"

It was like the limits list was a catalogue and this nondescript room was the showroom. Every impact toy, every restraint, ball gags, harnesses, tails, vibrators - everything she could think of and a great many things she couldn't possibly have imagined before that moment was available to them in that little room.

She approached the top drawer and examined its contents. Clamps, handcuffs, collars, chains.

She lifted a simple collar with an O-ring and held it up to the light, watching the white metal glint. She saw Dan's face across the room, inscrutable as ever, but something told her she should put the collar back. Instead she picked up a pretty pair of clamps with purple bows on them, "Can I try these, please?"

DANIEL FELT THE TENSION ease out of his body. He'd almost lost his self-control when he'd seen her holding the collar, but she'd left that where it was and picked up...some pretty nasty clamps, if he remembered rightly. Should he give her what she's asked for or suggest a more suitable pair?

She wasn't as alarmed by the room as he'd thought she might be. She looked curious, relaxed, not at all afraid of the extensive collection of playthings concealed in the furnishings. Daniel wanted to put that down to her trusting him. She'd learnt already that they'd only use things she agreed to or try things he promised wouldn't hurt. That was a good start.

"They're pretty, sure, but I think they're a little too painful for you, sweetheart. Will you let me pick a pair?"

She looked at them and frowned, the same shadowy look behind her eyes as had been there earlier. This sub had something going on that he needed to get to the bottom of. The frown was gone as quickly as it had arrived. "Yes please," she said.

He pulled her towards him and kissed her gently. "I'm going to undress you now, Maisy." She nodded, eyes wide, whatever had been troubling her moments before had been replaced with curious arousal.

He stripped her slowly, relishing the goose bumps that rose all over her skin as she met the cold air, relishing the soft curves that were just as lush as he'd imagined.

"Kneel on the bed for me." She touched his arm gently as they passed each other. He wanted to look back and watch her arranging herself on the bed, but he managed to keep his eyes on the top drawer. He wondered if she'd be kneeling up or with spread thighs.

He picked a pair of tweezer clamps, easy to adjust and still pretty. When he turned to see how she'd done he was thrilled to find she'd recreated the position he'd taught her when they'd watched William's demonstration on Thursday night.

"Beautiful."

She smiled her thanks. Apparently she'd learnt not to speak unless she was absolutely sure she had permission. What a fast learner she was turning out to be.

He gripped her hair and pulled her head back a little to give him clear access to her heavy breasts.

MAISY COULDN'T HELP but whimper quietly. There was something about the slightly unbalanced feeling she got when Daniel pulled her about by her hair that turned her on like nothing else. Such a simple gesture, but so potent with feelings of control and submission.

Daniel bent his head to suck and nibble her left nipple. Maisy was surprised by how hard and long her nipple became from his attentions, she was sure it didn't usually look like that during sex.

Daniel held up the tweezer clips so she could see how they worked. "Tell me when, sweetheart."

He applied the clamp and slid the tightening loop up, watching her reactions carefully.

Maisy hissed as the pressure turned into pain, "When!"

Daniel slid the loop a fraction of an inch higher then stopped. "How's that?"

Maisy took deep breaths and noticed the pain easing into something else, something sensual and strange. "It's good."

She wriggled experimentally and smiled as the beads that hung from the clamps danced.

"Next one," Dan bent his head again and Maisy nearly forgot that pain was due to follow his gentle administrations.

He was faster this time, sliding the clamp to the same tightness as the other in one smooth movement.

"Ow!" Maisy scowled at him and reached for the clamp. He grabbed her hand before she got there.

"Ask me, sweetheart. Do you need me to loosen that for you?"

In the seconds that had passed since he'd tightened the clamp the pain had become bearable. "No, it's okay now."

He kissed her forehead, "Good. Your job is to do as you're told, that's all. Communicate using the safe words or very polite questions. Okay?"

She felt a tension she hadn't realised was there ease. All she had to do was give control to him. All she had to do was follow instructions. That seemed like the easiest thing in the world. No worrying about when to move position, or how to please him, or how to ignore the hundreds of tiny thoughts and questions that usually distracted her during a sexual encounter. Just be there and let him worry about everything else.

Profound relaxation and arousal sound like strange bedfellows, but right then she felt more prepared and excited to be with him than she ever had with anyone else before.

When she looked into his eyes she thought she saw a similar peace within him.

The moment passed and the tingly, aroused excitement returned. He hadn't spoken for a long moment, apparently considering how to proceed or, more likely, drawing out the pause so she felt the pleasurable weight of anticipation.

"I want you to kneel on the bed with your arms down and your arse up, understand?"

She arranged herself as best she could, face and arms pressed down into the bed. He pushed her legs a little further apart, "Not bad at all, sweetheart."

She couldn't see him, but it sounded like he'd gone to the wardrobe on the far side of the room. She tried to remember what she'd glimpsed in there. Impact toys mostly. Maybe he'd use another flogger!

Something hard and thin tapped the back of her legs.

"Stick your arse out, sweetheart, there you go."

Was that a cane? She tried to turn her head to look, but a gentle tap on her thighs stopped her. "Keep your eyes down, Maisy."

"I won't hit you with this unless you're really bad, you won't like it," he ran it up her thighs, over her arse, and up her back, it was cold, unyielding. She shuddered, no, she would not like that. He tapped her bum lightly, just enough to make her jump. "I said stick your arse out."

She hurried to comply, arching her back and pushing her shoulders down as far as she could. The threat of the cane was somehow deeply arousing as well as motivating. The fresh sheets grazed her clamped nipples sending dark need rushing through her.

"You're very wet, Maisy," he remarked matter of factly.

She gasped. Something about his refined accent made him talking filth sound so deliciously wrong. She felt his appreciative gaze like the sun on her back and she arched even further, displaying herself for him.

She heard him step closer and she tensed. Would he spank her? Fuck her? Do something to her with the toys that filled every drawer and cupboard in this deceptively vanilla-looking room?

She trembled with excitement as she felt him kneel somewhere behind her. Small rustles and movements told her he was still there, but he didn't touch her. She forgot herself and tried to look again.

His hand landed on her arse with a loud crack before she even realised what she was doing. Thank goodness it hadn't been the cane.

She yelped. "Sorry Sir!"

"Not good enough, sweetheart."

She held still, pulling her elbows in and making herself as small as she could. Anxiety fed the butterflies in her stomach. His tone had become cold, strict, the very opposite of the laughter that had been there moments before. She held her breath.

"I shouldn't have to remind you of something so simple, but you're new to this, I'll show mercy."

"Mercy?" She whispered, staring determinedly at the bedspread even though every instinct screamed at her to look at the man who stood inches from her exposed body.

"Yes, mercy," he said. "How bad do you think you've been? Pick a number between one and ten."

"Um. One?"

"One?" He was incredulous.

"Three?"

"You said one, sweetheart. Let's stick with that. You get one." He brought his hand down hard on each arse cheek in quick succession. She gasped, but just about managed to stay in position.

"Hm. No, I don't think that counts, do you? You will thank me for your one blow, Maisy."

She whimpered as his hand, which had caressed her so gently moments before, cracked against each cheek again in exactly the same place. "Thank you," she said.

He stroked the burning patches on her arse and she let out the breath she'd been holding.

"Thank you who?" He said, his voice somewhere between playful and cold. He was definitely enjoying this. As his hands smoothed the pain into dark pleasure she realised she was enjoying it as well.

"Sir! Sir! Thank you, Sir!" She exclaimed through laughter, knowing now what game he was playing.

"Too late." His hand landed again stinging her already pink and warm flesh.

She growled softly and held back the torrent of swear words that she'd just love to unleash. "Thank you, S-"

"Too slow," he said. Maisy cried out as he spanked each cheek again, still on the same sore spot.

"Thank you, Sir," She said through gritted teeth.

"Attitude." He hit each cheek three times in quick succession.

She hissed and cringed away causing her clamped nipples to rub against the sheets, the faint pressure from the clamps briefly surged into pain before merging back into a more intense pleasure along with the heat on her backside.

"Give me your arse and take your one blow, Maisy." His voice was perfectly calm. She opened her mouth to tell him how unfair he was being, but stopped when she realised that he wasn't, not really.

They were playing the game she'd agreed to and she wasn't following the rules.

She took a deep breath and arched her back, sticking her arse up in the air and offering her pink flesh to him.

Crack, crack. "Thank you, Sir," She said. And she meant it. The sharp sting from the blows quickly faded into warmth and she smiled, proud of herself.

"Good girl." Without warning, his hand was on her, tracing wide circles around her clit. She moaned and spread her legs a little further, arching up into his touch, willing him to touch her closer, more intimately.

As if reading her mind he pushed one thick finger into her tight, wet hole.

"Thank you, Sir," She gasped without prompt as he stroked her inside and out. His left hand pressed down on her back as he added another finger. She stretched around him, wriggling between his strong hands as pleasure built in her core. The small tastes of erotic submission he'd given her up until now had served only to leave her in a constant state of arousal and she desperately craved release.

He stroked her most sensitive spot inside with firm pressure, sending her thoughts spiralling. Then, just as she was settling into the rhythm, he started rubbing her clit with his thumb. He circled the sensitive nub, holding her in place with his other hand as she began to quake.

He increased the speed and pressure, pumping her with his thick fingers and stroking her to wild heights. She clenched down on him as she felt herself near a peak, her breathing erratic, her cheeks flushed.

He pulled away, adding insult to injury by lightly spanking the back of her thighs.

She whimpered, pushing herself towards him, pleading with her body for her ruined climax.

"Were you going to come then, sweetheart?"

"Yes...No... I don't know."

"You don't know? You were certainly thinking about it. I give you a nice reward and you go and think about coming without permission? I don't know, Maisy, I don't think you're learning very quickly."

"No! I am, please, I would have asked, I -" Confused by her eagerness to please and the frustrated, pulsing sensations in her cunt she could barely string a thought together.

"Pick a number between one and ten."

"No! I...' She stopped and struggled to tame her confused thoughts. She wanted this, she wanted to be good for him. Why was she trying to avoid the punishment that would help her learn?

"Ten," she said.

"Ten?" He asked, quietly.

"Yes Sir," she said, determinedly pushing her arse towards him and trying to still the involuntary tremor in her legs.

"Sweetheart," he began, but seemed to think better of it and stopped. "Ten it is." She heard him walk away to the other side of the room, heard rustling and movement. She stared obediently down at the bed the whole time, never giving in to her temptation to look and find out what he was going to deliver her punishment blows with.

She cried out in surprise as he pushed his thick, long cock into her with one smooth, slow, and careful thrust. He was big and although she was wet and eager it'd been a long time since she'd taken anything other than his fingers.

His hand pushed down on the base of her back again, steadying her as he filled her entirely.

"Count," he said, before pulling out and thrusting back in. It hurt, but not for long as her long denied nerves twitched into full awareness.

"Count," he repeated.

"Two," she said, "Ah!" He had smacked her arse as he pulled out again leaving her painfully empty.

"It doesn't add to the total if you're not counting now, does it? Start at one."

Maisy was about to argue with his crappy logic, but all thoughts left her mind as his deliciously thick cock filled her again. "Ah! One," she said, wriggling her arse towards him, wordlessly begging him to fuck her properly.

He pulled out again and began to push back into her, but this time he went slowly - too slowly. She whined as he pushed his rock-hard length into her centimetre by centimetre. Her sensitive tissues stretched around him, waiting for the thrust she desperately wanted.

"Please," she said, pushing herself onto him as far as she could with his hands holding her in place, the moment the word left her lips he pulled out entirely again, causing a string of swear words to fall from her lips.

He laughed gently and reached around to play with her clit. "Be a good girl, stay still, and you'll get what you want soon enough. We're still on one of ten."

She groaned, but she nodded and straightened her back. He kept massaging her clit in tight, infuriating circles as he began to enter her with the same tortuously slow pace. Her breath came in short, desperate pants as she fought the urge to push down on his cock. "Please?"

He stilled, but didn't withdraw, "Please what, Maisy?"

"Please Sir!"

He eased in another inch and pinched her clit roughly, Please Sir what?"

"Please Sir fuck me, please, please, please," she said, shaking with the effort it took to stay still.

"Good girl," he murmured, before filling her completely with one strong thrust. "Fuck," his voice rumbled with obvious pleasure and relief - he'd been torturing himself as well as her.

All thought of counting was gone from her mind as he began to fuck her in earnest. It was all she could do to breath a ragged, "Thank you," as he drove into her again and again. He resumed stroking her clit, his other arm holding her up as she started to sag under his pleasurable weight.

"Please, please, please," mindless gasps fell from her lips with each stroke as she climbed towards release again. Her heavy breasts, nipples sensitive from the clamps, brushed against the bedspread. It felt like rough tongues laving at her sensitive flesh and that, combined with his hand on her clit and his cock filling her, urged her towards orgasm fast, quicker than she could control.

As she reached the top off the cliff she remembered she should ask permission, but he increased the speed of his fingers on her clit and it was too late.

She fell over the edge, every nerve in her body exploding with pleasure. She cried out her powerful release, the week's many erotic frustrations pouring themselves into pure ecstasy. Dan kept up the rhythm, holding her while she bucked and moaned, but as she came down from the overwhelming high she felt rather than heard him chuckle.

"Well, sweetheart, I'm glad you're enjoying yourself."

She froze, "I couldn't help it, it just happened. I'm sorry, Sir, I won't do it again, I-" she stopped as she felt him shaking with barely controlled laughter behind her. "You did that on purpose."

"Of course I did, and now I get to punish you for it, isn't that wonderful?" He turned her over so her tortured nipples pointed at the ceiling. She scowled at Daniel as he massaged her stiff limbs until she relaxed into the bed, her legs spread wide for him.

"I'd wipe that look off your face if I were you, Maisy," the laughter had retreated to his eyes and his voice had become darkly serious again. She swallowed her retort and smoothed her features as best she could.

"That's better"' Now she was allowed to look she drank him in. He tucked his sheathed erection back into his trousers where it bulged conspicuously, then shrugged his black t-shirt off as she watched with unashamed lust. The muscles on his broad chest rippled bewitchingly as he unfastened his black armband.

"Now, do you think you can stay very still or would you like to be restrained properly?"

She grinned up at him, made bold by post-orgasmic bliss. "Restrained please," she said, coyly.

His grin matched hers, "Good choice, brave little sub, you're going to be wriggling in a minute."

She stretched languidly as he tied her wrists and ankles to each corner of the bed with rope he retrieved from the wardrobe's bottom drawer. She was immobilised and it was somehow exquisite. She felt beautiful and helpless.

She'd almost forgotten that she was in trouble, until he picked up a large mains powered...something.

"What's that?" She eyed the bulbous head of the thing in his hand warily, it was much too large to be insertable, she hoped, but that didn't ease her apprehension.

He plugged it in and stalked back to her, an infuriating smirk on his face. "This is my favourite toy. It could be yours too, but unfortunately you're going to be punished with it the first time you meet it. What a pity."

She squirmed in her bonds, his words sending a pulse of nervous arousal through her, "Punished?"

"Yes sweetheart, punished. You need to learn to ask for your orgasms, because they belong to me right now." He climbed onto the bed and knelt between her bound legs while she watched with rapt attention. He covered the monstrous thing with a condom and placed it against her thigh.

He ran a finger down her slick folds, almost nonchalantly, and smiled when she shivered. "You stopped counting at two, yes? I won't make you start from one."

"Thank you, but-" she was interrupted by her own strangled cry as he switched the thing on and pressed the bulbous vibrating head against her clit.

"Thank me and count when you come. You will get to that ten you asked for." He pushed down on her mound with the palm of one hand and pressed the infernal vibrating thing impossibly close to her clit with the other.

It took seconds for it to push her over the edge again, he moved it away from her while she caught her breath enough to pant "Three, thank you, Sir."

"Good girl," he smiled approvingly, before pressing the wand against her far too sensitive clit again.

"No, no, no, please, it's too much, please," she strained against the rope and the big hand pressing her into the bed. The vicious toy relentlessly buzzed against her tender and protesting flesh until, somehow, the cruel sensations turned back into pleasure and she flew into another orgasm.

"Good girl. What do you say?" He brushed her clit with his thumb, holding the buzzing toy against her thigh.

She hissed at the rough sensation, 'Four, thank you, Sir.'

"Good. Watch the attitude next time." She screamed as he pushed the toy against her again.

"Please, no, pleeeease, I can't come again, I can't," she pulled against the ropes, unable to move an inch away from his unyielding attentions.

"Yes, you can," he said, before pressing something on the shaft of the toy that caused the motor to go twice as fast.

"Oh God, no," she cried out as it forced her to come again, the tidal waves of pleasure too intense, almost painful.

"Maisy?" He moved it to her thigh again.

"Thank you, Sir, five," she spat out through gritted teeth.

He slapped her right breast, rattling the clamped nipple and causing her to cry out again, then pressed the damned thing harder against her cunt, dialling up the intensity to even greater, more tortuous levels.

"I said watch the attitude, sweetheart. I'm giving you all these lovely orgasms, you don't even have to ask for them, and you can't even thank me nicely."

"Oh fuck, fuck, fuck," she went over in seconds, tears spilling over her cheeks, she was bewildered by the intense sensations. In a daze she heard him turn it off and she breathed, "Six, thank you, Sir."

He leaned over her and wiped a tear from her cheek gently, "Are you okay?"

She saw the concern in his eyes and forced her scrambled mind to consider the question properly.

Was she in pain? No. Was she really upset? No, just overwhelmed with the fierce sensations. Was she enjoying herself? Yes, the way he had taken control of her body in ways she'd never imagined was amazing.

This was difficult, yes, but it was a punishment, it was meant to be - and it was thrilling.

"I'm green," she said, kissing his hand.

"Are you sure? Remember, I need you to be honest with me."

She shook her head, "I'm fine. The wand is...It sucks, but I'm okay. I can take it."

He tilted his head as he assessed her intently, apparently making up his mind whether she was telling the truth, "Okay, you've got four left."

'Wait, no!" She said, but he'd already switched it on.

By the time she screamed, "ten", tears were running down her cheeks, her legs shook uncontrollably, and her clit was numb. He'd used every setting, every intensity, on the evil toy, and he hadn't let up for a second. He'd taken her from orgasm to oversensitive torture to screaming, impossibly intense, orgasm again and again.

He turned it off and she realised she was mumbling, "Thank you, thank you, thank you," the words running into each other in a mindless puddle. Maisy stroked her limbs as he loosened the bonds that tied her to the bed and she slowly regained logical thought.

After a moment of silence in which he watched her recover, she said, "Fuck me, Sir." He raised an eyebrow and undid the fastenings of his trousers, releasing his straining erection.

"You want more?" He pushed his trousers off and knelt between her thighs again, chuckling when she wrapped her shaking legs around his waist and pulled him towards her.

"Please Sir, fuck me," she desperately needed him to fill her, after coming on nothing again and again she needed to feel full.

"My pleasure, sweetheart." He didn't hold back this time, plunging into her with a guttural moan and setting a fast rhythm. Her own arousal stirred again and she groaned in response as every thrust of his thick cock pulled new nerves into play, nerves that hadn't been exhausted by the wand.

There was no way she'd be able to come again even if she wanted to, but she wanted him to find pleasure like she had.

She wanted to hear him come because of her, give him pleasure like he'd given her...so much more than just pleasure.

She clung to him and tried to match his frenzied pace, he had been denying himself the whole time and he was nearing his end quickly.

"What do you think, sweetheart?" He said with a breathless grin, "Do you have one more for me?"

She laughed and shook her head, "Fuck all chance, Sir."

She realised what she'd said the moment his eyebrow quirked. "I mean, I don't think so, sorry, um..."

He slowed the pace for just long enough to reach over and pick up the wand, before driving into her with as much force and speed as before. His forehead shone with the effort it was taking him to keep up the rhythm without coming, but he seemed determined to make her pay for her attitude before he finished.

Maisy tried to pull him down onto her so he couldn't use the wand, laughing in mixed terror and excitement, but he evaded her attempts easily and grabbed her wrists.

"Grip the bed post," he said, releasing her hands and glaring at her until she complied. "Good girl."

He was still fucking her with the same driving rhythm, eliciting small grunts of pleasure even as she fought to stop herself from pushing his arm away. He hadn't even turned the damn wand on yet and she was terrified.

He held her gaze and pushed down on the firm flesh above her clit as he fucked her. She started to forget about the menacing toy in his grip as she relished the feeling of him filling her, stretching her, owning her.

Held by his gaze and hands she melted into his control, wanting nothing more than to please him.

His thrusts became faster and more erratic as he neared release, his breathing becoming ragged. Just before he came he switched the wand onto full power and pressed it against her clit.

The dark pressure of his cock and the new assault on her exhausted clit forced her into a shuddering orgasm in seconds. She let go of the bed and clung to his shoulders instead as the aftershocks shook her, moaning at every thrust as he pumped into her once, twice, then stilled and gave a rough groan.

They lay for a long while in happy silence, a pile of sated limbs, the wand buzzing restlessly beside them. Eventually, Daniel opened his eyes and kissed her gently. "You're amazing, sweetheart."

She laughed, "I'm exhausted."

"So you should be. Sorry about this," he said. Before she could ask what he was sorry about, he unclamped her right nipple.

"Jesus fuck, why?" She exclaimed, trying and failing to wriggle away from him. He held her steady and took her abused nipple into his mouth, gently suckling the pain away.

"Hurt more coming off than going on, right?" He said, when he pulled away, "Sorry, probably should have warned you about that."

"Probably," she said through gritted teeth, eyeing her remaining clamp with deep suspicion.

"Come on, sweetheart. It's got to come off. You can hold my hand if you want."

She glared at him, hugely unamused. To his credit, Daniel didn't laugh, "Does it help if I say we're going to have spiked hot chocolate when we get out of here?"

Maisy sighed theatrically and offered him her left breast. He muffled the ensuing profanity speckled shrieks with a fiercely possessive kiss.

Chapter 18
Loose Lips

Maisy sat on the edge of the bed watching Dan gather the debris they'd left in the Boutique room. He insisted she didn't need to help, which she was grateful for because her legs felt distinctly wobbly.

There's something embarrassing about a condom wrapper, Maisy thought. The condom itself isn't embarrassing, it's vital and soon discarded after fulfilling its role. Condom wrappers though, strewn about on the carpet, emptied of their contents or, worse, hastily refilled after the act. There's just something a little slapstick about the toothless, un-erotic evidence of sex in the near past. Something that seemed antithetical to the screaming orgasms that the room had just witnessed. Too mundane. Too ordinary.

Daniel moved fast. He gathered their rubbish and his holdall, putting a 'needs cleaning' sign on the door after he locked it. "Claude would rather we use the cleaners he provides and take care of our subbies after a scene. Can't say I disagree with him there."

Cleaners? Wow. They had to be in the lifestyle. It'd be too mortifying for everyone involved otherwise, she thought.

They went back to the main atrium, both a little bedraggled. Daniel steered Maisy to a large empty booth, "Put your feet up, sweetheart."

She didn't need telling twice. The club was in full swing, so the main bar room was buzzing with conversation and laughter. Maisy could hear sounds of pain and pleasure echoing faintly from the many tunnels. Scattered about the room were many people wrapped in blankets and sipping hot chocolate or something stronger. Maisy wasn't the only one with her feet up on the substantial furniture. It was easy to feel at home here.

Dan returned from his expedition with a basket like the one Xavier had fetched for them the other night. "Budge up, then."

She scooted along the seating and allowed Dan to drape a blanket around her shoulders. She was grateful for it this time. The club was definitely chilly tonight. Damn stone floors...

Before she got too settled a sparkly waitress came over with two steaming mugs of hot chocolate. "Thanks," Maisy called, recognising the spiteful lady Jenna from earlier and wanting to smooth things over.

She just nodded, but Maisy could tell those feathers were still very much ruffled.

Dan pulled Maisy into his side, "Forget her, sweetheart. She's just one woman. I'll introduce you to some of the others next time. I shouldn't be keeping you all to myself."

Maisy nodded and reached for her hot chocolate. Jenna was an unpleasant distraction she didn't have the energy to think about at the moment. She sniffed her drink curiously -

almonds! It must be spiked with amaretto. Dan had guessed well; she loved the stuff. It was like drinking cake.

Dan stroked her shoulder, content with her leaning into his side, "So…"

Ah. That obligatory debrief.

"So?" She said.

"How do you feel?"

"Good," she said, honestly. Then, realising that probably wasn't enough information, "Drained. Tiny bit sore, too. Peaceful."

"Peaceful, hm? That's good. Me too. What do you think about the limits list now?"

Maisy sipped the rich, creamy hot chocolate, buying time to think. "Honestly?"

"Always."

"I'm even less certain than I was before."

"How so?" He held her patiently while she drank her hot chocolate and mulled his question over.

Eventually she said, "I just love it all. Everything we've done so far has been amazing and I don't know what to put on my checklist because I don't know which things are more brilliant than they sound, you know?"

"I certainly do," he grinned wickedly. "That's no problem. We can carry on talking and working our way through things. We can try anything you like, skip anything that you don't. And my limits, of course."

Maisy realised she hadn't even thought to ask Daniel about his limits. "I'm sorry, I was so busy thinking about me I didn't even -"

"Don't worry about it. I've got a big mouth and I'll speak up if I need to."

"Still, I feel bad."

He chuckled and hugged her closer, pulling the blanket further around them both, "You're sweet as they come, little Maisy."

She didn't really know how to reply to that, so she finished her hot chocolate and replaced her mug on the booth table.

"You'll have to tell me all about your limits, Sir."

"I'll be sure to," he said, "but rest now."

She snuggled into his side, cosy under the blanket and wearier than she'd expected. Resting here was a very nice prospect.

MAISY SHIFTED IN HER sleep. Why was she so uncomfortable? She rolled her shoulder and stiffened as the surface beneath her moved. Oh Christ. Had she fallen asleep on the train again?

Lowered voices rumbled around her. Some of them were familiar. That French one had to be - Claude! The club. How could she have fallen asleep at the club?

She screwed her eyes shut even tighter, not ready to find out who had witnessed her drooling, snoozing self. A hand stroked her shoulder firmly and she relaxed a little. She was still with Daniel. She must have fallen asleep in his lap when they were cuddling. Mortifying, but it could be worse.

A low female voice, possibly Matilda, piped up, "Why don't you just hire a professional? This isn't Dan's speciality - sorry Dan - and he has enough on his plate."

"Okay, okay, you are right." Claude sounded like he was surrendering after a sustained campaign. "But who? I can't just invite a stranger into our home."

A rougher voice, William? "Yeah you can. Just get them in when we're not here."

Dan spoke from above her, his warm tones comforting even when they weren't directed at her, "I'm not sure it works like that, won't they want to be there during the event?"

"Depends," Someone mumbled. In the silence that followed Maisy realised with some alarm that it was she who had spoken.

She opened her eyes to find Claude, William, Matilda, and a group of people who she presumed were other Drift Masters and Mistresses watching her intently.

"Crap," she muttered.

Daniel leaned over to meet her gaze. "Something to contribute, sweetheart?"

Still half asleep and not entirely sure what she'd wandered into, Maisy wasn't sure how to respond. "Kinda?"

Matt's big laugh came from her left, "Don't be scared, love. Let's hear it."

Claude and William sat side by side, heading up the informal meeting in the booth. In between William and Maisy was Matilda. Matt was looking down on her from the other side of Dan. She sat up and saw that there were two other women and a man she didn't recognise. They all wore black armbands.

The Masters and Mistresses of Club Drift. And every pair of eyes was focused on her. She pulled herself upright, even though curling up in Dan's lap and pretending she was still asleep was a much more appealing alternative.

"Sorry, everyone, I didn't mean to interrupt. I was just saying that some event planners stay through an event to the end and some just orchestrate ahead of time. Most would prefer to stay though. Especially with a new client. You want to make sure everything is running smoothly, you know?"

She was babbling, wasn't she? Definitely babbling. She clamped her mouth shut and glanced at Claude. His gaze had become…hungry. Like a cat spotting a plump and lazy bird.

"You are in the business, Maisy?"

No! Keep it all separate, Maisy. Come on, just tell him you're guessing and go back to hiding in Dan's lap.

However, lying in the face of Claude's eager and commanding expression was much easier said than done. "Um, yes. It's what I do."

"You're an event planner?" Matilda grinned at her, "That explains a lot."

Before she could ask what, exactly, her profession explained Claude continued, "I wouldn't like to pressure you, petite, but do you think you might…?"

He left the question hanging, as if he knew how big a jump it was for her to merge her professional life with the club.

"I can give you a business card? My boss never bothers turning up to the actual events unless there's free booze, so you should be safe with us."

Did you actually just offer Claude your business card? For goodness sake, Maisy. Abort! Abort! Tactical withdrawal!

It was too late.

"Can I help you home, sweetheart?" Dan helped her to her feet. "You still seem a bit…"

Drowsy? Half-witted? Like my head's off in the clouds with my screaming orgasms and there's no chance of it coming back any time soon?

"Yeah, thank you." she agreed, she wasn't feeling 100% yet.

She held Dan's arm as they approached London Bridge underground station. It was late, nothing but night buses and cabs around. Their journey was illuminated irregularly by passing vehicles and glaring streetlights. They could have been characters on a stage lit enthusiastically, if inexpertly, by a high school drama club.

They travelled down the escalator together, his hands resting gently on her shoulders. A subtly possessive gesture that looked like nothing at all to the passers-by, but to Maisy felt like a subtle leash tying her to him in that public place.

"I'm going East," she said as they reached the bottom of the escalators and the underground crossroad. She was loathe to break the silence that'd kept them enveloped in the club's comforting after-hours atmosphere even after they'd left.

"West," he said briefly, as if he was also aware of the intimate bubble of silence dissipating more with every syllable.

Maisy almost asked the question automatically. 'Would you like to come back for coffee?' That old cliche that seemed almost obligatory when you're this intimate with someone and you want to have them in your own bed.

He'd been inside her only hours before, but somehow she knew that this was a line she could not cross. Whatever this was between them, it wasn't the sort of thing where you wake up next to each other the next morning.

She knew that this was an intangible barrier she could not cross, so she said, "Thank you for a great night," instead.

Daniel kissed her sweetly, "See you soon, sweetheart."

Chapter 19
Firecracker

Emails needed answering, florists needed booking, transport needed cancelling, but all Maisy could think about was the night before.

She pressed her hands tighter around her mug, absorbing the heat, holding on until it was too much. She released the mug and looked at her reddened palm. Pain. Visible pain that she'd chosen.

There'd been small bruises on her ribcage where one flogger stroke had strayed a little too low. They looked a lot like the finger print bruises she had just above each hip on her waist. She didn't remember feeling those in the moment.

She ran a finger across the place where she knew the flogger bruises hid beneath her shirt. Properly covered up for her day at the office, but still so very present.

How does this work? She understood, in the most basic layman way, that pain and pleasure were both intense sensations. Mixing them to produce more intense results was logical, but to relish the marks left by passionate violence? Was that more of the same?

No, not quite. It wasn't about the firecracker intensity, the crackling electric connection between the players and the pleasure and pain they alchemised; it was something quieter. More simple and rich. Like kneeling by his side absorbing the atmosphere, protected and looked after by him.

It was being marked by the experience that had changed you a little, because it does change you. The more Maisy walked in Drift's world the more she realised that truth. It was a gentle sort of change, the kind that unpeels layers to reveal your core, the kind that leaves you more aware and sure of yourself. But it was a change.

Do people get addicted to this feeling? The sensual embrace of bondage. The intricate dance of power exchange. The rise and fall of pleasures and pains. When's the last time the average person got pushed to their limits? Some people climb mountains. Some people learn new skills annually. Some people find partners to trust and expand every inch of their mental and physical limits together.

It can be an adrenaline fuelled experience. A touch of fear like bitterness at the end of a drink. Just the very slightest edge, but unavoidable and indeed sensible if you don't know your companion.

It's thrilling. Like throwing yourself off a building with a thin bungee cord for life assurance or like running screaming through an empty field. It's baring every inch of yourself and giving yourself over to the unknown. A safe unknown, a negotiated unknown, but nevertheless a thrilling unknown.

You find yourself there, at the edge of trust and fear. At the edge of pain and pleasure and desire. Your limits shift and grow with time and experience, you might find addicts in the scene pushing further and further in search of more...something. But you'll probably just find yourself growing.

Additionally, if you were Maisy, you might find yourself offering your meagre professional services to one of the most effortlessly stylish people you've ever met.

Putting her empty mug aside, Maisy pulled her notebook from where it'd been hiding under her keyboard. She didn't know exactly what Claude was looking for yet, but she hadn't been able to resist sketching out a few ideas.

Anyway, the more she could get done ahead of time the better. Michael had a habit of swooping in and stealing the credit for other people's completed plans, but that was honestly better than him getting involved half way through. No, the best way to get Claude an event worth having would be to plan it all herself, tell Michael it was alcohol free, and let him take all the credit. It was more than likely that he'd leave Maisy to do all the work. Maybe she should cancel the whole thing.

No. This could work. The confidentiality required would be an extra challenge, but not an insurmountable one. Claude will have invited members already, so he might not even need invitations. Tables, chairs, any stage or set building they decided upon could be done well outside club hours.

The trainee subs were excellent waitstaff already and could probably be persuaded to step up for the evening. Hors d'oeuvres were easy enough to arrange and the trainees could also serve those. Their uniforms and the bar were already 1920s themed, maybe Claude would let her run with that.

They probably had refrigeration in the room behind the bar, right? She made a note to ask Dan what kitchen facilities they had, if any. However, if Claude was looking for a full sit-down meal, things could get complicated.

Her phone started ringing. Loudly. Club Drift. Claude. Crap. Why had she given him her card? Planning an event at the club was a terrible idea. She'd have to get work involved and Michael, the creepy sod, would figure out what kind of place it was and everything would go to pot.

Calm down, she tried to tell herself, you can manage Michael. Probably. Hopefully. Her phone was still ringing. It vibrated obnoxiously on the cheap pine-effect desk so she picked it up.

Still, answering it seemed a bit drastic.

Michael walked past, his eyebrow raised disapprovingly at whoever dared disturb the office peace. More like a tense and uncomfortable office atmosphere as far as Maisy was concerned, but Michael insisted it was peace. She answered, affecting her extra-chirpy customer service voice.

"Good morning! Maisy speaking, how can I help you?"

On the other side of the phone Dan chuckled, "You are too cute for words, sweetheart."

"Oh!" Maisy saw that Michael was still lurking nearby and bit down on the instinct to call Daniel 'Sir' or mention last night in any way. "What a pleasant surprise."

"Claude will be here in a minute. He wanted me to start the call so he could honestly say to the people he's conference calling right now that he's got someone waiting on the other line. Bless him, I've got no idea how he's done so well in business with that soft heart of his."

"That's great. Can I run through some details with you?"

"Is someone listening?"

"That's correct," she replied, keeping Michael's position in sight, as usual. She liked to know where he was so he couldn't sneak up on her.

"So I probably shouldn't start asking you for your thoughts on boutique hotels?"

Maisy felt her cheeks turn red, "No, no, that will not be necessary."

Dan laughed, "Don't worry, sweetheart. I wouldn't really. I'm Dan the business man today, anyway."

"There's a novelty," she said, just about resisting the urge to ask when he became a poet. "What's the deal with kitchen facilities at the club?"

"Non-existent. I mean, there's a big refrigeration unit and a sink in the utility room behind the bar, but that's as far as it goes."

"No problem. Speaking of the bar, have you already ordered anything for the event drinks wise?"

"Yeah, I managed that bit," he said, "I informally invited everyone who's been a member since the beginning and the regulars too."

"Good. Do you think Claude will want the formal invites?"

"That's where you lose me, sweetheart. There's a reason we need you. I think he wants to stick with the bar's Art Deco theme, but apparently that doesn't mean we can just do nothing for decoration." His good-natured tone reassured Maisy. He sounded grateful to be passing responsibility on to someone who knew what they were doing.

"Okay, how about -"

"Hang on, sweetheart. Here he is."

Maisy heard the men talking indistinctly for a moment before Claude spoke directly to her.

"Hello, dear Maisy! My apologies, I have had too many phone calls to make today before I got to this one, but this is the only one I wanted to make. Always the way, no? Has Daniel filled you in on his progress?"

"Um, yes, I suppose he has."

Claude laughed lightly, "Don't worry, I know it is not greatly advanced as of yet."

Maisy felt herself relax, Claude was just another client who needed a little help turning his ideas into a plan. She could do this. "So I'm going to need some information from you so I can prepare some ideas. The next stage is me walking you through what I come up with and then we decide together how to move forward, okay?"

"Perfect. I must thank you again for doing this, Maisy. It is good to be passing this on to somebody we can trust."

"It's fine," she said, "I'm looking forward to it." But inside her mind the twin demons of insecurity and shame were fighting for her attention.

What if you can't do something that Claude will like? What if you can, but Michael ruins it? What if Michael finds out about Maisy's connection to Drift? She pushed the unpleasant thoughts away.

"On second thoughts, Claude, it might be better if I email you this list of questions - it's getting long. For now though, what is it you want in a nutshell?"

"A big question for a nutshell, petite. What I want is, I believe, called a formal event in your business. There will be speeches, so a stage, perhaps. I would like to be able to serve a meal, but I understand there may be practicality and privacy concerns. I would like to show off my club at its best and celebrate everything that we are. I am sorry. It is vague."

Maisy had scribbled down notes as he spoke. Notes that covered far more than what Claude had actually said, "No, that's great. I just need a starting point. We can get specific next time we speak, when I have something to show you."

"Excellent. I can get Daniel to text you the appropriate email address to use?"

"That's perfect. It'll just be some logistical stuff for now. Rough numbers for attendance, facilities, stuff like that."

"D'accord. No problem at all."

"Great. So I should have something to show you by Saturday if you're available?" She meant 'if you're at the club', but she didn't want to say too much out loud, Michael was still lingering like a bad smell.

"Indeed. I look forward to seeing what you have for us, Maisy."

"Thanks Claude. Speak soon."

She put the phone back on her desk with her hand that was only shaking a tiny bit, really.

Claude had been reassuring and easy to talk to, as usual, so at least all she had to worry about was everything else going wrong, not the client being difficult.

"What account was that," Michael leaned on the back of her chair, looking over her shoulder at the notes she'd been making.

She pulled her chair forward slightly, forcing him to move to the side of her desk, "No-one yet. Just a query that I'm putting a proposal together for." She bent over her work and continued making notes, hoping he'd get bored and leave her to it.

"What's the company?"

"He wasn't specific." Maisy felt hot, as if the marks from the night before were glowing bright red, a brand for anyone to see.

Michael tutted, "Well, what's the name? Is it worth chasing?"

"Leroy. Mr. Leroy."

"Leroy?" He suddenly looked more interested than Maisy was comfortable with, "Not Monsieur Leroy?"

Shit. "I don't know," she said, keeping her tone light and disinterested, "He was French."

"For fuck sake, Maisy. Next time just come straight to me, yeah? We've got to get him in for a full presentation, all the bells and whistles. Saturday did he want it? Leave it to me, we'll land the whale." He clapped his hands together and grinned hungrily. Was there anything so repulsive as a talentless man with power?

Panicking internally, Maisy tried to appear calm, "Sure." There was still a chance Michael would be too drunk or disinterested to put a pitch of any sort together by Saturday, anyway. She could still get control of this.

"You should really be doing something else, you know."

She answered, "I'm sorry?" For a moment Maisy thought he was talking to someone else, but she knew nobody else had entered the office floor.

"This isn't really your thing, is it?" Michael said, smoothing his over-gelled blond hair back with an indifferent shrug. "You'd be better off as a waitress or something I reckon.

You're good with people and your arse is bound to bring in the tips. You'd probably make more than we pay you working down the pub if you wore a short skirt."

Maisy had heard people say their brain short-circuited before, but she had never really understood the phrase until that moment. Michael's sexist commentary definitely went into her brain through her ears, but it was so bizarre and outdated her software encountered a problem when trying to interpret the data input.

The unfortunate effect of this temporary malfunction was that she sat gaping at Michael like a goldfish rather than telling him where to stick his short skirts and 1950s management style.

"Send the details on to me when you get a chance, yeah?" He winked and made a clucking noise with his mouth. The one people usually use to persuade horses to giddy up.

"Bloody cheek," she said, long after Michael had stalked away to his office, because she really didn't know what else to say.

Chapter 20
Just A Client

It seemed to Maisy that as the rest of the world moved forwards in time, Michael went backwards. The longer he was the manager of the company, the further his attitudes seemed to regress. Maybe he was merely growing more comfortable in his position and expressing views he'd always had to a broader range of people.

It wasn't just the sexism and racism and...well all the -isms, to be quite honest, he was also bewilderingly old fashioned in his approach to the event planning business.

The company had a few huge sheds on Michael Snr.'s land an hour outside London. The kind of sheds you could happily store a small aircraft in; barns, really.

Over the years, any bespoke sets and props that the company had needed to produce rather than rent from suppliers had piled up in these barns. The thing is, the company had been running for 30 years in one form or another before Maisy turned up. Some of this stuff had gone out of fashion, come back in, then gone out again twice since it was first made.

Some of it was still usable for vintage or kitsch effects. Maisy had spent many happy hours perusing the inventory looking for wonders and browsing oddities.

She had been delighted to discover that the company owned no less than 20 giant toadstools. Sadly, there was no record as to why these had first been created, but they were wonderful for woodland weddings.

The problem with this eclectic treasure trove was that Michael Jnr. had no taste. He had no design or management experience either, but the taste thing was somehow more troubling.

He was the sort of man who would gold plate his penis if it was possible, especially if he could get a good deal on the job. This meant that he couldn't see the problem with pitching an 80s-style under-the-sea theme complete with moulding paper seaweed. To a major tech company. A tech company who'd asked for a sleek event to celebrate a new innovation in their area of expertise, no less.

Maisy had long since given up trying to push him towards more appropriate options when he made these proposals. He always just said, "I'm making an executive decision!", and grinned arrogantly as confused customers left one after the other.

Instead, Maisy quietly made her own plans that were... in the same thematic ballpark to Michael's outdated ideas, but better fleshed out and adjusted to modern tastes.

Sadly, many customers backed out before she got a chance to implement her plans, even longstanding return contracts, but every now and then she got enough alone time with the client to show them her work and beg them to let her try.

Michael rarely turned up to the events they put on anyway for fear of having to help set up. Even when he did show, he was usually too drunk to notice that he'd had different plans for this specific client.

This could all still work out. All Maisy would have to do is put an accelerator on her damage control and keep Michael's lazy arse away from the club on event night. She could do this.

If she told herself enough times, she might actually start believing it.

TEMPTING AS IT WAS to call Dan and cancel her night at the club, she decided against it. After all, if Michael managed to ruin everything in the newly arranged meeting tomorrow she might never be able to show her face in the club again anyway.

Maisy'd made a mistake before leaving work. She'd done a web search on 'Claude Leroy.'

She should have guessed Claude was as wealthy as the Queen as well as sweet and gorgeous. No wonder Michael was so excited about potentially landing the Leroy account. The company could use a big haul like that.

The bouncer who always hovered outside Drift and pretended not to know anything about it gave her a nod as she entered. One day, when she was less pre-occupied, she'd have to ask Claude why he hired this guy. He didn't interact with anyone that Maisy had seen. Maybe he only became useful if there was trouble.

Dan was waiting at reception. He pulled her in for a long kiss.

"It's good to see you sweetheart," he said, holding her firmly around the hips.

"Good to see you." She nuzzled into his neck. A big part of her wanted to explain everything. To tell him all her worries about the next day and let him soothe her fears away for the night.

A small and scared part of her soul held her back.

Dan took Maisy's hand and led her into the main room. The vaulted ceilings were still impressive even after a handful of visits.

"There's Claude, I need to - do you mind if I just say something to him before I get changed?" Maisy asked.

"Of course not, sweetheart, but you're here to have fun. Don't spend too long worrying about work."

She smiled at him gratefully, "Not going to happen." She was glad she hadn't cancelled tonight. Even if she wasn't brave enough to talk to him about whatever horrors awaited her tomorrow, Dan would take her mind off things for a while.

"Claude?"

The owner looked up from the incomprehensible table of figures he'd been perusing at the bar and gave Maisy a broad grin. "Good evening, Maisy. Dan. What can I do for you?"

"It's about the meeting tomorrow. It's not - I mean, this is very early stages, you know? Don't worry too much if you're not happy at the end of tomorrow's meeting. It's just a stepping stone to the proper planning bit." She clamped her lips together before she could babble anymore and let on about Michael's interference.

"I know, petite. Do not worry, okay?" Claude frowned, his pale blue eyes concerned. "You will do a wonderful job, Maisy."

She nodded, but she didn't seem convinced, "I hope so. I'd better go get changed. I can't stay late tonight. You know, things to get up for." She smiled weakly at Claude and went to find the dressing rooms.

PLENTY OF PEOPLE CAME to the club in normal dress and got changed once they arrived. They usually looked a bit happier about it than Maisy did in that moment, though. Dan watched her go, his own frown mirroring Claude's.

"What is wrong?"

"With Maisy, you mean?" Dan asked, glad that Claude had also noticed that something wasn't quite right.

"Something has changed."

"You're right, but I haven't a clue what." She'd been fine the last time they'd spoken. She'd been happily asking questions about facilities for the event. Questions she'd repeated and expanded upon in an email later that day. She'd been chatty. She'd even sounded excited about planning the anniversary, at least he'd thought she had.

Tonight, though, she was subdued.

"What are you planning for her tonight?"

"Nothing heavy. It'll take her mind off whatever's wrong though. Will you come back here after the meeting tomorrow? I want to know what happens."

"You think the problem will become clear then? Perhaps you're right. I'll make sure I get back here before Maisy comes in the evening, yes?"

"Thanks Claude."

"De rien."

Chapter 21
Wax

"Are you ready?"

Maisy's fingers tightened involuntarily around Dan's arm. She forced herself to relax. This was what she wanted.

The club was heaving tonight. People she recognised and several she didn't milled around the main room. It was early, so there wasn't much going on, but if you stopped to look for more than a second you could see the differences here from a normal bar. The clothes, the scents, the sounds.

"Maisy?"

"Yes?" Her eyes snapped back to Daniel. He stood calmly watching her as she watched the room. "Yes, I'm ready. Sorry Sir."

"Not at all, sweetheart." He squeezed her hand and led her away from the main room, to a quiet, darker tunnel.

He let go of her hand and pointed at a cushion by his feet. She knelt and watched as he lit several candles. Some in lanterns, some brightly coloured, some white.

As the gloom lifted she saw that the only furniture in the tunnel was a padded bench. What Maisy didn't notice, however, was the rings embedded in the floor and ceiling.

Daniel took a plastic wrapped sheet out of the storage cubbies where aftercare baskets and safe sex supplies were kept and threw it over the bench.

He knelt in front of Maisy, took her face in his hands, and kissed her gently.

"I've been looking forward to having you like this, little Maisy." He kissed her again and she melted into it. Ready to give, ready to take, ready to assume her place in their dance.

"We're going to experiment with wax today, sweetheart."

Maisy pulled back and tried to glance over his shoulder at the candles, but he held her in place. Wax? That sounded like more pain than she was willing to deal with.

"Eyes on me."

At the quiet command Maisy focused her gaze on Dan's eyes, feeling his quiet, composed attention calm her. They'd spoken about pain, about pleasure, about her desires and needs. Her Sir wouldn't be suggesting this unless he thought it'd be okay.

She caught sight of a luminous armband as a DM wandered past their tunnel's entrance. She was safe here.

"Is it going to hurt?"

He didn't answer, just waited, thumb brushing her cheek softly.

"Is it going to hurt, Sir?"

"Good girl. It may a little, but that's not why we're doing this experiment. This is for your pleasure, my Maisy."

"Okay then." She leaned forward and kissed him, trying to communicate the trust and desire she felt with the simple action. He kissed her back at first, tenderly and deeply, then she felt his hand fist in her hair as he pulled back. He held her immobile as she knelt, their lips an inch apart.

"What's your safe word, Maisy?"

"Red, Sir."

"Good," he brushed his lips against hers, a small reward, "And if you don't want to stop, but need to slow down?"

"Yellow, Sir." She smiled, parting her lips a little in anticipation of his kiss.

He smiled a cruel little smile and shook his head, "Greedy little sub."

"Yes Sir," she grinned and leaned forward a little more, reaching for the kiss.

He chuckled and kissed her briefly before biting her bottom lip. She squeaked and tried to pull back, but he held her in place a moment longer before releasing her.

"You get what I want to give you, understand?"

She licked her throbbing lip and closed her eyes as the little pain rushed through her body as raw heat. Oh yeah, she understood alright.

"Good girl. Up you get." He helped her stand and led her to the padded table. "Strip sweetheart."

She did so quickly, awkwardly, still unused to getting naked outside of her own home. Dan's appreciative gaze helped soothe her nerves

He offered her a hand and helped her get on the bench. The protective sheet that he'd placed on it was cold on her skin, but it warmed within seconds.

"On your front, please."

She obliged and lay as neatly as she could. He pulled her legs slightly further apart, then smacked her arse playfully, "Beautiful."

She grinned and relaxed into the table, this wasn't so bad.

She nearly jumped off the table when something cold and slippery splashed on her back. "Jesus!"

He bit back a laugh, "What was that?"

"Nothing, Sir." She replied through gritted teeth, trying to relax into the table again. He began massaging the oil into her back.

Her muscles softened under his fingers and she sank into a relaxed state, quite like how she'd felt kneeling with him the other day. "That feels good, Sir."

"Mmhmm. It'll protect your skin from the wax and make it easier to peel off after I'm done making you all pretty for me."

Oh yeah, the wax. The massage turned from sensuous to ominous in a heartbeat. She couldn't help tensing a little when he stepped away. Was it going to drop hard and fast like the cold oil had? Would it really hurt? What if she couldn't bear it?

"Stop all that worrying, little Maisy." Dan knelt by her head and ran a gentle hand through her hair. "If you really don't like it we'll stop, but I want you to try for me, okay?"

Suddenly she felt like she'd take a lot more than wax to please him, "Yes Sir."

"That's my girl. I'm going to drop a tiny amount from really high up at first, okay?"

"Yes Sir," She relaxed into the table properly, feeling slight excitement alongside the fear for the first time. Hot, smooth wax. There was something sexy about the way it pooled and dripped even before a Dom got hold of it.

Dan stepped away again and Maisy felt herself tense up. Frowning, she made herself relax. She wanted this. Wanted all the sensations he could give her, even if they scared her for now.

She took a slow and steady breath, listening to his footsteps behind her, letting the familiar noise be her anchor.

"Ready sweetheart?"

She nodded, then when he didn't answer - "Yes Sir."

"Good girl."

She tensed, waiting for the pain. She waited a few seconds, a minute, the tension in her back eased as she turned her head and began to ask "Sir-ah!" The first drop of wax landed on her lower back.

It burned for just a split second, then became a warm caress. She shifted back to the position she'd been instructed to stay in and felt the little rivulet crack.

"More?"

"Yes please, Sir."

"Stay very still, little Maisy."

She wriggled her arse, giggling when he smacked it, then settled into the position he'd specified, waiting quietly for the next drop.

He let her wait. Perhaps testing her to see if she'd break orders again and move or speak. No, now the fear of the unknown had lifted she was determined to take it like a good girl.

The next searing drop felt the same as the last. It landed and cooled in seconds. He let one, two, three the same drop up the centre of her back and she sighed happily. The light sting was well worth the warming caress that followed.

"Good," He said, "let's see how much you can take."

"Sir, I-" His hand cracked down on her arse with a stinging crack.

"Unless you're using a safe word I want you to be silent, little Maisy."

She huffed out a breath. Jesus fucking Christ, it hurt when he really spanked her.

He took her painful recovery time as silent agreement, it seemed. He rubbed an oily hand over the spot he'd spanked, then let three drops of wax drop on the pinkened spot in quick succession.

She hissed at the sudden, shocking sting. Dan rubbed her shoulder soothingly, and as he did so the pain eased into a more intense warmth than she'd felt with the other drops.

When she relaxed he started again. He concentrated on her arse at first. Letting one drop after another land on her glistening cheeks. He gradually upped the intensity, holding the candle closer to her body by millimetres each time then lifting it up again when she wriggled with too much discomfort.

Likewise, he sped up the drops until the stings barely had time to ease before the next one landed. Her arse was covered in dripping, warm, half set wax by the time he stopped the sensuous onslaught.

Maisy moaned softly when he stopped, pulled from the happy cycle of pain and pleasurable warmth. He knelt in front of her so she could see his face.

"Do you want more?"

"God yes!"

Dan chuckled at her eagerness. "I'm glad you like it. We're going to move you forward a little, that's it. Now roll onto your back."

She wrinkled her nose as she felt the wax on her arse crack. It wasn't an unpleasant sensation, just very strange.

"Lie back, there's my girl." He poured more baby oil onto her front - less shocking when she could see him coming - and began massaging her breasts.

All the sensual warmth she'd felt from the earlier wax suddenly became intensely erotic. Her sensitive nerves wakened under his hands and she felt herself grow wet.

Would he touch her today? God, she really hoped so, there was no way she'd get through tonight without coming. He smoothed the oil down onto her stomach and up her ribcage, then went back to her breasts. Playing with her nipples and enjoying the weight of her in his hands.

She smiled, men were predictable really, whatever their more obscure sexual preferences.

"Enjoying yourself, little Maisy?" He asked, noticing her expression.

"Not as much as you, Sir." She said, made brave by his obvious enjoyment of her body.

He grinned, "Is that right?"

She couldn't resist pouting a little when he removed his hands and moved back round to her head. He bent to kiss her briefly - too briefly - then said, "Open your mouth."

She did, obeying automatically before she'd had time to process the order. Her eyes widened when he undid his jeans and pulled out his hard cock. "Seeing as I'm enjoying my little sub's body so much I think she'd better do something about it."

She nodded eagerly and leaned her head back, opening her mouth as wide as she could. She'd fantasised about pleasing him with her mouth - she was good at it and something in her just wanted to give Dan as much pleasure as he gave her.

He gave her the thick head of his cock and she sucked it gently, trying to get as much of him in her mouth as possible. Slowly, too slowly, he pushed in until half of him was sheathed in her hot wet mouth.

She could see him watching her, assessing her comfort level. She could take more, she wanted to take more. She tried to tell him so by wriggling her body up.

"No darling, you'll be glad when you're feeling the wax too."

She stilled. He was going to carry on pouring wax on her while she had his cock in her mouth? What if he made her jump with the pain and she bit him or something awful. Her panic must have shown in her eyes because he grinned, "You'll be very careful, sweetheart."

He picked up a candle - purple - and held it high about her chest, not tilting it yet. Just holding it where she could see it.

"Suck," he ordered. She obeyed. Swirling her tongue around the head, lapping up the sweet salty liquid at the tip.

"Fucking hell," he growled, and began to thrust gently in and out of her mouth. He never went further than half way, which she discovered she was grateful for after all because of the angle her head was at. She closed her eyes and concentrated on pleasuring him. Relishing the taste of him and the thick, pulsing sensation when he thrust in. She moaned around his cock when his free hand settled on one oiled nipple, pinching it hard then rubbing the hurt away.

"Beware of wax, Maisy." He said, only the slightest huskiness in his voice giving away how turned on he was.

She sucked a little harder than she had been and opened her eyes, meeting his lusty gaze and hoping he'd interpret that as 'full speed ahead.'

"Good girl," he grinned, then the first drop of purple wax landed on her nipple. She felt the sensitive skin pucker under the slight sting, felt the ensuing warmth travel to her clit like a lightning bolt. He released the other nipple and lifted the candle above it, "Suck."

She realised she'd been so absorbed in the sensation of the wax she'd stopped paying attention to his cock. She closed her eyes and focused on licking and sucking him, moaning around him when the next drop landed, but staying on task.

He pulled away and she whimpered.

"Spread your legs." He walked to the storage cubbies and rummaged in a drawer.

She obeyed. Would he fuck her? Oh please, please let him fuck me, she thought.

The skin that wasn't covered in wax was just a little chilly, making every drop of warmth as comforting as it was erotic.

Cold lube drizzled between her legs, quickly warmed by his fingers. He massaged around her hole and clit, just titillating, not enough to get her off.

"Sir, I need you." She said, hating how whiny she sounded.

"Shhh. I know, little Maisy." He plunged one finger into her, then another, stroking her gently, stretching her just a little. The she heard the crinkly noise of a package opening. "I think you'll like this."

She lifted her head to watch what he was doing.

"Head down."

She obeyed and clenched her fists, desperately wanting to see what he was doing.

"You've been a very good girl, Maisy. That's why you get to try this." As he spoke he slid something hard and firm inside her. The 'C' shaped device fitted snugly against her g-spot and her clit at the same time. He put it in position then carried on fucking her slowly with his fingers.

"I think I'll fuck you like this one day. I wonder how you'd feel with a butt plug, me, and this toy in all at once."

She clenched around him and he laughed, "I think that's a yes. I'm almost tempted to change today's plans."

She nodded and wriggled on the table, wanting more, needing more stimulation now she felt full.

"No love, not today. We're going to see how hard this-" he withdrew his fingers and flicked a switch on the vibrator, "Can make my little sub come."

Maisy's back arched as the device sprang into life. The internal arm rotated slowly as it vibrated, keeping insistent, rhythmic pressure on her g-spot, keeping her feeling full, while the external arm pressed firmly against her hard clit.

It'd be too much if it wasn't vibrating in a wave pattern, making the sensations intense, but bearable. Building rather than overwhelming.

"Yes, I think you like that."

She gave a frustrated mewl and reached for him, needing him to touch her, fill her - to do anything.

"I think you've been moving around far too much, subbie."

"Hey!"

He attached long, wide straps to the rings on the floor around the bed and tightened them until her torso was firmly tied down. Her knees were still up, exposing her filled body to him, but her arms and belly were held down so she couldn't move, only wriggle.

When he stepped back and looked her bound form over she felt a rush of pleasure. Being bound by him, for his desire, was a heady rush she'd never get enough of.

"There's my good girl." He bent by her head and kissed her long and hard, then pulled away. She saw him pick up the candle again. "Open."

She opened her mouth and took his cock gratefully. Focusing on sucking as much of his length as he'd give her, running her flat tongue across the underside of his cock, teasing him so she didn't have to think about the insistent pulsing in her cunt.

She knew she'd come like this, but she wanted to get him off first, wanted to give him something.

She'd forgotten about the candle by the time she felt the next burning drop. She cried out when he let five drops land on her chest leading up from her navel. They were closer to her skin than before, but the pain drifted away almost instantly and the sensations merged with the intense pleasure that was coming in waves.

He lifted the candle a little and let drops land fast in circles around her left breast. She began sucking him again, feeling the heat and warmth and vibrations combine until she was all sensation.

Before the drops hit her nipple he switched to circling the right breast. She moaned and sucked him harder, her hips lifting against the bottom restraint in a useless attempt to get away from the driving vibrations leading her to inevitable orgasm.

He pulled out from her mouth and she moaned, her distraction gone. He poured a heavy puddle of wax over her right nipple. Not a drop, a wave of burning sensation. She cried out and arched, then felt the restraints holding her down and felt another wave of pleasure at being controlled, bound, his.

She looked up and saw him watching her, the candle in one hand, stroking his cock with the other. She heard his dark, guttural moan as he came, felt the hot spurts of his pleasure landing on her chest become cold as true burning heat landed on her left nipple.

The pulsing in her cunt reached a crescendo and she screamed her release as he poured the hot wax on her left nipple and it merged with the evidence of his pleasure. The vibrations were relentless and she shuddered for longer than she'd thought possible.

"Please turn it off, please, please, please."

He put the candle aside and walked round to her legs, taking far more time than was necessary, pausing to unclip the restraints. He finally got there and switched the vibrations off, pulled the toy out, and eased the loss by flicking his tongue over her aching clit. She jerked violently intense sensation. He stood and caressed her knee. "Look at you."

She lifted her head and looked down at her panting chest, covered in sensuous rivulets of drying wax and his come. She'd been used as a canvas for his pleasure, bound, used - and she'd loved every second.

"Thank you, Sir."

Chapter 22
Bad News

Maisy had been waiting in the conference room with Michael and John – Michael's university buddy and incompetent second in command – for far too long. She usually avoided spending any time alone with the two of them. They were not pleasant company.

Maisy was sure that Claude greeted the others the European way just so he could kiss her cheek and give her hands a reassuring squeeze. She'd never been good at hiding nerves, but Claude couldn't know what was causing them yet.

If Claude was surprised when Michael, not Maisy, stood to give the presentation he didn't let it show. He smiled politely and nodded as Michael began to lay out his pitch.

However, as the pitch continued and Claude realised that Maisy's ideas were absent, he wore a cold frown. Maisy kept her eyes on the projection screen as much as possible, monitoring Claude's reactions, but not wanting to get caught doing so.

She saw Claude shake his head in that disappointed way he had, she'd seen it devastate submissives in the club, so she wasn't surprised that Michael stumbled over his words momentarily.

"So, that's not the only option," he continued, finding his clueless stride again with the ease of the preternaturally confident. "We also specialise in charming retro themes."

Claude raised an eyebrow, apparently anticipating that he didn't share a definition of 'charming' or 'retro' with this man.

This was humiliating. Maisy shrunk back in her seat, no longer looking at Claude for his reactions because she could feel his eyes on her. The projector displayed garish images of 'Under the Sea' events the company had thrown with their ancient decorations. They looked even more cheap and tacky in the black and white photos that Michael had inexplicably chosen.

"Enough." Claude said, interrupting Michael mid-bullshit.

Maisy looked up and saw Claude looking at her expectantly. Oh God. She couldn't just say nothing, "Claude, Mr. Leroy, we have a team orientated approach here, but-"

"That's enough, Maisy," Michael said, the venom in his words echoed on his face for just a moment before he smoothed his features to the usual false grin.

Claude looked between the two of them, then at John who was texting under the table, apparently unaware that anything had gone awry with the presentation.

"What happened to your plans, Maisy?" Claude asked quietly. "I understood you had been working on something."

"Yes, yes I was, but as I was saying, we have a team orientated approach here and some plans never make it to the client."

"It's so you only get the best, Monsieur Leroy," Michael simpered, his affected pronunciation sounded like a sneer.

"I see." Claude smiled, but Maisy could tell he was annoyed, "Well, if it is okay with you gentlemen, I'd like to see Miss Bennett's presentation too."

Michael glanced at John who'd finally looked up from his phone, waiting for someone to return order to proceedings.

"If you insist," John said, his false smile dimming as he realised the wealthy Mr. Leroy was less than impressed with his company's offerings. "Go on then, sweetheart."

Maisy bristled at the unwelcome endearment, but brushed it aside along with Michael's poorly concealed smirk

Maisy gave her presentation with only the rough sketches and notes she'd made in her personal notepad. She steadfastly avoided looking at Michael and John, instead focusing on Claude, who was listening intently. If she focused on his kind eyes she could almost pretend she was at Club Drift, not in the old conference room that'd hardly been used since Michael Snr. died.

"That's it. I really must apologise for the lack of proper presentation, I didn't think I'd get a chance to show you and -"

"That is more than fine, Miss Bennett." Claude smiled at her briefly then stood, ready to leave the room. He shook Maisy's hand and said, "We'll speak later," so quietly that the other men couldn't have heard.

"Thank you, gentleman. I'll be in touch." He shook their hands too, but only out of politeness.

As soon as Claude turned the corner John rounded on Maisy, "Well, that was a waste of time. Remind me not to follow your leads again. A moment, Michael? I want to go over the Montague christening thing quickly."

They left Maisy sitting in the empty room feeling more embarrassed than she'd ever felt in her adult life. If only that idiot hadn't steamrollered her, if only she'd prepared something more thorough just in case, if only she'd never offered to help Claude in the first place.

She'd mixed the club, her sanctuary, with her shambolic work life. What if Claude thought less of her now he'd seen her colleagues walk all over her? Or now he'd seen her bare bones pitch?

3 p.m. Too early to slink away and hide in a dressing gown with a bottle of wine. Bollocks. Reluctantly, Maisy held her head high, pasted on a smile, and went back to her desk.

DIVING INTO WORK HELPED take her mind off things. She'd taken a handful of enquiries, received a card from a happy client, and sorted out most of the supplier admin for the week by the time 5 p.m. rolled around.

Maisy signed out of her email account and gathered her things. She was already thinking about seeing Dan at the club and, slightly more anxiously, seeing Claude.

What had he meant when he said they'd talk later? Was he disappointed in her for wasting his time? Interested in her pitch? Interested in Michael's pitch?

Unfortunately, what with Claude's inscrutable politeness earlier she wouldn't know until she'd spoken to him. She resolved to wear something that'd make her feel confident tonight, seeing as she wasn't sure what she'd find waiting for her at Drift.

The office was pretty much empty and the clock had reached 5:40. Huh, those last few jobs must've taken longer than she'd thought. She really needed to get a wriggle on if she wanted to bathe before going out tonight.

Her mental run through of getting-ready tasks was interrupted by Michael's pallid grin. He stepped out of John's office, reeking of whiskey, as she passed the door. She moved to pass him, not even bothering with the usual polite smile, but he blocked her way.

"Excuse me, please," she said, voice bright and louder than usual. She could see John's legs behind Michael in the doorway, was he listening? Asleep?

"You're fucking useless, you are. Good job you've got a good pair of tits"

Maisy blinked, taken aback by the crack in Michael's usually flawless city boy veneer. John must have been dishing out the good stuff today. She opened her mouth to respond, righteous anger rising in her chest, but was stopped by something in his face, or his posture, or maybe just in the intangible human scents that animals might understand better than she could. Something told her that she was tiptoeing around a sensitive tripwire.

"You should watch yourself, a woman like you-"

A loud, clear 'ding' rang through the hallway and he paused, the unspoken words heavy in the air between them. His eyebrow twitched involuntarily.

The cleaning lady, Roberta, an elderly and good-hearted woman that Maisy spoke to most evenings, stepped out of the lift and started towards them, pausing when she saw her way was blocked. Michael clumsily stood aside and Maisy walked on without another word, unspeakably relieved that Roberta had arrived when she did. The tension of the moment did not pass. She could still feel the potential violence rippling in the air between the three conscious human beings left on this floor.

"You can't even sell to that frog you're fucking." He called after her. Maisy froze, shocked by the naked vitriol in his voice. The cleaner's eyebrows disappeared behind her fringe.

Both women stared at the floor, caught in the apex of the flight or fight moment, waiting for the red-faced man to continue or stand down. He laughed at his own joke and stepped back into the office, slamming the door behind him.

Both women visibly relaxed and Roberta shook her rubbish bag soundly. "He's bad news, that one," she said, simply, before turning the vacuum cleaner on and drowning out all other noise in the building.

Chapter 23
A Proposal

Claude was waiting at the bar when she arrived at Club Drift that night a little before ten. Carl had been uncharacteristically quiet in reception, swapping his usual effusive greeting for a nod. Maisy'd raised an eyebrow at him, "What's up?"

He'd nodded at a roll of duct tape that had been placed on prominent display on the counter, then rolled his eyes. She'd let him stamp her hand in silence so as not to tempt him further.

Claude was deep in conversation with William, Matilda, and Daniel when she approached the bar. Daniel spotted her and smiled. Even though she was still feeling stiff from the tensions of the day, his smile soothed some deep part of her mind.

William and Matilda waved at her then left the bar, walking off in opposite directions.

"Evening sweetheart," Dan pulled her into a casual embrace that left her facing Claude.

"How are you, Maisy?" Claude asked, something a little different about his bright blue eyes tonight.

"Oh god, did Claude tell you how embarrassing our meeting was?" She laughed and hid her face behind Dan's arms, hoping that confronting it head on with humour would make any awkwardness pass faster.

"Mm. Something like that." Surprised by the cold note in his voice Maisy twisted to look up at Dan. He was frowning, but soon eased his expression. He kissed her forehead again, "Sorry sweetheart. Just pissed off with your arsehole colleagues."

"Oh, don't worry about that." She pasted a smile on, redoubling her resolution not to tell Daniel about Michael's behaviour as she was leaving work earlier.

If either man noticed her discomfort they didn't mention it. Claude cleared his throat, "I know this may be difficult for you, Maisy, but I'd like to put the offer to you all the same."

Maisy held Daniel's arm like an anchor. Whatever Claude said now could alter her relationship with the club forever.

"I liked your pitch very much and would like to hire you, but I cannot work with those...imbeciles at the company. Would you consider doing it yourself? Off the books? I know this is impolite to ask and could get you in trouble, but if you are interested please do let me know."

Maisy was stunned, thrilled, and started thinking of the possibilities. Long buried plans for a solo business began to rise to the surface of her mind, then fear of losing her job and failing to make anything of herself, then remembering Michaels venom.

In the end she said, "I'd love to."

Claude beamed and Daniel squeezed her arm gently in approval, "You don't have to decide now, petite, you can have some time to think or-"

"No." She said firmly, imagining squashing Michael the cockroach under the purple doc martins that she usually wore at outdoor event sites, "I'd like nothing better, Claude, thank you. Can we meet tomorrow, perhaps? Or Sunday? I'd like to get the paperwork and planning in order to show you properly. I might have to jiggle some logistics to get it to work without the company infrastructure, but there's no reason you can't get the same service with just me.

Claude grinned and placed a grounding hand on her shoulder, "Relax, little one. Tonight is for fun, work can wait until tomorrow, non?"

Chapter 24
Discovery

Maisy was still buzzing with ideas and anxiety when Dan returned with her water.

"You doing okay, sweetheart?"

"Yeah, totally. I'm totally fine. I wonder if Claude has strong opinions about the language of flowers. You know, whether he wants to keep traditional with the flower message or more contemporary. Have you ever seen him buying flowers?"

Dan raised an eyebrow and sat beside her, apparently happy to let her rattle away until she ran out of steam. "I can't say that I have."

"Never mind that now. I'll ask him tomorrow. Do you think he'll break the no photos rule so I can take some reference shots? I'll need the dimensions too, of course. And guest numbers. Are they having plus ones or is it members only? Dress code? Fetish or formal? Or fetish-formal!" She paused a moment, picturing all the fabulous things people like Xavier and Matilda would no doubt come up with if tasked to produce fetish-formal wear.

"Do you think I can do this? It's such a big event." She didn't leave a space for him to reply before continuing. "I mean, I've never done anything by myself before. I should have done a birthday party or something first. Maybe a cosy wedding. This is huge. This would be huge even if I was doing it for the company. Oh Christ, what if I ruin it? What if I ruin Claude's lovely event and he makes me leave and..."

"Okay, I'm going to stop you there." If Daniel wanted to laugh at her scatter-brained ramblings, he hid it well. He pulled her into his side and settled his arm around her shoulders, a comforting weight.

"Of course you can do it." Was the first thing he said. "I haven't seen your work, but I know you're thoughtful, diligent, and you have excellent taste in men, so I'm sure your taste in other areas is alright."

Maisy rolled her eyes at him, "But-"

"Nope," he squeezed her shoulder as gentle admonishment, "No buts. Not tonight. You've had a long, hard, weird day and you should put work out of your mind for now. Tomorrow. Tomorrow we can talk about the party and you can talk to Claude and plan to your heart's content. Tonight we'll take your mind off of everything, deal?"

Maisy thought through her anxiety that morning, the cringe inducing meeting itself, and the nasty confrontation with Michael that Dan didn't even know about. All of that with Claude's generous offer on top was quite a lot, really.

Maybe he was right. She should decompress tonight and return to her higgledy piggledy work life tomorrow.

"Okay sure. That makes sense." She drained her water bottle in one go then took his hands, ready for whatever he had planned.

"How do you feel about blindfolds?"

She shook her head, "Not right now. I need to see a bit or I'll -" She was going to say 'freak out' but she realised that

Daniel would probably worry if she did so. There was just too much going on in her head right now. She didn't know how to put that into words.

He gave her a piercing look, "Right. Follow me."

He led them to an empty booth and sat on the velvet seat before placing a cushion on the floor by his side. "I want you to kneel and face the wall."

She smiled, calmer already just from hearing the order. His straightforward orders had a way of calming even the most chaotic thoughts.

She bent her knees as gracefully as she could and settled neatly on the cushion.

"Most submissives remove their shoes when they're in role here," he said matter of factly.

She uncurled her legs and removed her heels, handing them to him with a coy smile.

"Thank you, sweetheart." He stroked her hair and took a sip of his drink, "Relax there for a bit. Don't speak or look around without permission. Matt, good to see you. Time for a catch up?"

"Dan! How's it going? Alright Maisy?"

She tensed, but Daniel kept stroking her hair and Matt didn't push her for a response. Apparently it wasn't strange for her not to reply. She smiled at him instead and leaned into Daniel's knee.

"Eyes, sweetheart," Dan reminded her gently.

She lowered her eyes and listened to the sounds of the club. Quiet conversation was everywhere. Some people, such as Daniel and Matt, were discussing club gossip. Who's been playing together a lot recently, how the trainees are doing, whether William had been turning up for his shifts (more than usual was the answer to that one, Maisy was glad to hear).

Others were talking about sex; negotiating scenes, or reminiscing like the laughing couple one booth over. The scent of leather and sex was less overwhelming than it had been when she first came in.

Somewhere in the distance she heard a loud female moan. This was a strange place. A good place. She placed a hand on Daniel's leg and smiled when he glanced at her.

This was okay. More than okay. Kneeling by his side as his sub, no-one to heed but him, no responsibilities, and his attention tangibly on her even when he was looking the other way - it was pleasant. Calming even. She realised that had been his intention all along.

She hardly noticed the time passing. It was something like meditation, sitting there peacefully. She didn't notice the conversation above her changing tone either.

"Maisy," his voice was quiet but commanding, "I want you to get on your hands and knees facing Matt. Get your back as straight as you can."

She began to obey his command before she'd even processed it. She smiled to herself, apparently her subconscious was obedient if nothing else. She arranged herself as he'd described and found herself face to face with a stranger.

"Hello," she said, bemused.

Daniel tugged her hair gently, "Neither of you have permission to speak right now, sweetheart."

The woman, a striking red head in trainee handcuffs, smiled at Maisy and rolled her eyes slightly.

"I wonder if you'd be rolling your eyes if Master Matthew could see you, Laura."

The red head gaped at Daniel as if she wanted to call him something rude then winced when Matt swatted her arse casually. "No Sir," she muttered.

Maisy swallowed the urge to laugh at the poor girl's plight; her sulky face really was a picture.

"Straighter Maisy."

She stretched as smoothly as she could, not sure how much straighter she could get.

"Good girl," he said, then balanced his cold tumbler on the small of her back.

"What the fu-"

"Maisy." The warning in his voice was clear so she shut up, but she scowled freely. Laura seemed to be used to this treatment as she was resignedly balancing Matt's glass of red wine on her back. Maisy wondered if that was why she was wearing a white dress tonight. It'd make for an effective punishment – balance this glass well or walk around covered in wine all night.

"I suggest you try a different facial expression, Maisy," Matt sounded amused rather than commanding, for which she was glad. She wouldn't have stood for a near stranger bossing her about, even if Matt was one the club Masters.

She schooled her features just as Daniel leaned over to see what his friend was talking about.

"Hmm. Careful sweetheart, you really don't want to spill that." She stiffened, recognising the threat. This wasn't something she'd ever imagined doing. It seemed harmless, but she couldn't see the sexual appeal.

Being a table was just pointlessly humiliating, surely? She was glad that there was someone else there going through the same thing because it made it seem easier to laugh at, but she did wish they could talk.

The men resumed talking as the women concentrated on staying still. Daniel lifted his drink to take a sip then placed it further up her back in a more precarious position. She tensed further. Might as well try to do this thing well if it was something he wanted.

Although the men continued talking about current affairs Daniel reached down and cupped Maisy's breast, teasing her nipple through her clothes. She gasped and pulled away, completely forgetting about the glass. Daniel had thankfully anticipated this and lifted the glass to safety.

"Last chance, Maisy," he said, calmly gesturing for her to resume the position. She glanced at Laura and realised that she was concentrating extremely hard and making strange mewling noises. Maisy was baffled until she saw the remote control in Matt's hand. Ah. Poor Laura. Maisy was getting off easy after all. She knelt back down with as much grace as she could manage and offered him her back again.

"Good girl." The approval in his voice spurred her on. He placed his glass on her back again and reached down to put his hand down her top so he could pinch her nipple a little harder. She remained still, very glad that her underwear wasn't full of something battery powered.

Poor Laura was shaking somewhere between ecstasy and agony as she fought the urge to come. Maisy watched transfixed. She'd never been with a woman before, so witnessing female arousal was a new and fascinating experience.

"Jealous sweetheart?" He whispered in her ear so as not to disturb Laura's concentration.

"No way," she said quickly, shaking her head as hard as she dared. The growing wetness in her underwear betrayed her real answer, but this was enough for the moment thank you very much.

"Hmm. Maybe next time," he ran his hand over her arse and under her skirt, toying with the elastic band of her underwear. "I'd like to see you balance this while I fucked you."

She laughed, "You'd be dry cleaning my dress, Sir."

"Would I now, little subbie?" He grinned and pinged her underwear strap hard causing her to jump. His other hand was ready to catch the glass, but she knew she'd failed the challenge. There was a pause while Daniel waited for her to acknowledge her mistake.

Laura moaned, frustrated, and Maisy felt an unexpected flush of arousal. She blushed red and turned to watch Daniel's stern gaze, waiting for his next command.

He placed his glass on the ledge above his head as he assessed her red cheeks with a pleased eye, "Over my knee."

She knew better than to argue. Glancing around to see if anyone was watching she stood and carefully arranged herself over his knee.

She looked down and saw the redhead trembling as Matt pushed a different button on the remote. Laura was obviously nearing orgasm, in fact Maisy was impressed she'd held on so long. Despite his affected indifference, Matt was ready to grab the glass when she went over the edge.

Daniel's hand landed on Maisy's arse with a resounding crack. Laura startled and looked straight up into Maisy's eyes as the second blow landed. Maisy blushed even redder and closed her eyes but opened them again with a gasp as a third hard blow landed.

Laura groaned loudly and shook into what looked like an extremely powerful orgasm. Maisy felt a jealous clenching in her cunt as she watched the curvy submissive buck and moan in the American Dom's arms.

"Not counting, sweetheart?" Daniel asked before spanking her even harder for a fourth time causing her to cry out loudly and squirm away.

She heard the smugness in his voice and realised that the men had planned every moment of what had just happened right up to Maisy's arousal tipping Laura over the edge.

"I'll start counting when I get an orgasm, Sir."

Loud laughter drew her attention to a breathy and flushed Laura who was now curled up in Matt's lap.

"Now you're for it. Master Daniel doesn't like mouthiness."

"Shh pet," said Matt, but he too was grinning.

She turned to look at Daniel and was met with a cold stare. Whoops.

"I mean sorry, Sir, I can count." She wriggled her arse as if inviting him to spank her again.

"I think you might need a stronger lesson, sweetheart, what do you think?"

As much as it was a threat it was a genuine question. They both knew how aroused she was and she could feel that he wasn't unaffected by their situation. The stresses of the day were entirely forgotten. She felt calm, relaxed, and extremely turned on. She'd come this far, what did she have to lose?

Chapter 25
The Bench

Daniel led Maisy to a thing that reminded her of her senior school gym class. It was solidly built from wood and leather. Anywhere else it would have been obscene, but in the cavernous otherworldly space of the club it just blended in with the staff uniforms from another era and the clientele who left their inhibitions at the door.

There were long adjustable leather straps with buckles attached to the frame and the floor around it. It was an intimidating piece of furniture, but she was still riding high on the surreal intimacy of watching a strange woman have an orgasm.

Daniel pulled her dress over her head and she was pleased to see his mouth drop open slightly when he caught sight of her embroidered under things.

When Daniel stroked her back gently from base to hairline she bent over the bench obligingly.

He moved slowly, deliberately, making sure that his tread was audibly heavy. His hands never left her skin unless their eyes were locked on each other's.

He fastened her hand to the side of the bench. She felt him tighten the buckles a little too much then loosen them. When she tugged at them her arms could only move half an inch in any direction. She let out a shuddery breath and wriggled her arse eagerly at Daniel.

"Are you being impatient little sub?" Daniel stroked her arse as he spoke. She'd heard the laughter in his response, but she was unsure how tolerant he'd be of her sass in this environment, especially as a few people were standing close enough to hear anything she said.

"No Sir - ah!" She cried out then stifled a giggle when he swatted her arse lightly.

"Liar." He whispered in her ear then kissed her cheek. Anyone who'd followed them or been intrigued by their process through the bar was blocked off by his torso as he knelt by her side and stroked her arm.

Ah. The talking bit. Maisy felt a tiny swarm of panic. Every time they spoke in detail about sex stuff she started to over think what she was doing, but she knew this was necessary. She still couldn't quite get past how naughty she was being, bad in a good way.

It was exciting, but this was still new and frankly a large part of her wanted to rush in head first, avoid the fear, and think about it all later.

Judging by the easy question he started with Daniel had more or less guessed her thoughts. "How do your wrists feel? Your back?" He murmured in her ear, no-one else could hear them.

"They're fine," she smiled and tilted her face into his hand.

"Remember what I've told you about safe words, sweetheart. If you want out you know what to do."

"Yes Sir," she kissed his palm then licked it, savouring the slight saltiness of his skin and his surprised laugh.

"Good girl." He stroked her cheek gently and held her gaze. "You taunted me into punishing you, so I'm going to do so. However, I'm going to do it my way."

She grinned at him and flicked her tongue out to lick his little finger.

"Lucky for you, sassy little sub, I'm in a giving mood."

He stood so she had to strain her neck upwards to maintain eye contact.

"You'll get more than you bargained for. That I can promise you."

A dark shiver ran through her at those words. She recognised the sincerity in his promise and she couldn't wait to experience its implications.

"Thank you, Sir," she said. He bent to kiss her lips briefly, barely concealing his smile. She grinned happily, his apparent pride at her obedience was hugely pleasurable to her.

He stood properly and released Maisy from his gaze before stalking away from her head. With him gone she was more aware of her surroundings. Voices whispering nearby, moans further afield, the prickle of eyes on her skin.

She inhaled deeply, determined not to panic herself out of something she wanted so badly. Daniel rested his palm warm and heavy on the base of her back. To a casual observer she was being used as his armrest, but just like kneeling by the wall, this action was meant to calm her.

She saw some bare feet shuffle closer in her peripheral vision. Was it the submissive she'd locked eyes with? She tried to twist her shoulders to look but there wasn't enough give in the restraints.

She could hear the low rumble of Daniel's voice conversing with another male behind her, but she couldn't make out their words. Their conversation paused when an attendant - Maisy heard her 1920s style beaded dress rustling - approached, then resumed when the attendant moved away.

Maisy shifted her feet and wriggled her arse, hoping that her underwear hugged her body the way she imagined it did.

"Oh Maisy." She could hear the amusement in his voice, "You so nearly avoided this."

"Avoided wh- Oh."

He knelt behind her and pulled her ankles closer to the bench with two smooth yanks. The shackles were lined with soft fur which she was grateful for. Her legs were spread further than they had been; she felt exposed.

The soft sound of rustling beads returning seemed to cause the ripple of quiet conversation that had been building around them to die out.

"Maisy?"

She arched her back, intensely aware of the newly commanding tone in his voice. "Why are you receiving this punishment?"

"Because I was cheeky, Sir."

"Yes. And you watched Laura after I ordered you to keep your eyes down." He trailed his fingers up her spine as he approached her head.

She nearly argued that he was being unfair, but it didn't matter that he'd planned it all, it was adding to the punishment fantasy she was enjoying so much.

Black silk enveloped her head and the murmurs, the feet, the floor were gone.

"Your gaze is mine. Your pleasure is mine. Your cunt is mine." He growled into her ear through the hood and she turned her head towards the sound searching for his lips.

"Maybe later, sweetheart." He brushed his thumb over her bottom lip. She felt his breath warm against her cheek, but then he was gone.

Where had the blindfold come from? Was that what the attendant had been sent for? Without her vision she had no way of knowing if she'd brought Daniel anything else from the club's no doubt intimidating reserves.

His calming touch was gone and she felt the weight of anticipation. A blow was coming, but from his hand or some other implement?

The slight fear just fed into the thrill. Here she was bent over some bizarre sex furniture in her lingerie about to be spanked in public.

"Count Maisy," he said, interrupting her thoughts before she had a chance to get lost in them.

Maisy stiffened. Moments before something broad and stiff landed on her right cheek with a heavy thud.

"One. Thank you, Sir," she said before the blow had even finished. She wasn't going to be tricked into receiving twice as many blows because she didn't count properly.

Daniel squeezed her glowing arse affectionately, she got the feeling that he'd be chuckling if they were alone.

"Good girl." The next two swats came almost simultaneously and this time she cried out. Whatever it was in his hands it was much crueller than his hand or the flogger had been.

"Two. Thank you, Sir. Three. Thank you, Sir." She raced through the words, tensing up as she heard him approaching her shoulders. Already the pain from the blows was turning into a pleasurable tingling. She yelped in surprise as he fisted her hair and pulled her head up so he could speak in her ear without kneeling. His voice was low enough for her to be the only one privy to his words.

"This is hard isn't it, sweetheart? Two more with the paddle then I'll move on to something you'll enjoy more. Nod if you're still green and speak up if not."

She nodded hastily and tilted her lips towards the sound of his voice again.

This time he did chuckle. "Greedy little sub," he gave her a quick peck.

"Four more with the paddle seeing as you're so needy today."

She gasped, "No! That's not fa-"

Her lips were stopped by his hand gripping her chin roughly.

"I'm sorry, little one? What were you saying?"

She wished she could see him; when his voice was cold and his entire demeanour was commanding he exuded an almost bestial sexuality that melted her.

"Nothing Sir"

"Quite right, sweetheart." He kissed her properly then, lingering on her bottom lip and only loosening his grip on her chin when he stood and stalked away.

"You've had three."

The next swats landed in quick succession again. She hissed through her teeth. The paddle really stung when it hit the places that had already been pinkened by earlier blows.

"Four. Thank you, Sir. Five. Thank you, Sir."

He hummed his approval and smoothed his hand over her warm arse. She wriggled in her restraints and stretched towards him as much as she could. His gentle touch after the sharp sting of the paddle seemed to transform all the confused and excited energy she'd been feeling into pure pleasure.

"Thank you, Sir," she whispered.

"You have to wait until I give you the blow, sweetheart."

She felt him place something on her back - the paddle? - at the same time as she heard a quiet female giggle to her right. This was immediately followed by a muffled cry and some shuffling as the giggler was taken away.

Whoops. Sounds like Laura was in trouble too. Maisy grinned - hopefully her trouble would be as fun as Maisy's own.

"I think we'll save your final paddle blow. What do you think?"

She hesitated, "Whatever pleases you, Sir?"

"Good answer."

She could almost feel his approving smile.

He traced a lazy pattern on her arm as he spoke his next words. "There are many benefits to membership at this club. The atmosphere, the exclusive clientele, the unusual furniture-" he pulled at her wrist chain to illustrate his point. "You also get access to brand new toys. It's a very expensive membership."

Her eyes grew wide under the blindfold.

"You want to keep your underwear on, yes?" She nodded, glad that he'd anticipated her lingering modesty despite the exhibitionist turn the night had taken. "That's fine, but I want to put something in your pretty little pussy. Is that okay?"

He paused, waiting and presumably watching for her reaction.

"I..."she stopped and forced herself to think. What did she actually think about his proposal? "Hang on... Sir!" She added hastily.

"Take all the time you need, sweetheart." He carried on stroking her arm while she thought about it.

She tingled from head to toe. Every nerve in her body was alive and desperate for stimulation, fuelled by his blows and caresses and jealously of Laura's orgasm.

Maisy's body wanted whatever Daniel was ready to give her. This was new and terrifying and more arousing than anything she'd ever experienced.

"Please Sir." She said firmly.

"Please what?"

"Please give me more."

He cupped her cheek and kissed her very gently, "Good girl."

Apparently the attendant had bought more supplies after all. She heard a soft buzzing behind her. She shivered as he massaged something cold and slippery around her entrance then pushed the buzzing thing inside her. The toy wasn't only internal. It was a clever C shaped thing that cradled her clit with strong pulsing vibrations even as it filled her with pulsing girth. Much like the toy they'd used the night before when they played with wax, but thicker.

"How does that feel?"

She tried to answer but only managed an incoherent moan as the vibration changed patterns. The bastard had a remote control.

"That good, huh?"

She nodded, "It feels great."

"I'm glad. What do you say?"

The vibrations suddenly intensified tenfold and she growled, pulling away from the strong sensations and finding that there was no-where to go.

The vibrations stopped entirely.

"I was looking for 'Thank you, Sir', actually."

She grinned; she did like these games, "Thank you, Sir."

"Good girl."

The toy was switched back on and she moaned happily as the steadily pulsing vibrations pushed her towards ecstasy.

Maisy started as she felt something against her lips then she realised it was his cock. She opened her mouth and sucked him hungrily. She moaned around him as the pattern changed to a faster frequency before licking him from base to tip. She was good at this and even if she was distracted by a vibrator she was going to make him feel fantastic.

It seemed to be working. She heard him muttering soft curses and he began to thrust very gently as she worked him. She relished the taste and feel, trying to ignore her building pleasure so she could finish him off first.

However, that was not Daniel's intention. The incessant waves of sensation caused by the toy were pushing her towards the edge quickly. She struggled to maintain a steady rhythm with her mouth and then he pulled away, sensing that she was nearing orgasm

The toy's rhythm changed again to an even faster one. She inhaled the scent of leather and sex and sweat and revelled in the freedom of submission. As she began to fall into climax she wished he would fuck her so she could come around his cock.

The tidal wave of sensation crashed over her and she moaned then screamed as the final blow from the paddle landed hard on her arse. The unexpected pain just intensified the clenching pleasure and she moaned over and over as the orgasm shook her from head to toe.

Maisy took a shuddering breath and breathed a final, "Thank you."

Chapter 26
Drop

Daniel removed her blindfold, releasing her from her private sanctuary back into the chaos outside.

"Maisy? Sweetheart?" Daniel's satisfied smile faded as he took in Maisy's depleted state. He cupped her cheek just as tears began to gather in her eyelashes.

"Bollocks." Daniel cursed under his breath and began unfastening her arms, signalling to an attendant to take care of her ankles.

"Just hold tight, sweetheart, you'll be down in a minute. You're fine. You're safe." Daniel murmured words of safety and comfort. She didn't respond, too far gone to form a coherent sentence, but he carried on speaking calmly as one might address a startled animal.

"Arms around my neck, there you go." She obeyed unthinkingly. She heard him and she felt him help her down from the bench. She felt his protective embrace around her, heard the comforting rumble of his voice as he spoke. Her awareness only stretched to him.

She wasn't quite there. All the adrenaline had evaporated along with the anxiety and arousal that had fed it and she'd been left empty. She'd just stopped being for a moment. Not sad, not anything. She was empty and overflowing at the same time. It was like someone had pressed the reset button and she was caught on standby.

She felt Daniel rubbing her wrists, checking for any signs of damage. She saw rather than felt as Daniel swung her up into his arms. It was like an out of body experience, or that one time she'd gotten high at university, or perhaps the come down afterwards.

"Daniel," she struggled to say even that one word and she wasn't sure what she wanted to follow it with. She realised she was crying. Tears ran down her cheek onto his white shirt.

"Shh, sweetheart. don't speak yet." Daniel settled them on the low back seating and cradled her close. She didn't hear - or rather didn't understand - what he was saying at first, but she watched his lips move and wondered why she was crying. She wanted to say thank you again, to tell him how happy she was, that the crying wasn't right at all, that she'd had a good time like she always did, but she couldn't.

Every time she tried to speak she sobbed instead so she just lay in his arms and focused on stopping the tears.

The attendant had tailed them to their nook and now knelt discretely by their side. Maisy watched the sequins of her dress dance in the candlelight and smiled. She thought she heard Daniel say something about chocolate as he slipped the woman a tip.

He resumed his low mutterings and Maisy realised that he was soothing her, saying meaningless comforting things and waiting for her to come back to herself.

"I'm crying," she said.

He stopped mid platitude and scanned her face. Apparently something he found there gave him cause for relief because his shoulders visibly slumped as the tension left his body.

"Yes sweetheart. You're crying rather a lot."

"I'm sorry about your shirt."

He barked out a tense laugh. "Forget about the shirt."

"I'm sorry. I - I don't know what's wrong with me. Christ." She tried to sit up, but he tightened his hold on her. His expression brooked no argument and she didn't have the energy in any case.

"Stay where you are until you've recovered please, Maisy."

The firm line of his mouth and concern in his eyes erased all thoughts she might have had of rising.

"What's happening?" She brushed ineffectually at the tears with the back of her hand, "Why can't I stop?"

"It's just something that happens after a scene sometimes. It's perfectly normal."

"Doesn't feel normal," Maisy nuzzled into Daniel's chest. The tears were slowing and her thoughts were coming in more or less the right order, but she still felt drained. This was an exhaustion unlike anything she'd experienced before.

"It's called sub drop. Your body and mind has been through a lot. Sometimes the endorphins rising and falling can cause a drop in mood or any number of other symptoms. Tiredness, shaking and so on."

"Ugh."

"Quite." He ran a finger down her cheek and smiled wryly, "I feel responsible. I shouldn't have done a scene with you, even a light one, after the day you've had. It was asking for trouble.

"But I wanted to." She frowned and held her tongue as the waitress Daniel had tipped came back over with a basket and an armful of Maisy's dress and shoes. Where had they even left those?

The woman in 20s beads, a brunette with a ponytail that brushed the bottom of her back, gave Maisy a sympathetic nod before she left.

"Are they all...?"

"Yes. They're mostly submissives. Some of them are attached to Doms who are members here, some of them just want to work somewhere with this atmosphere without the constraints of a relationship."

"Do they ever play?"

"Not while they're on the clock." Daniel winked at her, "I don't think you're up to round two anyway, sweetheart."

She just rolled her eyes at him. As they spoke he pulled a thick knitted blanket from the basket and wrapped it around her; that she didn't bother arguing was testimony to how used to Club Drift's idiosyncrasies she'd become in the last few weeks.

"They sometimes play with experienced Doms in technique demonstrations on open nights, that sort of thing."

"Huh. Interesting job." She curled further into his chest.

"Second job. The lovely lady you were just making eyes at, for example, is a lawyer in her other life."

"Wow. She's even more attractive now."

"I know, right?" Daniel pulled her hair gently and handed her the first of two bars of chocolate. "Eat this. Tea is on the way."

She sat up just enough to eat the chocolate. "Your sex bar serves tea?"

His loud laugh caused a number of patrons to glance in their direction. "Of course, sweetheart. We put our subs through a lot, they need something to get them back to themselves after a hard scene."

A cup of tea sounded just about right actually. Maisy hadn't particularly wanted the chocolate, but she remembered how much it'd helped before and once she'd tasted the rich, dark stuff she wolfed it down.

"I wanted to do a scene with you," she said quietly, sitting up a little straighter when the beautiful submissive lawyer came by to drop off her tea.

Daniel put two sugar cubes in her cup before handing it to her, even though he knew full well she didn't take any, "I know, but I'm meant to be the responsible one when you're in the submissive mind-set. I'm meant to watch out for times when you make decisions you shouldn't."

"I am perfectly capable of making decisions for myself thank you very much." She gulped a mouthful of too hot tea and glared at him.

"I know, sweetheart." He stroked her arm and gave her a moment with her tea.

"Maybe we should have waited until next time," she said quietly. It had been an intense day and they really hadn't needed to rush into a scene. They'd gotten carried away.

"Probably. I think you dropped so hard because of your confused emotional state beforehand." He looked her in the eye, "I'm sorry Maisy, I won't be so careless with your wellbeing again."

She handed him her cup before curling back into his chest. "I should think not," she said, in her snootiest voice.

He handed her the other unwrapped bar of chocolate, "That's my good girl."

Claude, his timing impeccable as always, chose that moment to approach their cosy nook.

"How are you feeling, dear Maisy?"

Her unexpected and dramatic mood flip hadn't gone unnoticed by the rest of the club then. More's the pity. Maisy's stomach lurched unpleasantly when she remembered Claude had hired her in a professional capacity earlier that very evening. She nearly dropped the chocolate in her haste to sit up and put on a bright smile.

"Absolutely fine, Sir! Nothing to worry about, just a little wobble. Shall I call you about noon tomorrow? We can just go over some preliminary details and then-"

"Of course, petite. You can call whenever you are ready. For now, however, I'd like you to consider staying in one of the member's bedrooms."

"Oh! Why would I stay here?"

Claude sat opposite them in the booth, pausing a moment before continuing carefully, "It is getting late and you've had a trying day. I'd feel happier knowing you were safe here than releasing you into the night when you're a little...what did say? Wobbly."

Maisy bristled at the suggestion, but something about the concern on Claude's lined face made her pause. She did feel strange and there's nothing particularly pleasant about late night tube rides home even when you are entirely in possession of your faculties.

"That's very kind of you, Claude," she said, pushing her prideful objections away, "I think I'll take you up on that."

Claude nodded and smiled as if giving thanks. His face seemed less lined now, Maisy thought, how strange.

Claude had just stood to leave them to their cuddle, satisfied with the knowledge his members would be safe that night, when Daniel, uncharacteristically quiet until now, spoke, "Just a minute, Claude."

Claude waited, an eyebrow raised questioningly.

Dan took Maisy's hands in his and said, "You could come stay with me if you'd prefer. I'm not far away and you'll be safe enough getting there with me, wobbly or not."

The serious intensity with which he asked this surprised Maisy. It was offered in much the same tone one would expect to receive a marriage proposal or notification of a birth. Her first instinct was to laugh, but she knew somehow that Daniel was offering more than a bed. It cost him to invite her to his home.

Those invisible guidelines that had restricted their relationship were more insubstantial now than they had been. The lines were blurring. To go to each other's homes, to spend the night, would have been out of the question even a week ago. Neither of them had noticed it at the time, but things had changed between them. Claude's rules weren't the only thing binding them together anymore.

"Maisy?" Claude was still waiting and Maisy hadn't spoken for a long moment. If Dan was pained at waiting for a response he did not show it, his expression was all stoicism.

"Sorry," Maisy said, "Yes, thank you, Daniel. I'd prefer that. Thanks for offering anyway, Claude."

"Bien." Claude's gave Daniel a long unreadable look then, apparently satisfied, nodded. "I'll speak to you both tomorrow."

Daniel seemed quieter now than Maisy had ever known him. He was deep in thought for a moment, then he smiled as if shaking off a tumult of bad thoughts and replacing them with something simpler, "Shall we go now?"

Chapter 27
House

Maisy looked around the spotlessly clean kitchen. Dan was apparently extremely organised. He had one of those herbs and spices libraries. Cookbooks in alphabetical order, clever pull out storage, and not a cornflake out of place.

Some mischievous part of Maisy couldn't resist switching Jamie Oliver with Nigella Lawson to see if he noticed. He returned from the adjacent room - she caught a glimpse of a washing machine and rows of cupboards, must be a utility room - with an uncorked bottle of red and two glasses.

"Let's sit for a bit."

She followed him through to a low ceilinged, cosy cottage style living room and took the glasses from him.

"You have a beautiful home," she said as she sat in the deep, tartan print sofa. It was the kind of huge and snuggly sofa that you could hardly help curling up in like a little kitten. She restrained herself for the moment, not wanting to appear rude.

"Thank you," he said, smiling warmly. "I must admit I'm proud of it."

"It's stunning. Like a catalogue."

He laughed and filled her glass with wine. "I'll be honest with you, sweetheart. There's a good reason for that."

"Mm?"

"This was when...when I had my old job, I paid a company to come in and do it like a show home because I haven't got the first idea about decorating."

She snorted, "Really? I didn't even know they did that."

"If it were left up to me we'd be sitting on cushions and drinking wine out of teacups. I've just got no taste or common sense, as Claude would say."

"Poor Sir," she smiled and took a sip of the wine. Warm, rich, and a little spicy. Delicious. "Well, your catalogue people have a lovely home then."

"Cheeky subbie," he kissed her cheek then pulled her to lean into his side. Her legs pulled up onto the squidgy sofa and they snuggled there for a moment.

"It's nice having you here," he said.

She squeezed his arm in response and tried not to notice how surprised he sounded. "So, how long have you known Claude?"

"Twenty years or so now," he said, "We were at university together. I was an undergrad and he was a mature post-grad. Lost contact for a bit when he went back to France. Met up again by chance around the time he launched Drift."

"You're close then?"

"Oh yeah. He was going to be my best man, after all."

Maisy's squeezed his arm again. He'd never really mentioned his engagement before. Or his previous job, for that matter. She'd guessed that it wasn't a tidy breakup, but she'd never heard it from him.

"Anyway, how would you like to see the rest of the house?"

She made a show of rolling her eyes, "Let me guess, the bedroom has the most impressive chandelier and a four-poster bed?"

"Right on one and a half counts, actually, but I was going to show you the basement." His evil grin told her all she needed to know about what kind of catalogue that room had been kitted out from.

"Sir!" She whined, "I'm meant to be recovering!"

"You look recovered to me, sweetheart." His eyes grazed over her black dress, which felt out of place in the quaint country room and she felt a shiver of arousal. Maybe a tour wouldn't hurt. "Don't worry. I only want to show you." She felt a little pang of disappointment. He helped her up. "Bring your wine."

Maisy took Dan's hand and followed him down a wide hallway. They passed the open plan kitchen and three closed doors before reaching an unusually big door at the end of the corridor. He opened it and revealed a set of concrete steps leading down into the gloom. Maisy felt suspiciously like a character in a horror movie.

Then Dan flicked the light on and she grinned. Curvy painted women in rope bondage adorned the bright red stairwell walls. Beautiful and kitsch and a little ridiculous. She gently stroked one woman's thigh as she went past. Definitely hand painted. That's something you can't get from a Laura Ashley catalogue. It was delightful.

The red theme continued past the stairs, but the paintings were confined to that one area. The only decorations in this room were mirrors, tool racks, and cabinets.

"Why bother going to the club at all?" She said, eyes wide with amazement.

"Fair question." Dan fingered the tails of a cruel looking whip that hung on a nearby wall while he considered his answer.

There was nothing the room lacked. Every piece of equipment she'd seen in Club Drift was here too, maybe even more than she'd seen in Drift. The basement must stretch the whole length and width of the house. The lighting was so dim she could only barely make out the spider's web contraption on the opposite wall from the stairwell. "I like public play," he said quietly, "and if truth be told, I'm a bit of a collector."

"Of sex stuff?"

"Of play stuff, look." He lifted the whip he'd been fondling and Maisy flinched.

He shook his head, "You know I wouldn't do that, pet. Don't forget, safe words work in here too, but I want to show you." He handed the evil looking thing to Maisy and she reluctantly took it.

"Oh!" The handle was of the most exquisite carved rosewood she'd ever seen and the leather fronds were all hand knotted and artfully attached. "This is incredible."

"I got hooked when I was helping Claude kit out the club. We went to all these auctions, show rooms. The equipment in Drift is great, but then there's this other artisan side that I found really exciting. You couldn't put this in the public club, it's a work of art. That bench over there is moulded to my height and my - Well, it's personalised anyway. I collect works of art that are also...useful."

Maisy glanced at the slightly asymmetrical imprint of a bum that was carved into the bench. It had surely been modelled from life. His ex-fiancée, perhaps? It must be. Carl had said Daniel never took subs home these days. Maisy thought it was probably best not to press Daniel for further details about personalisation.

Maisy handed the flogger back to him and approached the wall it'd come from. Hand carved wooden paddles with words embossed and embedded in them, ornately carved handles, canes with animal heads - what could be on the other walls? "Wow," she breathed.

"This I can be proud of without stealing someone else's hard work." He took her glass from her - she'd forgotten she'd even been holding it - and placed both on an oddly formed tall table by the door. "I think you're meant to put a plant on that, but it looked alright in here so I went with it."

She threw her arms around his waist and enjoyed the all-encompassing feel of having his arms around her. So, no idea about interior decor, but a collector of artisan and antique kink accoutrements - the place was practically a museum. She found the combination extremely charming.

"I love it, Sir" she whispered.

"Good," he kissed her forehead, "I look forward to playing with you in here another day."

She pouted, "But Sir, I feel fine!"

"Non-negotiable, sweetheart. I assure you I'm at least as disappointed as you are. Get the wine and go sit on that sofa on the back wall, I'll join you in a moment."

She stole a kiss and scurried away when he swatted at her arse.

She sat on a furry stole that was tiny compared to the plush leather sofa and sighed happily. The man had excellent furniture for sore bottoms. Maybe that was why this surprisingly vanilla section of the room was here, snuggly aftercare.

"Unfortunately for my non-kinky guests, the basement was also the best option for the home cinema." Dan returned with a box of DVDs and some remotes with far too many buttons. He passed the box to her in exchange for his wine and pressed something that made a projector style screen come down from the ceiling near the opposite wall.

"Whoa."

"Yeah." He put his arm around her and put his feet up on the coffee table in front of them. "Pick a movie."

"Aren't they all porn?" She eyed their surroundings then the box suspiciously.

"That's the other box, sweetheart." She wasn't sure if he was joking.

"I can choose anything?"

"Anything at all."

"No punishments for picking something you won't like?" She lifted *Pretty Woman* out and raised an eyebrow at him.

"Ha! Clever little Maisy. You might receive some extra hard blows during your next spanking if you choose something deliberately awful, yes."

She grinned; this was the sort of game she could get behind. "Hmmm. How about...*Mean Girls*?" She held it out with a sweet smile, sure she'd get those lovely sounding spanks.

"Good choice, go put it in the machine there, would you?"

She frowned but jumped up to insert the disc into the system, which was thankfully more low-tech than it looked.

They settled in, sipping wine and cuddling, both too tired to chat much. The movie was half-way through before she got anxious of waiting to find out when those spanks were coming.

He laughed out loud when she asked, "The mistake you've made there, sweetheart, is assuming I didn't know *Mean Girls* is a masterpiece."

She laughed, then stopped, noting a glint in his eye. Note to self - find out what Sir's taste in films actually is.

"You look tired," she said quietly, when the film was over and they'd sat in silence holding each other for a while.

"Just because I'm not going to play with you tonight doesn't mean I'm not going to fuck you senseless in the morning, sweetheart." He grinned and kissed her gently, the sweetness of the kiss belying his filthy promise. "Goodnight."

"Goodnight," she said. Maisy turned on her side and felt his warm arm drape over her waist in the seconds before she fell to sleep.

THE LITTLE MITE WAS out like a light. It'd been a long day for her, hell, for both of them. Dan was exhausted himself, but too in awe of the moment to let sleep take him quite yet. How long had it been? 5 years? More?

Having her in his home, in his bed – well, sofa bed - didn't just feel good, it felt right. He felt her chest rise and fall beneath his fingers, watched her lips part and her body relax as she fell deeper into sleep, heard the faintest rustles of what might become snoring. Damn, but she was cute. He'd screwed up at the club and she'd forgiven him in a heartbeat, with all the open honesty that had drawn him to her the night they'd met.

It'd be so easy to do this every night. For Maisy's beautiful smile to be the last thing he sees before he goes to sleep. He'd never imagined that love could feel easy again.

Chapter 28
Little Piggy

Daniel placed a plate of beans on toast in front of Maisy. "I'm sorry I haven't got anything else in, eggs or anything. The delivery is coming tomorrow." Daniel rubbed the back of his head self-consciously. "At least I've got fresh coffee. I get points for that, right?"

"No worries, I love beans on toast, I was just thinking yesterday that I haven't had this in months."

"Good." He placed the coffee in front of her, "Milk and sugar?"

"One of each please."

Maisy could get used to this. She'd been woken up late by the sound of a coffee grinder whirring away in the kitchen and the smell of the brewing drink had lured her in within minutes.

Coffee, breakfast, and a gorgeous man wandering around the kitchen in nothing but loose grey sweats - definitely a good way to spend a rare Sunday morning off.

They sat on steel and leather stools at the glossy black breakfast bar. If he'd noticed the rearranged cookbooks, he did nothing to let her know.

"What are you thinking, sweetheart?"

She picked up her knife and fork and started cutting her toast into neat squares, "That I'm really glad I packed normal clothes to travel home in last night." When she glanced up to give him a sly smile she was delighted to find that Mr. Perfect Dom had a faint trace of orange bean juice around his lips.

"What are you thinking?"

"That this feels good. More than good." He gestured at their spontaneous domesticity with his cutlery.

She nodded, not wanting to agree too enthusiastically because he was obviously still a little surprised by this homely turn of events. "It's nice. Thanks for having me."

He snorted, "You sound like a school girl when you say thank you, sometimes. It's adorable."

She gaped at him, "I do not."

"You do too." He wiped the orange gunk from his face and sat back to enjoy the last of his coffee. "Shall we go to the club together this afternoon? I've got work to do on the books and I know you're eager to speak with Claude now you've got that party to plan. It's only...um. This is why it's your job now, not mine. It's a month away, right?"

"Yeah, that's about right. It's going to be tough to get it all together in time, to be honest."

"You'll get there," he said. He sounded so sure that Maisy couldn't help but agree with him.

"Can I trust you to behave at the club today?" She asked, very much hoping the answer was no.

"I'm sure I'll be in bother with Claude if I put his event planner through too much strenuous activity while she's working."

"I'm sure," she said, with a wry smile.

"I don't think the kitchen counter is too much though, do you?"

She looked at the kitchen island which, now she thought about it, was suspiciously clear of debris while the surfaces against the wall were cluttered with empty cans and plates. "Seriously?"

"I never joke about sex, sweetheart."

He pulled her to her feet and wasted no time sweeping her up and taking her to the island. She shrieked with laughter as he put her down and her bare arse landed on the cold granite.

"So Maisy," he kissed her firmly and pushed her legs apart so he could stand between them. The shirt she'd borrowed from him slid up easily. "Do you want to be my good girl this morning?"

"Yes," she whispered and reached for his lips.

"Excellent." He fisted his hand in her hair and pulled away so she couldn't kiss him. "Enthusiasm is appreciated but greediness is not. Have fun figuring out the right balance."

He released her hair and she kissed him eagerly, shifting forward to the very edge of the counter so she could rub against his crotch with her own.

"That might be just the right balance actually," he laughed huskily and she felt him grow hard as she bucked her hips rhythmically.

He groaned softly, apparently loathe to stop her, as he shifted her arse back a little and pushed her down flat on the counter.

"Spread your legs wide and hold your ankles. I don't want to have to get rope, sweetheart. Stay still no matter what."

He pulled her underwear off and she obeyed his instructions eagerly.

He stepped back and assessed the sight in front of him. She tried to breathe steadily as he casually walked around her looking at every angle of her body.

"You look beautiful spread for me, Maisy."

Her breath caught and she gripped her ankles tighter, "Thank you, Sir."

"So pretty," he said, before bending between her legs and running his tongue down her slit.

"Jesus," she breathed, fighting the urge to close her legs.

"Sorry?" He said, lifting his head and raising an eyebrow.

"Nothing Sir," she tensed as he ran his fingers around her entrance and up to her clit, stroking her hooded nub with her wetness.

"Good girl," he bent his head again and circled her clit with his clever tongue in an infuriating and firm pattern.

She rocked her hips up and moaned and he stopped immediately.

"What did I say about greed, Maisy," he said, pushing his thumb against where his tongue had been. "Stay still."

She nodded and lay flat, determined to do as she was told.

He bent his head and resumed his attentions to her clit, but this time he pushed his thick thumb inside her. She moaned loudly.

"Now really, Maisy, it's almost as if you never want to come."

THEY DECIDED TO GO to the shopping centre on the way to Club Drift. It was closer than going to back Maisy's and they could grab a coffee along with a few planning supplies. Most of her work on the event was on her tablet anyway and that lived in her handbag. Always.

They walked arm in arm. It was nice to just wander together, in no rush, passing through the world in their own content bubble. They stopped at a window to peer at lingerie that caught Maisy's eye, but decided it was just too pink to suit her.

As they stood there contemplating skin tone and lace, Daniel's hand snaked up Maisy's neck and tightened in her hair before she could guess what he was doing. Taken by surprise by the possessive gesture, Maisy let out a high-pitched squeal causing several passers-by to turn and look. Maisy batted his hand away, unsure whether to blush or laugh.

"Maybe I should make you wear a gag when we're out, little piggy."

"Mm, maybe I should get a curly tail butt plug too."

Daniel's eyes brightened.

"Oh no, mister. That was definitely a joke."

"We'll see."

"I mean it!" She thumped his chest gently to emphasise her point. He laughed and covered her small fist with his big hand.

"You're fiesty today."

———◆———

BEFORE MAISY COULD reply a bellow came from the fountain area adjacent to the food court.

"Oi! Get your fucking hands off her."

"Wha-fuck me." Daniel ducked, but the fist still connected.

"James! James stop it, what the hell are you doing? James!" Maisy pulled at the stranger's arm while Daniel tried to make sense of the situation.

An angry young man had thrown himself at Daniel, fist swinging. Maisy evidently knew him and she was really, really cross with him. A woman holding a baby hovered anxiously nearby, torn between intervening and protecting her infant.

The angry man swung at Daniel again and Maisy stepped between them, catching a glancing blow to her shoulder. Seeing Maisy put herself in harm's way finally shook Dan into action. Split lip forgotten, he pulled her behind him by her good arm and looked back to check on her, not wanting to turn his back on their assailant.

"You alright?"

Her lip wobbled and she held her arm, but Dan knew the misfired blow couldn't have really hurt her. Daniel looked at the other man and saw that his face held a similar expression to Maisy's.

"I'm so sorry. Maisy, I didn't mean to – Christ. I am so sorry," the man said.

Maisy just shook her head, eyes wide with shock and anger. Daniel wasn't sure who this man was or why Maisy was affected this way, but he needed to get her somewhere safe and hold her until that look disappeared from her face.

"I think you should leave." Daniel said.

The woman with the baby stepped closer and hissed, "For God's sake, come on."

The man, James, looked between them. He had the bemused expression of a person who'd wandered into a casino looking for a nunnery. "I heard you cry out. He was hurting you. I heard you cry out."

Apparently unable to articulate her thoughts Maisy groaned, "You bloody... you...." She groaned again.

"Take a breath, sweetheart. Who's this idiot?"

"Oi!" James objected, but nobody paid him any attention.

"This is my idiot brother," Maisy said, "Oh God, look what he's done to your face. Look what you've done to his face!"

James's face, already ruddy by nature, was turning positively beetroot as the scale of his mistake gradually dawned on him. "Look sis, I heard you shriek and saw red. You'd have done the same."

Maisy scoffed, "I might have asked you if you were alright before I punched a stranger. In front of Connor for Christ's sake." She gestured at the infant, whose happy gurgling didn't really illustrate her point.

The baby's mother, Maisy's sister-in-law apparently, stepped closer now things had calmed down, "I'm sorry, Maisy, I couldn't stop him in time. Bloody fool."

"Oi!" James said. Everybody ignored him.

Behind the clenched fists and fiery eyes, Maisy looked close to tears. Daniel knew he couldn't leave it like this.

"Look, let's just sit down and meet properly, what do you say? Coffee?" Maisy looked at Daniel as if he'd grown two heads, but James's beleaguered wife agreed heartily and ferried them towards the nearest café before James or Maisy could put up too much of a fight.

Chapter 29
The Difference

Daniel slammed his front door, wincing at the sound of glass rattling in the antique frame. He'd kept it together well enough while they smoothed things over with Maisy's brother. The brother's wife, Anne, had been so furious with her slap-happy spouse that she'd come across as rude to begin with, but she turned out to be warm, intelligent, and witty. He could see why Maisy liked her.

The kid was charming too. He was barely able to string two words together, but he'd worked his way into Daniel's good books in a flash.

Daniel had even kept in good humour while he and Maisy finished their shopping and travelled to Club Drift, but as soon as they'd arrived Dan escaped to the office, leaving Maisy working in the club with Claude.

He'd stolen away home before they emerged from their meeting too. He rationalised this by reminding himself he needed to get changed before his evening at the club anyway, but really he just wanted some time alone.

Before he'd left, he'd passed by the nook they worked in, concealed by the bar. Claude had been bent over a checklist and Maisy had been on the phone. Dan gritted his teeth just remembering it, "No, no, I don't know much about Mr. Leroy's business. No, I haven't seen him. I don't know anything about a fetish club, of course I don't. Who do you think I am? Alright. No, I'm not dating him and I don't appreciate the assertion. Do you have anything to ask that's actually about work?"

Daniel had left then, Maisy's phrasing ringing in his ears. *Who do you think I am?* She'd sounded disgusted.

Daniel picked up a beer on his way to the living room, not even pausing to look at the washing up from breakfast. He needed to stew.

Maisy's James was just looking out for her, of course, Dan couldn't begrudge him the split lip too much. They'd even parted, tentatively, as friends. James was still embarrassed by his overreaction, but overall it'd been smoothed over. Maisy was teased for being noisy. They'd all blushed when Maisy said that she squealed because Daniel had pinched her arse.

Daniel knew in that moment what a big mistake he'd made inviting her into his home. Into his life.

Did it matter? That she'd confess to having her arse groped but not to having her hair tugged? Not really. But Daniel knew what the little white lie was hiding.

Everything they were to each other, all the D/s compatibility that had driven them into each other's arms despite each of their best efforts, it'd all fall to pieces if anyone else knew. That's why she'd said one thing and not the other, because if anyone 'normal' knew what they were to each other they'd be disgusted.

If that beautiful nuclear family knew that Maisy was willingly his, knew what they were behind Club Drift's doors, they'd do more than throw a punch at him.

So it was a secret, a little white lie to hide a bigger sin. So they'd smoothed it over for now. What about next time? What about when someone she loved, her brother or her roommate, found a note or a text message or a collar that told them everything? Would they force them apart? Would they call the police? Would Maisy -

Not again. I can't do that again. Daniel gripped his untouched beer so hard his knuckles turned white. He'd been an idiot. He'd kept away from attachments for years because he knew: this is how it happens. He couldn't see Maisy hurt like that. Worse, he couldn't see Maisy turn against him like that. He put the beer on the coffee table, still unopened, and picked up his phone to dial the Club. There was only one thing to do to prevent that. However hard it would be for him, he had to pull away from Maisy before he fell for her any more than he already had.

———⊙———

MAISY CONTEMPLATED her uncharacteristically shiny backside in Harry's full length mirror. She was glad her roommate was out for the evening, because this was a sight she needed more than the tiny bathroom mirror to fully appreciate.

The latex skirt had come with a free aerosol can of 'Spray Shine,' but Maisy wasn't sure what to do with it. Was she meant to spray the skirt after she'd got it on or before? She scanned the label again and, having found no pertinent information, shrugged and sprayed one arse cheek.

She rolled her hips experimentally and grinned when she saw an astonishingly shiny, almost sparkling, patch glinting in the bedroom light. Yup, definitely more of that on both arse cheeks, thank you very much.

She'd almost forgotten she'd ordered the skirt. Harry had signed for the delivery while Maisy was out with Dan and, luckily, hadn't thought to ask what was in it. Not that the skirt was particularly obscene; it was just very obviously fetish wear and that was a conversation she wasn't ready to have with her oldest friend quite yet.

Maisy had never been made to feel unwelcome at Club Drift, but the more time she spent there the more she felt her clothes lacked something. Despite wearing increasingly revealing outfits every weekend, she'd still felt out of place in the sea of flamboyantly dressed guests. Last weekend she'd realised what was missing: exclusivity. Not exclusivity in terms of expense or uniqueness, but in her own life.

She needed to own something that was only to be worn to Club Drift; an outfit that only existed in the hours she was being herself, being submissive, with Dan. So, after a tortuous hour of online shopping, she'd bought her first item of fetish wear.

She hadn't mentioned it to Dan yet, so watching his reaction when she arrived at the club was going to be fun. Hopefully, she'd get a chance to take off her outerwear in the changing room first so he could get the full effect all at once.

She'd decided to wear a lacy, black longline bralette, which looked like it'd been paired with the skirt deliberately, but really she'd just given up finding a top in her wardrobe that looked alright with the latex.

Dan had left her alone with Claude almost immediately after they'd arrived at the club that afternoon. He said something about needing to talk to some suppliers upstairs in the office. She hadn't even seen him to say goodbye before she came home to get changed, but it hadn't seemed worth it to distract him seeing as she'd be back soon anyway.

Polishing plans with Claude hadn't felt like work at all; he'd been a model client by anyone's standards. They'd settled on Maisy's fetish-formal dress code idea, mostly because they were both curious to see what the regulars would come up with.

They were inviting Claire's friend's band to play and measuring the bar to see if it could safely serve as a stage. All the suppliers that Maisy had contacted were absolutely fine with Claude's privacy terms and none of them had batted an eyelash at familiar caller Maisy opening a new business account.

One of them, the florist, had even asked whether she should play dumb if she had to talk to Michael or a company representative at any point. Bright lady; Maisy had always liked her.

Claude still hadn't decided whether to risk anonymity for the sake of a sit-down meal instead of hors d'oeuvres, but everyone agreed they needed to make the decision as soon as possible. Preferably tonight, actually. Aside from an intriguing sounding suspension demonstration by Matilda, Maisy wasn't sure what she and Dan were doing at the club tonight. Hopefully, she'd get a chance to get Claude's final decision on the anniversary event refreshments, even if they had to flip a coin to make their minds up.

Chapter 30
Detached

"Oh. My. Stars," Carl exclaimed, gesturing for Maisy to give him a spin. She complied, feeling more confident than usual in her new outfit.

"Darling, I cannot in good faith let you into this club. You're Dom bait. Just look at you! They'll flock to you like flies to shit and you know that'll make Master Dan even grumpier than he already is."

"Dan's grumpy?" Maisy frowned, he'd been fine earlier. Maybe he'd had trouble with one of the phone calls he'd rushed off to make.

"That's the only part you heard wasn't it, honey? Well, you'd best go cheer him up then, come here." He bent to mark her off on the attendance list and then stamped her hand.

Where did Claude get handcuff stamps anyway? She'd have to ask him. That would be a supplier contact well worth having. She saw that Carl's roots were dusted with gold glitter today to match his shining red and gold hot pants. He was always so coordinated.

"Thanks Carl. See you in a while, yeah? Matilda said you were helping her with a demonstration."

"I am permitting her to dangle me from the ceiling with her very own naturally produced spider webbing, if that's what you mean." He winked and waved her away because a group of trainees had just arrived and needed his attention.

Maisy heard him say, "Well, I am entirely in love with everything about that wig..." as the door to the main club shut behind her, blocking out the mundanity of London Bridge and replacing it with another world.

Dan was over by the bar talking to Claude. Why was Daniel wearing a fluorescent armband? He hadn't said anything about having DM duty tonight; maybe someone had called in sick. Maisy selfishly hoped it wouldn't stop them enjoying each other's company. It'd be a shame to waste the skirt.

Claude looked upset from where Maisy was standing by the door. She hovered there a moment, watching Claude gesticulating at Dan. Should she leave them to it until they were done or distract them from whatever disagreement they were having?

She decided to interrupt. They were both Club Drift Masters, if her presence wasn't welcome they'd soon ask her to give them a moment to themselves. Dan's back was to the door Maisy had entered through, so he hadn't seen her yet. When she reached the bar she threw her arms around his waist. "Guess who, Sir?"

Dan froze for a moment, as she'd thought he might, but the moment went on too long. He turned and placed his hands on the outside of her forearms, pushing her away as civilly as possible.

Claude backed off a few feet without greeting Maisy or saying anything to pause his conversation with Dan. The strangeness of the moment chilled Maisy's blood, "Sir? What's wrong?"

He still held her forearms gently. He didn't kiss her or take her in his arms. His eyes didn't meet Maisy's the whole time. At first she thought he was unwell; he was so unlike himself. But then he spoke. "Sweetheart, we need to talk."

The world slowed and Maisy's stomach lurched. She remembered this feeling from years ago, when her car once skidded out of control on a busy road. As Dan spoke, just as in the moments before her car crashed, Maisy's senses processed what was happening faster than her thoughts could catch up with, so she felt like she was witnessing the event in slow motion.

This had come in quite handy after the car crash, when the police had asked what had happened in those thirty seconds between the everyday and the catastrophic. When it was something more personal and infinitely more painful, though, Maisy found there was no real use for this biological quirk at all. The phrase 'we need to talk' coming unexpectedly from a partner's lips is one sure way to trick a brain into feeling that the world is about to come crashing down.

"What's up?" she asked, fixing her smile in place while she scrambled to make sense of his strange behaviour.

He met her eyes now for the first time since she'd approached. He looked tired, older than he had when they parted a few hours ago. "I'm sorry, Maisy, but I have to stop mentoring you now."

"Mentoring...?" She frowned. Oh! The six weeks mentoring thing that Claude had insisted on when she arrived at the club. How long had it been? Four weeks? Less? It felt like a lifetime. "That's okay, I kind of assumed we weren't doing that anymore anyway."

"No, sweetheart, I mean…" He looked so pained that Maisy automatically reached up to touch his cheek, the urge to comfort him temporarily taking over from the strangeness, until he gently pushed her hand away.

She shook her head, overwhelmed by the coldness of the gesture. His grip on her arms grew firmer for a moment, his expression unreadable, then he let her go entirely.

"We can't see each other anymore. Matilda or William or any of the house crew will be happy to help you find a Dom of your own. I'm on duty now, excuse me."

He turned and started walking towards the shadowy tunnel where some of the bigger public scene areas were located. Claude took a step towards Maisy, unnoticed by her or anyone.

"Wait!" She called out before she knew what she was going to say, but all she could think was one word, "Why?"

He didn't even turn around, just glanced over his shoulder, "I told you I don't do anything beyond casual play. You knew not to get attached."

Chapter 31
Office

Maisy felt the strong arm settle around her shoulder before the first tear fell.

"Come with me, petite."

She let Claude guide her through the bar, past the main entrance to the staircase in the corner that led to a door marked 'private'. She'd never been through here before. Any other time she might have been fascinated by the lush décor and unmarked doors they passed, as it was she could barely put one foot in front of the other.

"I told you I don't do anything beyond casual play. You knew not to get attached."

His cold eyes, the careless tone with which he'd dismissed their relationship as nothing. Could he have chosen any way to hurt her more deeply?

She was vaguely aware of Claude settling her on a deep sofa and patting her arm. He crossed the room to use a landline that was sitting on a commanding desk.

This must be his office. Deep green walls, dark wood and leather furniture – its old-world sophistication suited him. She'd have to ask if they could have event meetings in here in future. That's if she went ahead with planning the event after...

"You knew not to get attached." She shivered, the icy tone becoming icier in her mind. Of course. He had warned her, Carl had warned her, she'd warned herself.

Men like Daniel didn't want to be in a relationship with girls like Maisy. She'd known that from the start and he'd been clear. Just because they'd spent that time together, just because she thought it had taken a different direction doesn't mean that things had suddenly changed. How could she have been so stupid?

"Maisy? Oh, sweet little one. I am so sorry." Claude sat in a leather armchair that was angled towards her sofa and offered a tissue. "You must not give up hope. He is just having a moment, I am sure."

She laughed through her snotty tears, "Thank you, Claude, but he's made himself very clear."

When she'd wiped away the majority of the tears she could see that Claude was frowning and not merely at her distress.

"You have to understand; it is a difficult situation."

"I know, it was all explained to me before. Daniel doesn't date. It's fine, I shouldn't have let myself get carried away."

"No, no, no, sweet Maisy. You should have. You had to. Please don't think it was not real. He just has a past. Who doesn't, no?"

She sniffled and nodded.

"This is my fault. I am sorry."

She frowned, "How -"

Matilda threw the door open and stormed in, "You meddling fool."

To Maisy's great surprise, the all-powerful owner of Club Drift's response to this attack was merely to look sheepish.

William followed Matilda, every muscle in his usually languid body taut with anger. His silent glare at Claude was far more cutting that anything he could say. The two house Masters sat either side of Maisy like guardian lions.

"Thank you for coming. As I was saying, Maisy, this is somewhat my fault," Claude said.

He ignored William's snarled, "Somewhat, my arse."

"I don't know how much gossip you've heard about Daniel's past, but I think it's important that you know the truth now."

Maisy nodded, bewildered but comforted by the anger being shown on her behalf.

"Some time ago Daniel was in love with a woman called Alicia."

Matilda sneered at the mere mention of her name, when she saw Maisy's curious face she interrupted, "I do not forgive easily."

"Indeed," Claude continued in a measured tone, "She is not in favour here. Anyway, they were very happy, very involved at the club, they were even engaged near the end. She was a submissive who fitted as perfectly with Daniel's needs and desires as he fitted with hers."

Maisy shifted uncomfortably in her seat, it was bad enough that Daniel had dumped her in front of the whole club, did she really need to hear about how amazing a fit his ex was?

William squeezed her shoulder gently, "Get on with it, Claude."

"Oui, forgive me. One day, somehow, Alicia's family found out about the nature of their relationship and everything changed."

Matilda, ever impatient, interrupted again, "The idiots thought Daniel was abusing her and she never told them the truth. Instead of explaining that she was 100% on board with the kinky bits of their relationship she pulled away, let them believe it was all him, let them go around telling people he was a sick bastard. The police were involved as well, you know? He even left his job because his firm got wind of the trouble."

"Oh God," Maisy felt a pang of sadness for Daniel so strong she nearly started crying again. "What happened?"

"She left him." William said, bitterly. "Just like that. Turned up at their door with her brothers to get her stuff, told him she 'Didn't want anything to do with his filth anymore.' Cold as fuck."

"Jesus," Maisy said, imagining how that would have hurt him, "That's horrible."

"Telling me he was her soulmate one week, pulling that shit the next," Matilda's anger could melt steel.

"Yeah. She's a bitch." William was staring at Claude, waiting for him to continue.

"So, now you know why Daniel had a policy about dating or even playing outside the club. It was easier for him to limit his relationships so he wouldn't be burned again. I encouraged, well, I forced Daniel to see you exclusively for your first six weeks as a member because I saw a spark between you and I wished to blow on it, so to speak. I had hoped that Daniel would overcome his aversion to dating when choices were removed from him. I still believe this is the case. He just appears to have hit a road block."

Maisy spluttered, too baffled and angry to speak or even cry anymore. She couldn't quite make sense of what was happening. William and Matilda were here, furious on her behalf, because Claude had forced Daniel to date her?

"So, he never wanted me in the first place? He was just doing what you told him to do?" Maisy spoke slowly, barely able to believe that the words she was saying could be true.

"No! Petite, that's not the case at all. I merely encouraged what was already there, you see?"

"Shut up. I'm sorry, but shut up. I can't believe you people. What is wrong with you? You can't just meddle with people's lives like that."

"I told you so," Matilda said, glaring at Claude.

"You're just as bad. You knew. You nominated me too, why didn't you say something? You just let me be a pawn in this weird bloody experiment?"

William grabbed her other hand, "Maisy, pet, it's not like that I promise. Claude's a bloody idiot, but it's not like Dan never liked you, I reckon he even l-"

"Stop. No. I can't do this. I can't do this." Maisy stood, grateful that her legs were steadier than she'd anticipated they'd be. "I'm sorry, but I really have to go."

Chapter 32
How Does It Feel?

Maisy got home somehow, she didn't really remember. All her brain space was used up thinking about Daniel and the rest of...whatever that mess was back at the Club.

"Hello!" Harry called across from the sofa in the next room when she heard Maisy open their front door. Maisy nearly turned around and left again, but she no longer had anywhere to go.

Reluctantly, she closed the door behind her and started towards her room. If she was very lucky she could get to her bedroom and get cleaned up before Harry noticed anything was wrong.

Unsurprisingly, however, Harry had sensed something was amiss the moment Maisy didn't return her greeting, so she was looking over the sofa waiting for her when she entered the living room.

The playfully stern face she'd worn, prepped for an interrogation, melted to soft concern for a split second before being replaced with scowling fury. "Who is he and where is he? Do I need to have a word?"

However diverting the image of tiny Harry squaring up to six foot plus Daniel was, Maisy couldn't laugh. Instead she managed a feeble sniffle and gestured at her bedroom door.

Harry ignored that and did what all the best people do when their friends are sad and trying not to cry. She took Maisy in her arms and told her everything was going to be okay which, of course, gave Maisy the space she needed to let the tears fall freely.

Sometime later, when they'd held each other until Maisy's tears slowed down and her shoulders stopped shaking, Harry asked what she'd been dying to ask from the moment Maisy had got home.

"What on Earth are you wearing?"

Maisy looked down and found to her horror that her coat had flapped open at some point during the roommate hugging-and-crying-fest and her skin tight, unnaturally shiny, and obviously fetish inspired skirt was out for all to see. Also available for Harry's inspection was Maisy's longline bra which was still masquerading as a top.

"Um..."

"'Um' isn't good enough, missus."

"No, I suppose it isn't." Maisy wrapped her coat back around herself and tried to think of any way to explain her turning up in floods of tears and fetish gear that was less complicated than explaining the truth. In the end, she decided the truth was more than good enough and all she could manage in the state she was in, anyway. If Harry didn't like what she heard, well, that'd be a conversation for another day.

So, she told her. She hugged a cushion to her chest, sat on the sofa they'd gotten for free off Harry's mum when they'd moved in, and she told her best friend about her new, secret life.

She told her about the forums, how she'd gone for the introductory session at Club Drift and met Dan, how they'd gifted her a membership.

Harry interjected with a question here and there, "What's a single tail?" being the first with, "What the fuck?" following very closely on its heels. Mostly though, she held Maisy's hand and she listened. Maisy told her about the awe-inspiring tunnels and vaulted ceilings, the equipment, about the tea and the blankets in the baskets, about the wonderful people she'd gotten to know.

She told her about Claude's over-protectiveness, William's teasing, Matilda's wit, Carl's interminable gossip. She told her about how things had developed with Dan, her night in his home, this morning at the shopping centre and, finally, she told her about tonight. Dan's complete change of tune and the story about his past she'd been told in Claude's office.

When she'd poured it all out and she couldn't think of anything more to say to prevent the inevitable any longer, Maisy stopped and waited for Harry's reaction.

"He's an idiot." Harry pronounced, "And you can do better. No, don't look like that, you can. It's not your fault he's been burnt before, why should he get to treat you like that? I get it's a shit situation, but seriously, screw him."

After a long, thoughtful pause Harry added, her eyes wide with curiosity, "What is it you like about it all?"

Maisy thought about how she'd felt when she'd first met Dan, how thrilling and momentous the smallest touch or command had felt. How much more aware of her body she was when he teased her or flogged her or kissed her sweetly.

How strangely peaceful she'd felt over the spanking bench, how protected and complete she'd felt in his bed once she'd recovered from the sub drop afterwards.

"It's so much. It's everything-" She began, reaching for a comparison point in her mind.

"You know when you're young and someone holding your hand feels like a declaration of love? Or the way you get a crush on some guy in some one-hit-wonder band and it's all consuming? Or just the way we felt when we were teenagers in general."

Harry raised a cynical eyebrow, but Maisy was just getting into her stride, her eyes still sparkling with moisture, "No really, Harry, listen. You remember being a teenager and full of hormones? We didn't know whether we wanted to run away from everything or fight the world or fuck or-" Maisy groaned aloud, "I don't know how to say this. I'll get there eventually, just humour me, okay?

Harry waited patiently as she watched her usually eloquent friend scramble for the words to describe something indescribable.

Maisy was talking faster now, "You know the way music changes you when you're a teenager? No, it doesn't change you, that's not right. You know the way music gets inside your soul when you're young? The way it speaks to you and makes you feel in ways you can't explain in your own words yet? The way it gives you a space to put some of the excess feeling you're doing? All that everything that makes every moment feel so impossibly full?" Harry nodded, not really sure what Maisy was going on about, but loathe to let her stop now she was speaking rather than crying.

"Remember the way music used to make you feel? You don't notice when it stops, really, you're too busy being relieved that living has spaced out a bit. You haven't had time to grow bored of the spaces between living yet." Maisy paused again, well aware that she'd stopped making sense a long time ago.

"Go on," Harry said, "I won't laugh."

Maisy scoffed, "You probably should." She tried to find some sense in her jumbled thoughts. She remembered the last time she went out clubbing with Harry and their university friends. How a song had come on and it was a song that spoke to her soul at that moment and she could have wept. She could have wept for who she was last time she felt that way and who she was then on that dance floor and how horribly rare it is to feel like you're so overflowing with life you need a space to put the excess.

"That's how it feels. That's how D/s feels. Done right, the balance of power and pleasure and pain and all that...muchness, it makes you feel as overflowing as music did when you were young." She said, tongue thick with the unspeakable nature of the feelings she was trying to express. What she'd begun to feel with Dan, even in its nascent stages, it was incandescent. It was so much more than it seemed.

"That sounds worth going back for, to me," Harry said, quietly.

"To him?" Maisy asked.

"No, to that place. To the club. He's not the only Dom in London, is he?"

He might be, Maisy's bitter inner voice opined. "No," she said, "he's just my first one."

"I know, but your first kiss wasn't your best, you get me?"

Maisy laughed for the first time since Dan had pushed her away, "You're not wrong there."

"Ryan Wong, right? Over the Easter holidays? Tasted of chocolate?"

Maisy gaped at her, "How do you remember that?"

Harry shrugged, "Nearly the same as mine, isn't it?"

"You never told me that!" Maisy peered over the cushion she'd been cuddling.

"You never told me you like whips and handcuffs, but I guessed."

"I do not like whips!" Maisy began, then, "Wait, what do you mean you guessed?"

Harry's cheeks pinkened, "I might have been borrowing your books. Sometimes. When you're not in. Sorry."

Maisy was far too tired to be cross about the invasion of privacy, "You're incorrigible. I thought you'd stopped thieving after the empty tea caddy incident."

"Not thieving! Borrowing!" Maisy could tell that Harry believed that 100% which was as amusing as it was scary, really.

"You noticed I'd been sticking to a theme then." She reluctantly changed the subject back from Harry's pilfering to her proclivities.

Harry shrugged, "Yeah, it all went a bit romance and ropes for months and months. Not my thing, really, but I still read them. Pretty hot as a fantasy."

Maisy didn't know what to make of that. "So, you don't mind then?"

"Don't mind what?" Harry looked perplexed, "Oh! That you're a kinky weirdo? Of course not, you daft sod."

It wasn't that Maisy had been expecting her open-minded friend to shun her, but after the tale she'd heard in Claude's office she was half expecting some level of rejection from anyone she told about her submissive adventures.

She leaned into Harry and smiled when her roommate's arm settled around her shoulder. There was nothing wrong with her or what she'd started to love sharing with Dan. Now, with the tears dry and her heart full, it seemed horribly sad to Maisy that Alicia, however cruel she'd been to Dan, didn't have anyone like Harry in her life to love her unconditionally.

Instead she'd been faced with judgement and rejection from her family and she'd lost her lover as a result. She'd hurt Dan - that much was clear - but Maisy couldn't find it in herself to be cross with either of them, not tonight. There'd been quite enough fire and fury for tonight.

Chapter 33
Airborne

Maisy entered Drift with less of a spring in her step the next week. She was glad that Harry had persuaded her to return but knowing that she'd probably see Master Dan for the first time since they'd ended it last week made her insides do somersaults.

And she'd have to get used to thinking of him as Master Dan again. Not Sir, not her lover, not - ugh - whatever he might have been.

Still, she was here. She had the event coming up and if she waited any longer before coming back it'd be too strange and too painful to come at all, even to work. Claude was waiting in reception with Matilda when Maisy arrived.

"Wow!" Maisy took in the mistress's outstanding red leather catsuit. The bright colour contrasted gorgeously with her mahogany skin and her lips were painted bright red to match.

"You see Claude? How can I be on reception duty all night if I look so good subbies pull that face?"

Claude chuckled and Maisy realised she was gaping at the beautiful woman. Hell, maybe she'd see if Matilda wanted to use her for a demonstration of some sort, that was one way to avoid Dan. Sorry, can't talk, busy being immobilised by an actual goddess.

"Sorry Matilda, there's no-one else for the first shift. Laura will take over at midnight."

Matilda gave a good-natured sigh and waved Maisy over to sign the attendance list. "Fine, fine, I'll just entertain myself with scaring newbies."

She flashed a fiendish grin and Maisy was shocked to see fake pointed tips on her teeth. She'd have scared the hell out of Maisy if she didn't know the Mistress was a warm-hearted and welcoming woman beneath all the costuming.

"Stop staring and go inside, sub." Her tone was harsh, but the wink she gave Maisy showed it was all in good fun. "I'm glad you came back to us."

Maisy smiled, hoping Matilda understood that all was forgiven, and hurried after Claude.

"I'm glad you're here, petite," he said, "I must apologise again. You do not deserve the way I treated you."

Maisy kept her smile firm, "Water under the bridge, Claude. Really." Her heart still stung from the events of the week before, but she was determined to find her place in Club Drift again and holding grudges was no way to do it.

"Good," Claude was visibly relieved, he really did seem to be sorry for what he'd done. "Would you like you to do a demonstration with William tonight?"

"Oh, Claude, I don't know. I was kind of counting on a quiet night what with, you know, everything."

Claude slowed and put his arm around her shoulders. "I understand your reluctance, but if you can find a way it'd help us out and, I hope, help you too."

"Help me?" They stopped as they reached the bar, Claude kept his conspiratorial closeness to her, his arm guarding her from the eyes of Club Drift.

"It is my fault that you are only used to being around Daniel at the club. I am sorry for that. You and William have a friendship of sorts, yes? I had hoped you'd let him show you the ropes, if you'll forgive my pun, as an easy way back into things. Think about it, yes?"

Claude let her go so he could walk behind the bar. The trainees on duty were standing at the other end of the room gossiping, but it was early and a weeknight, so Claude didn't bother reprimanding them. Maisy didn't mind, of course, because who could resist a drink poured by the illustrious owner of Club Drift himself?

He passed her a gin and tonic. She was touched that he remembered her favourite, but she really must tell them all she liked other drinks too.

He leaned down on the oversized bar so they could hear each other speak from either side despite Maisy's diminutive height. He might look a bit less noble doing so than the Master in Chief should look, but Maisy reasoned it served him right for putting the gargantuan bar up in the first place.

"How have you really been, petite?"

No-one on this Earth could lie to Claude when asked a direct question face to face. The customary, 'I'm fine,' died in her throat and she answered that question honestly for the first time all week.

"I'm not doing great to be honest, Claude."

He nodded, "That is about as frank an answer as I can expect from the British, I suppose."

She grinned and, feeling like her Austen heroine namesake, said, "Such prejudice is unbecoming in you, Sir."

He grinned back, his pale blue eyes sparkling with humour, "You have not lost your wit, then? Good. So long as you have laughter, all will be well."

Her grin faded when Dan stepped out from the Bar's utility area.

Seeing him in the flesh was every bit as painful as she'd feared. He nodded at them, his expression inscrutable, then went to herd the waitstaff.

Maisy took a long gulp of her gin and tonic and focused on the ice-cold sensation of the drink sliding down her throat, the aromatic scent of bitters, the spicy notes on her tongue - anything but the way her heart ached when Dan looked at her like she was a stranger.

"Ready love?" William appeared from behind her, his usual relaxed smirk in place. Somehow though it wasn't the same. He was still thinking about that horrible conversation in Claude's office too, he had to be.

She nodded and held out a hand, hoping he'd lead her away from the bar. She was sure that she'd cry if Dan looked at her in that detached way again.

William looked at Maisy, then over to Dan, and scoffed. "Come on, pet." As he led her to a booth she was sure she heard him mutter, "Pillock."

He sat facing away from the bar and pulled her in next to him. She was shivering a little, so he put an arm around her.

Her friend William: the one who made them all laugh, the defender of subbies, the guy who got a little too excited about kicking arseholes out.

That was why she liked coming here; people like William. She took a deep breath and really relaxed for the first time since she'd got there.

"There's brave Mistress Maisy," William grinned and squeezed her arm and the sense of belonging that Drift usually gave her started to return.

"Is Claude alright? He seems a little...reserved?"

"Nothing for you to worry about, love. He's just got an even bigger stick up his arse than usual."

Maisy snorted, there was nobody like William to take the stress out of a situation. "He feels bad?"

William nodded tersely, "He does. Bloody right to and all."

Maisy wanted to look back at Claude to see if he was watching her, but she couldn't stand coming face to face with Daniel again. Not yet. So she turned to the other anxiety in her immediate future.

"Claude said something about a demonstration? Listen, I don't want to do anything too involved, okay? Claude said I should do it, but I'm still feeling a bit edgy and-"

"He didn't say you had to, did he? Bloody hell, he is in a bad mood. He didn't mean it, pet. You don't have to do anything."

"No, no, not like that, I'd have left if I thought you'd make me do anything I didn't want to do. He just thinks it'd be good for me and I'm inclined to agree, but nervous anyway."

"Fuck him. Do it if you want to, but not because he said so. I'm meant to be doing a rope demonstration to go over basic safety stuff with the newbies. You've got suspension listed as 'want to try' so we thought we'd see if you fancied it."

"Oh yeah, I did put that down, didn't I?" Maisy glanced over her shoulder at the bar and saw Claude deep in conversation with Daniel. Oh, bloody hell.

"Mistress Maisy," William's eyes were gentle when she turned to meet them, "Fuck both of 'em, yeah?"

She laughed, "Yeah. And I'd love to be your bunny for the evening, Master William."

"Glad to hear it." He pulled her closer so her head rested on his shoulder. "I'll string you up real good and you'll forget about the rest of it."

She sank into the friendly embrace and tried to forget that her Daniel was barely more than ten metres away. "Thanks William."

AN HOUR LATER SHE WAS questioning her sanity. Suspension looked fun from the outside, but it was absurdly intense to experience first-hand.

She loved bondage, loved the freedom that came with having everything taken away, of giving the control to someone she trusted. Maybe that was the problem. She trusted William, liked him a great deal, but that electric zing that she'd experienced with Dan just wasn't there.

Maybe it was because he wasn't Daniel or maybe it was just because she knew this was just going to last the evening, but she couldn't get her head in the right space.

William knew it too. He adjusted a loop and showed a newbie Dom how he'd redistributed Maisy's weight, taking the tension off a potential problem area. He ran a hand through Maisy's hair and give it an affectionate tug. "Comfy pet?"

"Mmhmm." She gave him a warm smile and wriggled in her bonds, showing him how effectively he'd tied her. "Good job, Sir!"

"I know that, love, but I've missed your mind completely, haven't I?"

Maisy bit her lip, knowing that lying to a Drift Master was a hanging offence.

He laughed and pulled lightly at the rope at her chest, causing her to sway gently, "It's alright, Mistress Maisy. I won't take offence, I know you're not the instant submission type."

"It's really not you, Sir."

"I said I know, pet. Don't fret. You can stop the demonstration if you'd like, I'd hate to keep a sub bound when she's not getting anything out of it."

"No! No it's fine. I feel like I'm helping out and it's...nice." Truth be told, if she could stop thinking about Daniel for five minutes she might have really enjoyed it. William was an extremely commanding presence as well as a massive flirt and he really knew his way around ropes. She felt like a baby in a sling up there in the air.

"Right then," William nodded, apparently satisfied. He turned away to answer an enquiry from a softly spoken Domme. Her mousy female sub eyed Maisy with curiosity.

After a moment, the sub approached William, spurred on by her Domme. His eyes lit with mischief.

"Be nice!" Maisy hissed. He turned to roll his eyes at her before turning back to the small woman who was stealing herself to speak.

"Excuse me, um, Master William, was it? Can I... I mean, if you don't mind..." William held his hand out and the woman took it instinctively.

Maisy saw the Domme quirk an eyebrow, then suppress a laugh as William bent to whisper in the sub's ear. The mousy woman squeaked and pulled her hand away, then scurried over to Maisy. William approached the Domme, know-it-all tutor mode clearly engaged. The man was insufferable...

"Sorry about him," Maisy said, as the blushing sub reached her.

"He's...intense. I don't know how you let him...you know. I'd just melt."

Maisy laughed, "Fortunately for me I'm not his. He's all bark and no bite though, honest."

The woman looked doubtful. "I just wanted to ask you what it feels like up there, does it hurt?"

"Oh, no! It was getting uncomfortable on this side earlier, but I told him and he fixed it. If you're getting strung up by someone who knows what they're doing it's really quite comfy."

"And...well, how does it feel?"

Maisy knew what she was asking, but she wasn't sure what answer to give her. She knew that if she'd been tied up by someone she connected with, someone who cared about her, who she submitted to eagerly, she'd have been hypnotised by his movements, turned on by every loop, every second as the freedom was taken away, but with William it was just a demonstration. Fun, but not exactly mind blowing, especially not with how distracted she was.

"Hey, why don't you two come to the workshop on Thursday night? Then you can try it for yourself."

"Yeah, maybe. See you," she looked unsatisfied, but she went back to her Domme. William said his goodbyes and left the women deep in conversation.

"Behaving yourself?"

"Only as much as usual," William grinned back at her. This was okay. With friends like William and dozens of interesting people coming in every week, Maisy would find a place here again. Maybe seeing Dan would stop hurting after a while too.

Chapter 34
Heist

Maisy stretched her shoulders again, "You owe me a massage."

William laughed and passed her another gin, "I'll get Carl right over. Did he tell you he's a qualified masseuse?" Maisy shook her head. "Strange. He tells me at least twice a week." He flashed a cocky grin which made her laugh. The man could make anyone feel at ease.

"Thanks William," Maisy said, "That was a good thing to do first time after... I appreciate it."

"No worries, Mistress," He came back round to her side of the bar and pulled her into a firm hug. "We look after our own, yeah?"

"Yeah," she mumbled into his t-shirt.

"Enjoying yourself, William?" A terse voice interrupted their friendly embrace.

Maisy jumped back, the warm feeling of safety and kinship vanishing at the sound of Dan's voice. Anger welled up inside her. How dare he? He'd shoved her out of his life last week without so much as a by-your-leave and now she'd managed to come back and enjoy herself with her friends he was being a jealous arse about it? How dare he.

"Excuse me a moment, William," she said, her voice as calm as the waters of a frozen lake.

William glanced between them. He took the measure of Maisy's tone and stern expression and, reasoning that she was more than capable of dealing with this herself, stepped back behind the bar.

"You absolute arse."

Daniel was lost for words, "I'm sorry?"

"Do you really think that I'd let what other people think effect how I feel about you?" Daniel blinked, like he'd been expecting her to say something very different.

"It's not that, it's just that-"

"I am not Alicia."

He froze mid-sentence, "How..."

"Claude told me. You don't even know my family and you obviously don't know me very well. Did it ever occur to you that Alicia was a complete shit for not standing up for you?"

He stepped back like her words had punched him in the chest.

She continued, too furious to hold back, "You need to stop beating yourself up for something that was never your fault. Christ, I thought you were brighter than this."

He was silent and, although his eyes held no rebuke, he looked pained.

"Sorry. No, actually, not sorry. Somebody needs to tell you that you're being a complete-"

"Pillock," William said, from the bar.

"Piss off," Maisy said at the same time as Dan said, "Fuck off, William."

"You have been a pillock though," Maisy said, more gently this time. "Her family didn't understand kink, right? It happens. This looks weird from the outside. But instead of defending it, or you, or just explaining anything she lets them think it was all your idea and makes you look like an abusive creep? That's not a problem with her family finding out, that's a problem with her being spineless and not caring about you."

Daniel shook his head

"I'm sorry, I know I'm being mean, but I'm so bloody angry with you, with her, with her family, with this whole stupid situation."

"It's okay."

"It's not okay, Daniel. It's really not okay. I didn't even find out what the issue was from you, you know? I had to rely on second hand gossip to even get an idea why you'd hurt me like that."

His expression hardened, "Maisy, I swear, I never meant to hurt you."

"Of course you hurt me, you..." Maisy took a deep breath and blew it out slowly through pursed lips. "It's fine. I understand."

"You don't understand. It was – everything was so right and then it was like I was an abuser, a criminal, dirt on their shoe. You don't understand what it is to have somebody you love look at you like that."

"No?" Maisy looked Daniel up and down and shook her head. "No. I suppose I don't. I think it's time for me to leave. And don't you dare have a go at me or William or anyone for being friends. You have no right."

"Don't go, alright? I'm sorry I've made such a mess of things, but I'm really just trying to make everything easier on you."

Maisy laughed, a cold sad laugh that didn't reach her eyes, "Well, thanks so much for that."

"Maisy-"

"No. You're just a coward with a half-decent excuse. Stay away from me, Daniel."

LATER, DAN GLOWERED at the young Domme who'd spoken. "What?" He snapped.

"Jesus, Dan, I just asked for a glass of red." She gave him a look that could wither a bouquet in seconds.

Shit. "Sorry, Chloe, don't mind me. Distracted." He poured her a glass of the pricey stuff before turning his attention back to the door to reception.

Maisy had been gone for a while now, but he kept expecting her to walk back into the bar.

"Daniel." The owner's soft voice interrupted Dan's raging inner monologue.

"What do you want, Claude?"

"May I have your armband?" Claude asked gently.

"Why? Oh. Saw that, huh?"

"I heard Chloe asking people what had – uh – 'crawled up your butt and died.'"

Dan scoffed humourlessly, "Fair enough." He unstrapped the armband and passed it to Claude, his attention still elsewhere.

"Daniel, forgive me, but I really can't ignore my friend being in pain. Would you let me-"

"You've done enough."

Claude didn't pursue the matter. He couldn't, really.

The fridge door in the bar's concealed utility room slammed shut, rattling the bottles within violently. Matilda stepped out, freshly off reception, a bottle of wine in her hand. She glared at the Masters at the bar then went to find herself a clean glass.

"What's your problem?" Dan asked.

Instead of replying, Matilda kissed her teeth and poured herself a generous glass of wine. It was at this point that, unnoticed by Daniel, Claude made himself scarce, because he knew the signs of a furious Matilda and he wasn't keen to be on the receiving end twice in a week. Daniel, however, was shoulder deep in self-loathing and had no such functioning self-preservation skills.

"Spit it out, Matilda."

"You're a damned fool," she said, fixing him with a hard stare.

"Good to know."

"You need to fix this, Daniel. You're not doing anyone any good moping this way, least of all your own sorry self." Matilda's accent definitely got stronger when she was cross.

"I can't. You know I can't. I made a mistake and that's the end of it."

Matilda regarded him for a moment then sighed and passed him the bottle. "Join me."

"Only if you stop nagging," he said, hesitantly picking a glass from the rack.

"Never."

Dan shook his head and poured himself a glass anyway, "I didn't have any choice, Tils."

"Don't call me that, Danny boy. And you did, you had the choice to not be a damned fool." The determined angle of her eyebrow was enough to deter most from continuing the argument at this point, but Daniel was at least as headstrong as Matilda and probably less patient.

"You were here when Alicia left; would you put yourself through that again?"

"Five years. It's been more than five years since that girl waltzed out of here with your heart. Are you going to let her keep it 'til you're dead or just until you're too old to care anymore?"

"Matilda-" He tried to interject, but she'd warmed to her theme.

"You might be waiting that long for a woman as right for you as Maisy anyhow! You think chemistry like that grows on trees? I got news for you, big man: it doesn't."

Dan huffed resignedly, sensing he wasn't going to get the upper hand any time soon. "Look, she was ashamed of us, ashamed of me, it would've ended the same way. I heard her on the phone the other day, swearing blind she had no idea what sort of business Claude ran here and that she had nothing to do with us - it."

"You mean when she was on the phone to that rancid boss of hers?" Matilda's incredulous expression tilted her eyebrows to the point of being anatomically implausible.

"I don't know who it was. It doesn't really matter, does it?"

She tutted, "You heard Claude when he came back from that meeting. The man is an ass. I wouldn't trust him with a pet rock, let alone with any private information, you see, genius?"

Dan nodded begrudgingly, "Right, but that's not the only thing and you weren't there the other time so you can't just shrug it away."

"Alright then, big man, you tell me what she did, hm? What did that sweet girl do that made you believe she'd stab you in the back?" Matilda folded her arms and regarded him confrontationally.

"We were out in public-" he began.

"Right."

"I pulled her hair-"

"Mmhmm," she interrupted again even as he began his next word.

"And she said-"

"Yes?" Her derisive stare could freeze lava.

"Would you stop doing that?" Dan bristled. Matilda hadn't been there at the shopping centre, but she was making his well-reasoned argument sound ridiculous.

It wasn't ridiculous. Maisy had denied the nature of their relationship at least twice and he just couldn't take the risk.

Unless she was on the phone to her boss, he supposed, that would be a legitimate reason to be discreet. And maybe, just maybe, introducing Daniel to an irate brother as the man who ties her up and fucks her until she cries in a public dungeon wouldn't have been the most tactful decision. Oh.

He sounded less certain when he spoke this time, "Still, I can't take that risk again, Matilda, I can't -"

She held her hand up to silence him and interrupted a final time, "I've said my piece. I'm done. Drink your wine, hm?"

Dan regarded his glass glumly. Having Maisy in his life and in his home, however briefly, had been remarkable. Having her around for longer would undoubtedly be an experience worth having, but what could he do? Could he really put his neck on the line for what could be and risk a repeat of what had happened five years earlier? He'd had so much more to lose then, but what he had now was precious and fiercely guarded. Could he survive losing everything a second time?

Before he could think any further about Maisy and the decision he'd made so hastily, Claire came hurrying towards them from the dressing rooms.

"Matilda! Glad you're still here. Listen - Oh. Hi, Master Dan."

"Evening trainee," Dan looked at Matilda, who shrugged to indicate she was none the wiser either.

"How can we help you, Claire?" Matilda pushed her glass to one side and sat up taller, automatically more a Mistress in the presence of a sub.

Claire glanced at Dan nervously. His presence seemed to be giving her some reason to hesitate. He considered excusing himself to allow Claire to speak freely, but she gathered herself and began, "You should probably hear this too. I just overheard Jenna on the phone in there and I think she's up to something."

"Up to something?" Dan scoffed, "Is she planning a heist?"

Claire rolled her eyes and shifted all of her attention to Matilda, "Seriously, Ma'am, I'm worried. I don't know who she was talking to, but she mentioned Maisy by her full name and gave the starting time for the anniversary party."

"What did she say about Maisy?" Dan asked, suddenly much more interested.

Claire ignored him in favour of Matilda, who was also looking concerned, "It might be nothing, but I trust her as far as I can throw her, you know?"

"I know, sweet thing, you did well telling us." Matilda stood and took Claire's hand. "We'll talk to the boss man, hm? See if we can't keep an eye on Jenna this weekend."

They started towards Claude's office. "Matilda!" Dan called after her. She stopped and looked back over her shoulder. "Thank you," he said.

She nodded sagely and continued on her way, leaving Dan staring blankly at an untouched glass of wine.

Chapter 35
Trespass

Maisy tugged her bronze armband up for at least the twentieth time. It had been Claude's idea to give her the armband for event night, so the trainees and staff would know who to take orders from. It was a fine idea, but Maisy wished she'd realised how uncomfortable the damn things were.

The Masters and Mistresses milling about doing last minute jobs still wore their black bands. Maybe you get used to them if you wear them for long enough.

William came out from behind the bar with a case of champagne under each arm. Maisy bit back the desire to tell him to be more careful. Last time she'd given him an order he'd called her Mistress Maisy in front of everyone and now they were all saying it, much to William's delight.

Just a metre or so to the left, at the same height as William's head, an impatient foot tapped. The violinist it belonged to had been the first member of the band to arrive, the first to set up, and the first to begin exuding symptoms of extreme boredom.

If truth be told, Maisy was glad she was wearing the armband when she approached this sour faced man and his band mates, it certainly made her feel more confident in her authority.

"Okay, guys, thank you for your patience. Would you begin the cocktail hour set, please?" The swing band struck up a medium tempo number, something to get toes tapping, but not so loud or fast as to distract from conversation. That set was for after dinner when, hopefully, there would be dancing.

Maisy took the last opportunity of the night to step into the middle of Club Drift's main hall and take in her work all at once.

The band, neatly dressed in vintage style tuxes that matched the staff uniforms, were the focal point of the room up there on the oversized bar. Maisy had remarked to Claude that the bar was finally worth whatever money he'd paid for the ridiculous thing. Claude had raised an eyebrow at her 5'2" frame, but said nothing. Maisy wasn't the first diminutive submissive to object to his bar.

The stage-come-bar was opposite the main door. Maisy could just about hear voices coming from reception. They were almost ready to begin. The bulk of the room was empty and ready to become a dance floor. Maisy had been absolutely thrilled when Claude allowed her to install a huge chandelier. It would have been such a shame to settle for a glitter ball in a room like this.

Her light technicians had set the atmospheric lighting hours ago, soft orb like reflections from the obscenely expensive crystal chandelier covered the room in otherworldly light, as if a thousand tiny moons from a thousand tiny worlds had been borrowed to illuminate the great event.

Large round tables were arranged in a semi-circle facing the bar. Maisy automatically counted chairs and glasses from her vantage point in the centre of the room.

Her favourite company to hire dinnerware, tables, and chairs from always set up before the event anyway. Getting the event set up within Club Drift's exacting privacy standards had been easier than she'd expected. It'd been a close call to get everyone out though, with Maisy's old friend, the florist, only leaving fifteen minutes before the first eager guests arrived.

The red carpet had been laid behind the tables, so that people entering from reception were guided around the room and funnelled into the central dance floor instead of immediately sitting down. William's staff were waiting with trays of champagne and hors d'oeuvres.

All the service staff were house Masters, regular employed staff, or trainee subs and all of them had volunteered. There wasn't a St. Andrew's Cross or a whip in sight. There was equipment set up back in the tunnels as usual, but to stumble across anything untoward an unwelcome guest would have to wander very far indeed. That is, unless they saw the guest's outfits first.

Maisy signalled to Matt, the bearded American Master, who threw open the reception door with a flourish.

First through the door were Xavier and Mistress Chloe. Even though she'd been expecting some magnificent outfits, especially from these two, Maisy's jaw dropped. Chloe was stark naked, her coffee coloured skin covered by thousands upon thousands of stick on diamonds. From a distance you might think she was wearing an elaborate ball gown, but up close there was no mistaking the nature of her non-existent dress. She grinned at Maisy's astounded expression; she knew she looked radiant. Maisy immediately regretted not organising a best dressed prize.

Xavier was even more naked, he wore only black gems stuck on around his throat in the shape of a bow tie with some shockingly tight latex under things. Luckily for him it was warm in the Club tonight. Behind them she saw glimpses of collars and leads, tassels and handcuffs, latex and lace.

Maisy resisted the urge to stand and watch all the guests arrive. She'd have plenty of time to see their interpretations of Fetish-Formalwear later. Besides, at some point Dan was going to walk through the door and she'd rather not be gawping at it when he did.

Instead, she sought out the service volunteers not currently weighed down with trays.

In the end, Claude had decided on a sit-down meal and Maisy had been left with the task of providing full catering services without any external staff needing to see inside Club Drift. It had seemed an impossible ask at first, but the solution had become obvious the moment Claude mentioned that they had a car park out the back.

Having always arrived by foot, Maisy had never known it existed. She could bring in the same travelling caterers she used for rural weddings in woods or fields.

The catering truck could work out in the car park and she'd have the service volunteers ferry food through to the main room. So long as they were speedy, the food should arrive to the tables hot.

And if someone forgot to take their uniform handcuffs off before going out there? Well, maybe the chef would think it was a new fashion thing. Collars have been going in and out of vanilla fashion for years, after all, handcuffs aren't that much of a jump.

Maisy gestured at her gang of workers to follow her. "Let's just run through the route one more time, check for obstacles, then say hello to the kitchen, yeah?"

The all followed her without question. In fact, none of them had questioned her authority all day, which was a relief. She'd thought that as a newcomer and a submissive she'd be laughed at when she took control, but it hadn't been a problem.

Of course it hadn't, she chastened herself for the thought. She'd been a submissive when she was here with Dan, but tonight she was working. Tonight she was just Maisy Bennett, event planner extraordinaire, about to knock it out of the park with her first solo contract.

"Grab that for me, please," She gestured with her clipboard at a box that'd been left in their way. Someone picked up the box and flattened it ready to go in the recycling bin on the other side of the car park.

As they approached the back door that led the patch of asphalt where their caterers were currently located, Maisy saw that it'd been left ajar.

"Bloody hell," She muttered, glad that Claude wasn't here to see, "Don't forget, everyone, keep the door closed or guarded at all times. Okay?" They all murmured their assent, several of them frowning at the open door. They were all members and workers here, they valued the club's privacy as much as Claude. What clumsy arse had left the door open?

Maisy led the group out to the kitchen to check on the first course. She didn't notice Jenna watching the open door from the nearest tunnel.

Chapter 36
The Main Event

When she re-entered the main room it was heaving with the sound of laughter and corks popping. These must be nearly all the guests on the list by now.

She glanced to the reception door again. When either everyone who'd RSVP'd had arrived or the sit-down meal was due to begin, Matilda would come and join the party, leaving security to deal with stragglers.

Carl whizzed past with a tray of smoked salmon bites. Maisy did hope the black glitter in his roots was secure, nobody wants glittery salmon. His uniform was more glitzy than usual too, the usual amount of sparkle on the male trainee uniforms being none at all. She couldn't wait to see what Claude made of his alterations.

The door to reception swung open and Matilda strode in wearing a spectacular red latex evening dress with a plunging back. Before Maisy could cross the floor to meet her, she was stopped in her tracks by the swing band striking up a loud rendition of 'Waltzing Matilda.' There was a moment of shocked silence, then the gathered guests fell about laughing.

Matilda, icy faced, scanned the room to find the source of the prank. As far as Maisy could see, Carl and William were the only people not laughing or playing an instrument.

In fact, both men were extremely focused on their work. Always suspicious from either of them.

Matilda fixed the band with a hard stare and they decided unanimously to revert to their swing set. Maisy saw the Mistress glance at William, but if she suspected him she let it drop and continued on her path to Maisy, who was very careful to keep an extremely straight face.

"You have done so well, Maisy." Matilda kissed Maisy on each cheek, "I think everyone is here already. Shall we let Claude begin his speech soon?"

Maisy nodded, ignoring the fact that 'everyone' didn't seem to include Daniel. She'd wondered if he'd turn up after everything. If truth be told she would have liked him to be there, however awkward it might become. Maisy was proud of the work she'd done for tonight. Dan would have been proud too, back when she was someone for him to be proud of.

"Ready when you are. We've got about half an hour until the dinner service starts. Think he'll be done by then?"

Matilda gave her a sly smile, "I will make sure he is done, I am starving." She turned and sought out William, found he was deliberately not catching her eye, tutted, and turned to Matt instead. Matilda gave him a discreet thumbs up and the event began in earnest.

The servers who'd been circulating with trays went to fetch fresh bottles with which to furnish the dining tables. Matt and William began offering their arms to ladies and leading them to their assigned places Matilda floated through the crowd, smiling and shaking hands, gesturing at the rapidly filling tables.

Soon, everyone was seated and Claude was left alone in front of the bar. The staff, including Maisy, filed behind the tables so they could hear the owner's speech.

She thought the line looked sparse. Who was missing? Carl? Jenna? They definitely weren't all there. The musicians stopped their background music. Club Drift fell silent.

The door to reception creaked conspicuously as Daniel arrived, his hair in a typically dishevelled state, but not a line of his suit out of place. Realising immediately that he was interrupting, he held up a hand in apology and started to make his way around the staff - towards Maisy.

Maisy looked dead ahead. Determined to focus on the task at hand. Frustratingly, Claude became distracted by watching Daniel's progress. This did mean, though, that when Dan reached her side Maisy was able to catch Claude's eye and signal for him to get on with it.

"Right then," Claude gathered himself and smiled benevolently at his guests, "Here we are. For fifteen years we, Club Drift, have had this place as our home here in London. And what marvellous years they have been, non?"

The guests, already merry with champagne, cheered and clinked glasses with their table mates. It was a diverse mix of people. If you'd been unaware of Club Drift's nature and invited to guess the connection these people had to one another, you'd struggle.

There were older couples, some of whom Maisy had seen passing time in the bar, some who she'd yet to meet.

One silver haired pair caught her attention, their hands had been entwined from the moment they'd arrived. They wore understated black formal wear and leaned on each other when walking in and now again as they watched Claude speak. One wore a delicate gold collar and the most serene smile Maisy had ever seen.

There were men and women wearing black armbands. She'd been informed were previous House Masters and Mistresses. No longer active enough at the club to perform the role often, but always welcome to wear the armband when they visited.

There were people of all ages, of all professions, of all races and abilities. The striking Domme who she'd first seen holding court from her wheelchair weeks ago was there with a male sub Maisy recognised. Xavier and Chloe sat together and Xavier was actually allowed to sit on a chair, rather than kneeling by her side, in honour of the occasion.

Maisy estimated she'd seen about half the guests in the club before. The others were known to her only by name, by brief anecdotes Claude had shared when they were arranging invitations. "Marie," he'd said, "Oh, Marie. I would have married her, you know. If only she'd deigned to leave America."

"You could have followed her there," Maisy had offered. Claude had shaken his head, "I have moved far enough from my homeland, petite. I could not be an ocean away."

Despite several leading questions since, Maisy had failed to get any further information about Marie. But she was here. She'd flown in for the anniversary, as Claude had known she would. She sat on the centre table, her tightly curled mop of hair like soft fire in the artificial light. Striking was an understatement. Maisy could easily see how, once upon a time, she'd stolen Claude's heart.

Maisy realised she'd zoned out of Claude's speech entirely. Not surprising, really, she'd been helping him write it and was a bit sick of it. Not that it wasn't lovely, but she'd heard it ten times already on this day alone. There was a lot of gratitude and warm friendships and incomparable connections and so on.

"Maisy?" Dan spoke quietly from beside her. She startled, she'd been so busy watching the guests she'd temporarily forgotten he was there.

She gave him a tight smile and turned her attention back to Claude. Had he done the baguette joke yet? He would be finished soon after the baguette joke.

"Sweetheart, can we talk?" He touched her elbow gently, as if suggesting he lead her to somewhere private.

She jerked her arm away, "I'm working."

"Later then? I need to apologise. Beg forgiveness might be more like it."

Despite herself she smiled at the thought of him begging for anything, "I don't know, Daniel. Let's say maybe, okay?"

"Maybe baby." A smarmy voice chimed in from her other side. She grabbed Dan's hand instinctively then let it go almost as soon as she'd taken it. It wasn't possible. He couldn't be here. He couldn't be in her sanctuary tonight of all nights.

Sick to her stomach she turned to face the voice, knowing who she was going to see, refusing to believe it.

Hair slicked back, sneer fixed in place, larger than life and twice as arrogant. Michael. Her boss. And he looked extremely pleased with himself.

Chapter 37
One Of Us

"And there I was thinking you were frigid," Michael's grin was unnaturally wide and stiff. This wasn't the same as when he was drunk, this time he was sober and high on ugly rage.

"Who's this?" Dan asked, stepping closer to Maisy in a protective stance.

"Is this one in addition to the frog or is he the new squeeze?" Michael asked, looking between them gleefully. "Here, why aren't you naked like these other tarts?" He waved his arm at the guests.

Several of the guests had already noticed a disturbance, but this insult made several of them turn around and stare at the interloper.

"Maisy, are you okay?" Dan took her arm, "Maisy?"

She couldn't respond. She heard him, just like she'd heard Michael's crude comment and she was now aware that Claude had stopped his speech and was heading towards them. However, it was like she was watching these things happen to somebody else. She'd checked out the moment she heard Michael's voice.

Claude reached them and whispered something in Dan's ear, both men looked at Michael with disgust.

"You're leaving," Dan said, "Now."

Most people who were subject to Claude and Dan's united disapproval would make themselves scarce as soon as possible. Michael, however, had such an inflated opinion of himself he didn't notice when others were disgusted by him, so he continued. His eyes were as wild as his grin and they didn't stray from Maisy's stricken face.

"I'm not going anywhere, mate. My employee and I are going to have a little chat about sordid sex clubs and external contracts. And maybe we'll go into how nobody in the industry will ever work with her again after I tell them about this shit hole and how Miss Prissy Bennett is actually a massive slut. That'll be fun, won't it, hmm?" He leaned in closer to Maisy's face and she snapped out of her disassociated state enough to shove him backwards.

"Oh ho!" Impossibly, Michael grinned even wider and licked his lips, "Spankee or spanker? That's a fun game. John loves to be smacked around by escorts in leather boots, shall I move your desk into his office for Monday?"

"Excuse me, sir," The older man who Maisy had noticed holding his wife's hand earlier stood up. "Did I hear you correctly? You intend to blackmail this person?"

Michael looked him up and down then turned his malicious gaze back to Maisy, "What's it got to do with you?"

"I suggest you retract the threats, boy, if you know what's good for you," His hand rested steadily on his wife's shoulder. He might look frail, but he wasn't a pushover by any measure. His voice wasn't forceful, but it did not waver.

Michael laughed and reluctantly tore himself away from Maisy to look at the man again, "I suggest you fuck off and mind your own business if you know what's good for you, old man."

The man smiled and nodded, "Very well."

A man and a woman seated at the older man's table stood at the same time. Both were more conservatively dressed than most of the other guests. They both reached into a pocket to pull out a police I.D. and held it up for Michael to see.

He scowled at them, but didn't back off, "So I tell your boss he's got coppers hanging out in a brothel, or whatever the fuck this is, and you both get the sack too. You can't touch me."

The older man, still smiling, said, "Their boss is my daughter and I assure you she will not fire them for being at a party."

Maisy saw Michael's eyebrow twitch and took a step back. That always happened before he really lost his temper. It'd happened in the corridor the other day, after the meeting. Michael glanced around at the rest of the guests, no doubt wondering who else had witnessed his tantrum.

Monsieur Leroy, esteemed businessman, was looking at him like anyone might look at a slug in their cabbage patch. William, unnaturally still and quiet, was clearly ready to pounce and just as clearly able to overpower Michael easily. Matilda and Matt stood between Michael and the door to reception.

Slowly, it seemed to dawn on him that he'd walked into the lion's den and, what's more, attacked a cub. He needed to change his tune if he wanted to emerge unscathed.

He stepped back from Maisy and put on his best city-boy grin, "No need for all that. I'll go. You're still fired, by the way. Have fun being unemployed without a reference."

Matilda spoke up, her accent stronger than usual in anger, "Did she not tell you, little man? She is booked solid these six months. She doesn't need you or your *chaka-chaka* firm."

Michael sneered at Matilda and opened his mouth to respond, but her patented 'get your arse away from me before I beat it' stare shut him up completely.

"You heard her," Maisy said, voice steadier now, "I don't need you. Now get out."

His eyebrow twitched again, "You think you can boss me around, slut?"

"Watch it," Dan growled, but Maisy held up her hand to signal to Dan that she had this under control.

As far as Maisy knew, Matilda was very much exaggerating the amount of solo work coming her way, but that didn't matter. Maisy was standing in the middle of her first solo event, which had been going very well before Michael turned up. Actually, it had been going perfectly.

She'd pulled this off. She hadn't just survived her first solo event, she'd excelled. Surrounded by friends from Drift and illustrious guests, who had her back even though they didn't know her, she realised she didn't need Michael or the firm in the slightest.

Finally, after months of putting up with Michael's incompetence and abuse, she was ready to strike out on her own. Not because she needed to get away, but because it was what she was meant to be doing. She was good at her job, really good, and she didn't need the company to support her anymore. Or, more accurately, she couldn't let the company hold her back while she worked her arse off to kept it afloat anymore.

She smiled. Michael's smug expression faltered. Perhaps he saw that he'd lost all power over Maisy, that he couldn't make her feel uncomfortable anymore.

Whatever it was, he was shaken enough to stammer when he spoke next, "You're nothing without us."

Even he sounded unsure.

"Please leave, you're spoiling the party," Maisy gave him her best customer service grin and gestured to the reception door. Matilda and Matt stepped aside, clearing his path in a way that told Michael exactly where to go and to do so quickly.

He started on his way to the door then, gripped by the insanity that sometimes springs from an inadequate chauvinist being outdone by a woman, turned and slapped Maisy clear around the face.

The force of the blow knocked her into Claude's arms. The whole room gasped as if they'd been slapped themselves, surprised by the chaotic violence in this usually safe place.

Daniel moved first as the shock of the moment faded. He grabbed Michael's collar, pulled him forwards, and punched him square in the face. His nose broke with a satisfying crunch. The resultant spurt of blood splashed across the floor, sinking into Maisy's red carpet without a trace.

Michael staggered backwards, somehow surprised that his actions had brought consequences with them. "My nose," he spluttered, spraying blood unattractively around his face.

Daniel turned back to Maisy and Claude as if to dismiss Michael altogether. However, as soon as he saw Maisy's red cheek, he turned back and punched Michael again, this time catching his cheekbone. He hoped it was enough to give him a black eye.

"William," Daniel said. He didn't need to say anything else. William stepped up, grabbed Michael by the scruff of the neck, and shoved him towards the exit where the taciturn bouncer was waiting with open arms.

Silence followed in their wake as every guest watched them go, then turned their eyes to Maisy, Dan, and Claude.

Chapter 38
Bad, Bad, Bad Cop

Maisy rifled through the first aid box, tutting every few seconds. She knew full well that there was gauze in there somewhere because she'd restocked the box herself in anticipation of the event, but it was proving elusive now she needed it.

Matilda re-joined them, having detoured to get a bowl of ice and water from the utility room. "You okay, sweet thing?" Matilda said, eyeing Dan's bloody knuckles askance.

Maisy grabbed a packet of gauze triumphantly, "Yeah, I'm fine. It was only a slap." She was surprisingly unshaken. In fact, she felt full of energy and a sense of accomplishment. It was probably just adrenaline, but she felt pretty good at the moment and that was what mattered.

"Mm." Matilda put the bowl on the table of the booth they'd retreated to, "You put ice on your cheek, you hear?"

Maisy nodded, distracted by mopping up Dan's hand. Unheeded, Matilda backed away to the entrance of the tunnel, protecting their sanctuary from intruders and giving Maisy and Dan some privacy.

"Thank you," Maisy said, dabbing his cracked knuckles with an ice cube wrapped in damp gauze.

"What for?" He'd given up trying to tell her his hand was fine. Maybe she just wanted to torture him with this sadistic cleaning process.

"You know, for Michael. For standing up for me. Getting rid of him."

"You did the hard bit," he said, grimacing as she sprayed him with some stinging disinfectant stuff.

"Yeah. Still, thank you."

"I haven't had a chance to say congratulations. The place looks incredible." She nodded her thanks, concentrating on wrapping his hand with a clean bandage.

"And congratulations for getting out of that job," He continued. "I wish I'd known how bad things were," he said.

"I needed to do it myself," she replied.

He nodded, "You did a damn fine job, sweetheart."

She felt a little pang when he used the pet name, "It was a long time coming."

He took her hand, ignoring her protests about the bandaging, "I'm proud of you. I know that doesn't mean anything coming from me, but I am proud of you."

Maisy paused for a moment, not sure how to react, then brought their hands up to her lips and kissed his palm. "Thank you," She said. And she meant it.

"I'm sorry," He said.

She smiled, "I know."

"Can I ever make it up to you?" His eyebrows furrowed, his sincerity was clear, but Maisy didn't know what to say.

She could tell him again what a fool he'd been. She could give him a hard time. She could tell him all about Harry's benevolent reaction to her kinky secrets. She could tell him he didn't deserve another chance to explain or make things right. She could tell him how none of it mattered anymore because she'd forgiven him as soon as he apologised.

But, for now, all she said was, "Yes."

The look they exchanged then contained everything that had been between them and everything that might yet be.

If they hadn't been interrupted, that look might have gone on forever.

William had found them in their quiet tunnel and he'd brought Jenna with him. Matilda abandoned her protective position by the entrance of the tunnel to join them all. Jenna winced when she saw Matilda take a seat next to Maisy. Two angry Drift Masters and a Mistress to boot, no wonder she looked unhappy.

Maisy looked between William and Jenna and understood instantly why the trainee been brought to them. For some reason known only to Jenna and Michael, she'd let a stranger into Club Drift. She was a member here too. She'd violated her own privacy with this reckless act. It didn't make any sense

Once again, all Maisy could think to say was, "Why?"

Jenna remained silent, not meeting anyone's eye. William tutted loudly. "Speak now, pet, you know you're better off talking to us than Claude."

For the first time since Maisy had been at the club, she saw an expression other than arrogance and frustration on Jenna's face. She was unmistakably afraid. "Will he throw me out?" She asked, looking between the three senior members of the club and getting nothing but hard stares from any of them.

"Maybe," William said, "Maybe not. Depends what you tell us, doesn't it?"

Jenna shuddered, "Fine, but I don't want her listening."

Maisy pointed at her own chest incredulously, "I'm 'her,' I take it?"

Daniel took Maisy's hand, "You just deliberately let a stranger into our club on a night when our most publicly recognisable members are here en-masse. A stranger who you knew could impact Maisy's outside life considerably. She will be here while you confess your reasons and you will beg forgiveness from her."

Maisy nearly interrupted to say that, actually, she wasn't sure about all this begging for forgiveness lark, but Dan looked very cross, so she just nodded for now.

Maybe she should get all the people who needed to beg forgiveness from her to line up in a neat row and express their regret through the medium of interpretive dance.

Or maybe she'd been awake for far too long today already and she was likely to miss out on dinner because of this ridiculous interrogation.

"Look, can you just spit it out, please?" She said, "I know these three will get it out of you eventually with their bad, bad, bad cop routine, but I'm really hungry and can't be arsed to wait all night."

Jenna gaped at her for a moment before her features contorted in ugly rage. "See?" She said, gesturing furiously at Maisy, "She doesn't even take you seriously. Why her and not me? Or any of the others? Why have you been chasing after a charity rat when you haven't even helped with the trainees for months? Why didn't you just leave the club when Alicia did if you weren't even going to look at any of us, hm?"

Dan was as surprised as everyone else was by Jenna's outburst. For a moment nobody said anything, then Dan said, "But you and Alicia were friends?"

Jenna groaned as if he'd said the stupidest thing she'd ever heard. She completely ignored the reproving glare Matilda gave her. Whatever power they had over her as a trainee was void at this moment. She was running on emotion alone.

"Alicia was my friend. Exactly!" she said. When she realised that none of the other people in the room had understood what she clearly saw as an obvious fact, she sighed. "You're all as stupid as her."

"I'm 'her' again, if anyone was wondering," Maisy said, rummaging in a subbie basket under the table for water. Or chocolate. Hopefully there was chocolate in this one. Or maybe some painkillers, her face was starting to hurt after all.

Matilda hid a smile behind her hand while Dan, flummoxed, tried to regain control of the situation.

"So," Dan said, "You're punishing Maisy because you wanted to...what? Play with me? You've never even approached me."

Jenna huffed, "Of course I haven't. Everyone knows that you don't play with anyone properly. Not even the trainees."

William, also looking lost, said, "How is that Maisy's fault?"

"Why did he choose her if he'd suddenly changed his mind? There's loads of more experienced subs here. Most of us pay our fees too," Jenna glared at Maisy.

Maisy, unimpressed, rolled her eyes and held up three fingers at Matilda while mouthing "Still 'her'."

Daniel looked more pissed off than confused now, "So you think you've got some sort of prior claim on me because you're a trainee? Or because you were Alicia's friend?"

"Or because I'm a real member, not some wannabe who wandered in off the night bus one night." Jenna stood tall, one hand on her hip, clearly comfortable in her righteous indignation.

Matilda laughed out loud, all attempts to maintain composure flying out the window after Jenna's explanation.

"You ridiculous woman," she said, shaking her head and struggling to contain the laughter enough to speak. "He is not an escort! You don't pay your fees to get his booty, do you now? As for the rest of it - well- I would not dignify your nonsense with an answer, I'll let these three decide what to do with you, I think I can hear the first course coming now."

"Wait!" Maisy said, "I'm starving." She stood and went after Matilda, not even bothering to look at Jenna.

Dan and William glanced at each other briefly, then followed the women, leaving Jenna standing alone with a bowl of melted ice and a bloodied lump of gauze for company.

Chapter 39
Cards

Maisy took Matilda's hand and leaned in to whisper, "What will Claude do about Jenna?"

Matilda frowned, the laughter gone now she considered the serious nature of Jenna's actions. "I do not know. She is a daft and spiteful woman, but it is not in Claude's nature to throw someone out, you know? Maybe she can be helped"

Maisy nodded. Although Jenna had tried her best to ruin the event and Maisy's life, she couldn't bring herself to hate her. Not in the shadow of Dan's ex, Alicia, and how she'd lost everyone she knew because she'd been foolish in a crisis.

Maisy didn't want Jenna to be outcast by the club because she'd done something cruel and thoughtless. Then again, if she did anything like that again she'd happily wave her out of the door. Mostly, her overwhelming feeling for the woman was pity.

Dan caught up with them and took Maisy's arm. "Shall we walk in together?"

Matilda released Maisy's hand and stepped aside, doing a very bad job of pretending she wasn't interested in Maisy's answer.

Maisy leaned into Dan's arm, letting herself feel the safety and comfort he offered for a moment. A moment that neither of them could bring themselves to punctuate with words.

"I'll go stop Claude waffling." Matilda said, striding across the main room towards Claude without a backwards glance.

"Come on," Dan said, following close on Matilda's heels. Maisy saw an anxious member of the dinner service staff standing nearby. She wasn't entirely sure how late things were running, but from the look on the waiter's face the first course was going cold on the pass.

They reached Claude as a final round of applause rang around the main room. "Merci, mes amis." Claude said, too overcome with emotion to even notice his complete lapse into French.

"One moment of everyone's time, if you don't mind, Claude?" Daniel shook Claude's hand and stepped up to centre stage, one arm still around Maisy's waist.

Claude stepped back, waving Dan forward through misty eyes.

Daniel stood in front of the waiting band, over a hundred pairs of eyes waiting eagerly for his speech because it was holding up their dinner apart from anything else.

"I won't be long," he said, flashing a smile at the increasingly anxious member of the service team who still stood nearby, waiting to give the kitchen the go ahead for the first course.

"I would like for us all to take a moment to thank our wonderful event planner, Miss Maisy Bennett." Dan said, pulling Maisy closer to his side. The applause that followed was all the more enthusiastic because they'd witnessed the ghastly scene with Michael. Whatever mark the slap had left on her cheek, she was sure it was now obscured by her profuse blushing.

When the applause faded, Dan continued, "It was, misguidedly, originally my job to arrange this event. I'm sure we're all grateful I was relieved of my duties before it was too late."

The guests tittered politely, but many of them were fidgeting in their seats. They had been prepared to let Claude drone on, he was, after all, their host, but they were getting restless now.

"As you may have overheard, Miss Bennett is going to be flying solo from now on. Now, I won't lie, the regular house crew have each got at least one event in mind, so you'll have to be quick if you want to get booked in with her."

Maisy could feel her cheeks burning, "Okay, let's get your meal started," she said, fighting the urge to drag Daniel away from the microphone.

"Enjoy your evening," Daniel said to the crowd.

They started towards the hovering waiter who was eager to get service started.

"Wait a moment!" The older man who'd stepped into the disagreement with Michael earlier waved for their attention. "How do we get in touch with you? Do you have a card?"

Maisy realised then that she didn't. Her business cards had the company information on them.

"Yes! Yes, she does," Claude stepped up, his emotions now in check. "I hope you'll forgive the presumption, petite. I had some simple cards printed with your number, in case anyone here wished to hire you off the back of this. I did not think you'd be so...drastically in need of new clients, but I am especially glad I did this now."

"Thank you," Maisy said, overwhelmed by his thoughtfulness. "Um, I'll get you a card after your meal, Sir," she called to the man who had enquired.

Maisy could have been knocked over with a feather when several other voices called out "Me too!"

LATER, WHEN THE MEAL was over and the majority of the guests were dancing to the swing band, the house crew and Maisy sat at one of the abandoned tables, exhausted by the exertions of the day.

"I wasn't just saying it for the bastard's benefit, Maisy," Matilda said, waving a glass of champagne for emphasis, "You're going to be booked solid. Claude didn't want us to tell you and overwhelm you before tonight, but we all have things we want to talk to you about. I'm turning...well, I have a birthday coming up that I should probably celebrate. Chloe and Xavier want a collaring ceremony slash wedding planning, think you can handle it?"

"Matilda!" Chloe hissed, "We haven't told everyone yet, watch your gassing."

"Sorry, sorry," Matilda said, refilling her glass, "Still, it's about time you made an honest boy out of him, nobody will be surprised."

Chloe's stern features softened, "Bah. You're right, I suppose. I already have your card, Maisy."

William gave Maisy a wink from across the table, "You'll be alright, pet. We've got your back."

"Thank you, everyone. Really. Thank you so much." Maisy felt tears well up, not for the first time that night either. She'd only known these people for a couple of months, but they'd taken her under their wing and given her so much support. She could never have guessed that she'd make friends like this the first time she walked into this strange underground world, but she was so glad she'd had the courage to keep coming back.

A new business, good friends, and...Well, Daniel hadn't let go of her hand since that speech.

"Sweetheart?" He didn't need to say anything else.

Maisy nodded then turned to the rest of the table, "Excuse us for a minute."

Most of them focused on their own conversations. They were all undoubtedly curious about Dan and Maisy's current status, but they were generally too polite to ask or even to notice their entwined hands. William and Matilda, however, stared openly at their retreating backs.

"Think they're talking about us?" Dan asked as they navigated their way to a quieter tunnel, far away from the hub of the party.

"Definitely," she replied, "We should probably be talking about us, shouldn't we?"

"Definitely," he said, squeezing her hand a little tighter.

They sat in a booth in an empty tunnel, sliding onto the long bench together rather than sitting opposite each other by unspoken agreement.

MAISY'S KEEPER

Maisy leaned into his shoulder, feeling the familiar sensations of warmth and safety that his presence used to inspire welling up, waiting to be allowed in.

"I'm so sorry, sweetheart," Dan kissed the top of her head reverently, "I swear I will never, ever, do you wrong like that again."

"You were a dumbass," she said, simply.

"I was."

"I forgive you."

"I don't deserve it."

"Nope," she said. After a moment she laughed, "You do. You're forgiven and that's the end of it."

"You're amazing, you know that?" Dan sat back so he could look her in the eye, "Today has been - no, these last few weeks have been turbulent beyond belief. You're still sitting there smiling."

"What else should I be doing?" She said. Maybe that was understating things, and she had been in a state a few days over the last month or so, but really things were alright.

Work changing was going to be an enormous upheaval, but she had Harry and her family and her friends here at Club Drift and, unless she was very much mistaken, she had Dan.

"Will you take me back," he asked, his uncertainty clear in his expression, "No messing about this time. If I'm with you I'm with you. No hiding behind Claude or anything else. I want you in my life more than I've ever wanted anything. Will you let me make all this up to you? Will you take a chance on me?"

She reached out and touched his cheek gently. She'd never seen his dark eyes so conflicted. Daniel hadn't mentioned what it was costing him to offer himself like this, but Maisy remembered what a significant thing he was doing. Dan had been torn open before and because of the scars Alicia had left he'd hurt Maisy, but now he was inviting her back in and putting his heart in her hands.

There was a part of Maisy that wanted to hold back, to stay in the safe, if slightly icy, realm of friendship with Dan, but tonight wasn't a night for safe choices. Tonight was a night for taking a leap of faith.

Maisy wanted so badly to feel the highs and lows of submission with Daniel again. More than that though, she wanted to find out what else might happen if they reignited the intimacy between them. Her heart told her it was worth the risk.

"Yes," she said.

"And will you wear this?" Dan's words bled together as if he was afraid of pausing, "I wouldn't dream of asking you to accept a collar after the way I've behaved, and I don't expect you to say yes to this, but I thought maybe, while I earn your trust back...Well, would you?"

He pulled a slim box from his inside pocket and opened it for her to see. Inside was a stunning bracelet in the Art Deco style; white metal and stones that had to be diamonds.

Maisy was glad he hadn't offered her a collar, she wouldn't have known how to take it. This, however, was ideal. A discreet promise that could sit on her wrist during the day to remind her where her handcuffs would be when she was next with him.

That the bracelet looked as if it could have grown naturally in Club Drift, where Maisy and Dan had shared so much, only made it more perfect.

"Yes," she said, "Yes, I will."

Then she kissed him.

Epilogue

If she hadn't been looking for her client's wedding announcement in the paper, Maisy might have missed it entirely.

The picture of Michael beaming incongruously took up more space than the article. 'Local Business Collapses', the headline read. A few short lines followed detailing the embarrassing timing of the collapse, just over a year after Michael Snr.'s death and Michael Jnr. taking over.

Maisy fiddled with her bracelet nervously. She still felt a pang of guilt when she thought about her kindly mentor, but it was just a quiet pang now. She'd put everything she could into the company. Michael Snr. would never have expected her to hold herself back.

Her work phone rang from the kitchen where she'd left it plugged in. The Delia book she'd been browsing still lay open beside it on the counter. Daniel sometimes lamented the lived-in clutter Maisy always left lying around his home when she visited, but she was sure that he was secretly pleased to get rid of the cold catalogue sheen that had prevailed before.

"Hello, Bennett Events," she answered the phone with the customary greeting, "Oh, hi Claude. I don't know, isn't he with you? Okay, I think we'll be at Drift tonight, but if anything changes I'll drop you a line. Okay. Bye."

The front door slammed behind Dan as she hung up on Claude.

"You still here, sweetheart?" Dan called out.

"In the kitchen," she replied, "Sorry about the mess. I did make cake for us though."

"Well, that's okay then," he said, raising his eyebrows at the flour that dusted every surface in the kitchen. "Come here."

She stepped into his arms, frowning suspiciously, "What's up? You look sneaky?"

He laughed and squeezed her tight, "I'm a Dom - I'm always sneaky."

"True," she kissed him slowly, savouring the cold that lingered on his lips from outside.

"Hold your hand out," he said, pushing her back gently. "Close your eyes."

She did as she was told and smiled when Dan ran a finger over the bracelet he'd given her that night at Club Drift, still their own precious version of a collar.

"Have you been to that shop again? You're running out of storage in the play room. Oh!"

The small object he placed in her hand was very cold. Metallic?

"Open your eyes," he said, his excitement audible in his voice.

In the palm of her hand was a highly polished key.

"What-" She began.

"For this place," He interrupted, unable to wait. "If you want it. I mean, you've been here more than not and it's been great and I thought you might-"

She silenced him with a kiss.

"Of course I want it, dummy."

His shoulders visibly relaxed, but now he was more certain of himself he noticed her disrespectful form of address, "Who now? Dummy was it?"

She laughed and pulled away from his playful grip, knowing that she'd get a spanking for being so rude and horribly excited to find out what he's spank her with. "Sir! I said, Sir. Didn't you hear me?"

"Mm. Sure you did, sweetheart." He pulled her into a tight embrace, surrounding her with strong, immovable arms.

She gave up her playful resistance and relaxed there in the simplest form of bondage. Who knew a hug could give her such warm, deep, submissive feelings?

"Thank you, Sir," she said, the key growing warm in the palm of her hand.

The End

Next time: William's Story

Sign up to the newsletter at www.saffronhayes.co.uk to keep up with upcoming releases

About the Author

Saffron Hayes is the British author of 'Romance and Ropes' novels set in Club Drift. She lives near London with two dogs and many, many books.

Her work features inquisitive subs, communicative Doms, SSC realistic BDSM kinky stuff, and a side helping of laughter - just like all the best sex, right?

Look for Saffron at www.saffronhayes.co.uk, on Twitter, and Facebook.

Printed in Poland
by Amazon Fulfillment
Poland Sp. z o.o., Wrocław